About the author

Josephine (Jo) Wallace briefly explored the academic life, studying music at Oxford University for a year before decamping to the Mediterranean in search of adventure. Soon based in Antibes, she became a cordon bleu cook on luxury yachts along the Med, adept at catering to wealthy and demanding charterers in the confined space of a yacht's galley.

In the early 1980s she met her husband Dennis, and together they crewed yachts for another 20 years, before celebrating retirement with a six-year circumnavigation of the globe in their sailing yacht *Aurora of Polruan*. They finally settled on the Aegean coast of Turkey, by which time they had crossed the Atlantic four times and the Pacific once, visiting over 60 different countries.

A gifted musician, in later years she indulged her passion for singing, and delighted audiences of friends with her renderings of arias from Italian opera. She also wrote a number of travel articles which were published in yachting magazines, and several works of fiction. *Lanzarote* is her first published novel.

LANZAROTE

J.H. WALLACE

Aurora Polruan Books

The estate of J.H. Wallace would like to thank Nicholas Fry, Justin
Higham and Alexandra Sellers for their many hours of work in
bringing this project to fruition, and all the members of the family for
the donations which have made it possible.

First published by Aurora Polruan Books 2014
in association with eBookPartnership.com
Cover by Ana Grigoriu, Books-design.com
Printed by CreateSpace

For Dennis
Goodbye to all that

Background note:

Lanzarote has always been an active volcanic island. From 1730 to 1736, there were multiple eruptions more or less continuously from the thirty or so volcanoes which developed on the island during this period. These eruptions covered most of the arable land with lava and forced the majority of the surviving population to flee to other islands. Many returned when the eruptions ceased.

The original inhabitants of the Canary Islands were the Guanches, who are believed to originate from North Africa. They were physically different from the later Spanish invaders and they had their own language and customs. Their numbers were drastically reduced over the centuries by Spanish conquest and marauding pirates from North Africa in search of slaves, but traces of a pre-Hispanic heritage can still be seen in the islands today.

Prologue

September 1st, 1730, a day like so many other days in Lanzarote, dry, windy, rainless. Night had fallen now on the cornfields of Timanfaya and the corn rippled in the bright moonlight. A faint cooling breeze blew across the overheated land, but that was not what was stirring the corn. The ground itself was in motion, bulging upwards and subsiding again as if some living thing were trying to escape, some wild beast imprisoned underground.

A crack appeared in the dry soil. Foul-smelling smoke billowed out, and suddenly the earth gave way. It had been no wild beast confined underground but a deadly brew of magma and poisonous gases—Lanzarote's evil soul, one might say—which had been searching for a weak point in the earth's crust for a long time. Now it had found one, and a great column of fire shot up in the middle of the fields with an appalling noise, louder than a thousand claps of thunder.

The villagers in the nearest houses stumbled shocked and horrified from their beds, staring in disbelief as their cornfields flared and blazed. The fire spread so rapidly that it seemed like only seconds before whole fields were consumed. There was nothing they could do; water was so scarce in the summertime that there would not have been enough to dowse even a small corner of one field. In the centre of the blackened stubble a monstrous mound was growing under the fiery column, growing higher and higher as the stunned peasants watched. From its peak, red streams began to flow, spreading in all directions, red-hot and smoking, setting fire to everything that was not already ablaze.

Men and women ran to and fro, beating vainly at the burning edges of their fields. All too soon, they realised that not only were their fields lost, but they were going to lose their houses to the blazing red torrents as well. Hardly anyone had the wits to do anything sensible. They were like frightened animals before a bush fire and only a few thought to grab some belongings before their homes began to blaze and crumble in their turn.

The forces of nature were relentless, the islanders' livelihood gone in what seemed like an instant—crops, houses, personal possessions, livestock, everything. They fled. The earth shuddered violently under their feet and the scarlet torrents of lava moved fast. Those who stopped to help any stragglers or who delayed too long to seize a few of their possessions died horribly in the burning tide. Some of those who were speedier on their feet died also, overcome by the fumes and smoke or struck down by the hail of red-hot rocks which followed the initial explosion.

The unexpectedness of the disaster, its awful wholesale destruction, made it only too clear to the doomed villagers that God was punishing them. What terrible sins they had committed they could not tell, but they prayed as they ran—*Oh God, let me live, I repent, I repent, spare me, spare me*—panic-stricken pleas for a mercy which was not forthcoming.

There had been signs, of course, there had been physical signs, but who was there in barren, impoverished, backward Lanzarote to read such signs? The cauldron of impending disaster had simmered and smouldered for years, belching out foul-smelling clouds and trickles of lava from time to time, but those who lived in the west of the island had become accustomed to these demonstrations of lurking malevolence, to feeling the earth tremble beneath their feet. Babies and puppies would wake in the night and whimper during the stronger tremors, but everyone else would turn over and go back to sleep. Till tonight.

Don Andres tolled the bell in the little church in Yaiza, the nearest village to the initial eruption. A forlorn gesture: it was hardly likely that any of his flock could have slept through the noise of the explosions. He asked God every day of the year to send rain to fill their cisterns before they dried up completely;

he asked Him to protect the crops from too much sun and wind; he asked Him also to keep the pirates away as long as possible—but it had not entered the priest's head (and God had not mentioned it to him any more than He had to his parishioners) that a much greater catastrophe was at hand than all these, one which would change the island for ever.

*

The church bell tolled in Arrecife, too, and Milagro woke out of a fitful doze. She had not been sleeping well; her husband—or the man she liked to call her husband—Felipe was away fishing and she was five months pregnant. Her fourth pregnancy, though she was only nineteen, but that was how life was. The baby in her stomach, sensing something untoward even in its cocooned isolation, kicked feebly, and through the glassless window of the small stone hut Milagro could see an unusual, ominous red glow in the sky. A fire, but a really big one. What was there that big which could burn like that?

Pepito, her four-year-old, her only surviving child (life was harsh in Lanzarote), howled with fright; she picked him up to comfort him and went outside. In the streets, men and women surged aimlessly around, hysterical with fear, and the ground beneath her feet quivered as she walked. Pepito had stopped crying and was staring in amazement at the fire in the sky.

Milagro began to make her way down to the port; she felt, though she could not tell why, that they might be safer near the water. Many townspeople were flocking towards the church and she almost fell over a woman kneeling in the street, skirts trailing heedlessly in the dust, swaying on the trembling ground and gabbling prayers, crossing herself over and over like a windmill. Milagro joined the desperate throng but she could hear Don Miguel's habitual thunderings about mortal sin and hell-fire before she got anywhere near the doorway. The priest, standing on the church steps, glared balefully at Milagro.

[11]

'This is God's punishment for the sins of such as you.'

The girl did not reply. She was used to such castigations, but she hesitated all the same. Even black Caterina from the brothel, who had never been known to go near the church, was one of those jamming the doorway, fighting to reach a place of sanctuary. Milagro turned away again; Felipe's boat might have returned, and dying without seeing him again seemed at that moment a greater evil even than eternal damnation.

She reached the harbour, which seemed bizarrely peaceful and deserted, the sea calm and dull as pewter, slapping gently at the rocks. There was no wind tonight and a thick pall of smoke had spread over the whole sky, obscuring moon and stars, giving the scene a grim and lifeless air, heavy with impending doom. There was no sign of Felipe's boat, nor of any of the other fishing boats; the sea was empty, a leaden grey blanket.

'Home, Mama, home.' Pepito pulled at her skirts and she turned reluctantly back towards the town. Every few minutes, there was a rumble like thunder and a dazzling flash of red, lighting up the sky more terribly than the brightest lightning.

Then came an explosion bigger than all the rest. Even here in Arrecife, ten miles or more from Timanfaya, she could feel its power, and she gaped in terror at the flaring western sky. A great fountain of smoke and flames rose up, illuminating the whole town and the hills behind it as she cowered in the street, clutching Pepito so tightly that he screamed. She, too, was screaming, the hot blast burning her face as she watched the familiar landscape crumble and crack and disintegrate, only to reform into a series of hideous, blazing cankers. The lid had come off Hell in Lanzarote.

Chapter I – The Amateur Vulcanologist

A number of years later, on another volcanic island, though one with a less dramatic history than Lanzarote, two men are poking around on a hillside. At least, one of them is prodding the ground with his walking stick, while the other one is standing well back, ready to run at the slightest sign of trouble. He has a handkerchief pressed to his face to ward off the awful fumes of sulphur. They have made their way up the mountain through the trees, which have given way to the black sand and arid wastes of the slopes leading up to the caldera. The rocks are yellow, reeking of sulphur, the choking fumes working their way through Fernando's handkerchief. But his master, Don Rodrigo de Perez y Manzara, Spanish grandee and enthusiastic amateur vulcanologist, does not seem to notice. He crunches his way over the uneven ground, slides down the sand dunes, taps the rocks, prods the fumaroles, and makes copious notes and drawings in his sketch book.

At last, Fernando can bear it no longer. 'Sir, the boat is leaving at six. Perhaps we should make our way back down to the port.'

'Nonsense, we have plenty of time. It only took us an hour to climb up here and it will be much quicker going back down. Look at this fumarole, look how delicate the edges are, like a piece of lace, or a fern.'

He peers into the fumarole, marvelling at the pale yellow tracery of its orifice, and is rewarded with a foetid blast of sulphuric gas. A fragment of rock breaks off under his stick, yellow, very smelly and friable. He bends down to pick it up carefully—in his gloved hand, for it is hot. In a mischievous moment he takes his leather water bottle and pours some water down the smoking cavity. There is a small explosion and Fernando leaps into the air with a scream.

'Sir, sir.' His nerves are fraying by the minute. 'I can see the harbour from here and there are already people going on board. If we miss the boat we shall be stuck here on Vulcano for weeks and you will miss M. Buffon's lecture in Paris.'

Rodrigo sighs. As if in revenge, another blow-hole fires off a blast of steam very close to where he is standing and he jumps back himself. Clouds are gathering on the horizon, the wind is getting up and they will have a lively voyage tonight. Fernando is half way down the hill and breaking into a run— away from the hellish, stinking slopes and towards the safety of the trees below the crater. Prolifically green, they seem to have no difficulty growing in such a hostile environment. Perhaps it is time to go. He stuffs the still warm piece of rock into his leather satchel, already clinking with an assortment of specimens. Santorini, Vesuvius, Etna, now Vulcano, another miracle of geology crossed off the list.

*

The journey to Paris is long and tiresome—a bumpy and sickmaking sea voyage to Naples on a boat little better than a basic trading schooner. Then, much to Fernando's disgust, another hot and stinking day revisiting the lower slopes of Vesuvius. The subsequent journey by land through Italy and France seems interminable, over vile roads, stopping at vile inns full of rats and bedbugs. Bruised all over, bitten by every imaginable insect, when they at last reach Paris, Fernando is seriously thinking of finding a master who wants to stay at home. Why can Don Rodrigo not be content with managing his estates, appearing at court, doing the occasional stint of modest fighting for his king and country, like every other sensible Spaniard? Travelling far and wide in extreme discomfort, climbing reeking mountains, risking a terrible death at the hands of Nature— none of this is is a suitable occupation for a nobleman.

The condesa, Rodrigo's loving spouse, is of much the same mind as her husband's manservant. She sniffs as Rodrigo bursts noisily into the bedroom of their elegant rented hotel on the rue de Rivoli and stares pointedly at his sulphur-stained boots. 'I hope you will be changing before you dine.'

'I am sorry to disappoint you, my dear, but I have to attend M. le Comte de Buffon's reception, so I will not be dining with you.'

'So you have barely returned from your travels and have no time for your wife.'

Rodrigo contemplates his wife's ballooning figure in its ballooning dressing gown. She has never shown the slightest interest in his passion for geology. Or done anything more than submit, sighing, to his exercise of his conjugal rights. Even after several months away, the thought of physical contact with her does not arouse him at all. Anyway, they have three children: he has done his duty and he has no qualms about devoting himself entirely to geology.

The condesa does not give up. 'Surely you are not planning another expedition and wasting all our children's inheritance on more pointless nonsense?'

Rodrigo refrains from reminding her that her own family money is more than enough to support their children. The eldest, no longer a boy but already in his twenties, is defending Spanish land claims in the Americas, while their twin daughters have both, for reasons he has not yet got to the bottom of, elected to become brides of Christ, thereby sparing him the cost of providing them with dowries. He changes his clothes and sets off for his evening's entertainment, dismissing family concerns from his mind.

The evening goes well. M. de Buffon listens to his account of Vulcano with interest, murmurs appreciatively over his sketches and rock samples, and allows Rodrigo to enlarge upon on his latest plans.

'I have heard, M. le Comte, that the eruptions have recently stopped in Lanzarote after six years and I feel sure the island would be more than worth visiting. No one, as far as I know, has paid it the least attention for many years. Everyone believes it to be a barren, unproductive Spanish colony, but

I am sure such a long period of volcanic disturbance must have produced many geological marvels. I intend to go next autumn, when the trade winds are suitable, and I should like to report back to you on what I find there.'

De Buffon nods approvingly. 'Let me know what you find. Six years of volcanic eruptions, what a tragedy that must have been for the population. A volcano is a cannon of immense volume, you know, whose opening is often more than half a league across. This broad mouth of fire vomits torrents of smoke and flames, rivers of bitumen, sulphur and molten metals, clouds of ash and stones. Unimaginable devastation for miles around.'

Rodrigo thinks this a touch poetical but bows to the great man's superior descriptive powers.

M. le Comte expatiates on his theories. 'I shall let you have some rough drafts of mine concerning the causes of such eruptions but, briefly, the subterranean fires can only act violently when they are close enough to the sea that the great volume of water can produce enough force. Lanzarote is a small island, I believe, so there is a more than adequate supply of water surrounding it to fuel the eruptions.'

'I have never thought of such a cause.' Rodrigo finds the theory strange but keeps an open mind. 'Now I come to think of it, all the volcanoes I have visited so far are next to the sea. I shall be sure to explore the matter thoroughly when I get to Lanzarote.'

'You have read Pliny, I take it.'

'Of course. My first introduction to vulcanology. I was made to translate his letters to Tacitus as an exercise in Latin when I was at school. I did not appreciate his prose style but I became fascinated by the subject. I cannot tell you how amazing it was to visit Vesuvius with his letter in my hand, seeing with my own eyes what he was writing about.'

De Buffon sighs. 'Sometimes I wish I had not embarked on such an ambitious project as my *Histoire Naturelle*. The task is so demanding I have no time any more for field work. How I should love to travel to Lanzarote myself, to see what conditions are like there now. You will have to be my eyes, mon cher ami.'

Chapter II – Milagro

A beauty like Milagro did not go unremarked in Teguise. Once the capital of Lanzarote before being superseded by Arrecife, it was rapidly becoming a backward provincial town, but men and women continued to live their lives there, particularly men, who went on behaving as men do everywhere. The youth of Teguise stared at Milagro as she walked down its streets and she even revived long-forgotten sensations in the old men who sat in the shade, waiting for their days to end.

Milagro was beautiful but she was also naïve. It took her some years to realise why men stared at her, why, in church, the whining priest would address his sermons on lust and fornication directly at her. She would cringe with embarrassment, not understanding his words at all, thinking there must be something wrong with her appearance—dirt on her face or a tear in her skirt. Large dark eyes, an unmarked skin, a voluptuous figure—at twelve and then thirteen, she was not aware of these as being assets. She asked her mother once, after a man had pinched her in the market and made a remark which she failed to understand,

'Mama, a man pinched me really hard here,' pointing to her breasts, 'and he said he wanted to take my clothes off. Was I doing something wrong?'

This earned her a slap and no explanation at all.

By the time she was fifteen, she had more or less put two and two together, but still she did not see the point of good looks. They were as much a nuisance as anything, since men would not leave her alone. Her innocence and ignorance were not entirely her own fault; the fact that she was, to all intents and purposes, an only child had much to do with it. Her mother, Doña Constancia, a cold and unfeeling parent with few natural maternal instincts, was thirty-eight when she became pregnant with Milagro. Having seen seven of her nine children—all girls, not a single son among them—die young, she was not eager to bear yet another child at such an age. The idea of starting on motherhood all over again had turned her against the unfortunate baby even before it was born.

The accidental pregnancy was followed by another unpleasant surprise when Doña Constancia's husband was killed three months before the baby was born. He died, like so many men of Lanzarote, defending their crops and their homes against yet another band of pirates—Berbers this time rather than the usual Ottomans. The Ottomans, though the inhabitants of Lanzarote did not know it, were having far too much trouble in other parts of their empire to bother with unprofitable slaving expeditions to far-flung islands, and had left the field free for the Berbers. As far as the islanders were concerned, pirates were pirates; they did not ask them what language they spoke before taking up arms against them.

The pregnant widow gratefully accepted a proposal from Señor Perez, one of the wealthier men of the town and a widower himself. After marrying off his last daughter, he was looking for a housekeeper, and he struck a better bargain than he realised. Doña Constancia proved to be efficient in the house and a surprisingly enthusiastic bed companion, though this did not prevent Perez from lusting after his stepdaughter later on.

Milagro understood only too well that her mother would be glad to see her married and gone and that her stepfather looked on her as a piece of marketable merchandise, though one he would dearly love to sample first. Her cursed beauty again; if she had been plain and flat-chested, he would have left her alone. Mercifully, Perez did not generally dare to do more than ogle her lustfully; he knew only too well that fulfilling his fantasies would result in serious trouble with his wife. In any case, the girl was very useful about the house.

Milagro's surviving older sisters had left home to be married before she could be truly aware of their existence; they had moved to other islands, in fact, so she could not know whether

her mother had disliked and resented them as much as she appeared to dislike and resent Milagro. She was difficult, she was told, but then it was difficult to be the child of such a critical mother, and she would wonder whether her older sisters had chosen to marry men from other islands in order to escape from Doña Constancia. It was not that she was really unhappy, more that she longed for escape from the dreariness of her home life. She fretted with impatience during the tedious round of daily tasks, at being at her mother's beck and call, her only future seemingly that of a breeder of sons for some older man chosen for her by her mother. She dreamed of a life that would hold more than that, one of freedom, though what kind of freedom she was not sure. Her longings were vague, unformed feelings of general discontent.

The few friends that she had, girls of her own age, the daughters of neighbours, in general, seemed to have no such doubts; their inevitable future of marriage and children did not dismay them, and if Milagro ever mentioned her desire for something different, they looked at her as if she were slightly mad. Life was what it was, why try to change it? But then they all came from large families, living in homes swarming with children of all ages, and solitude such as Milagro's was hard for them to understand. Little motherly love came their way either, Milagro would notice: slaps and scoldings were the order of the day for them, too. At the annual Easter reunion with Perez's extended family, an interminable lunch with relatives whose names she did not even know, with stepbrothers and stepsisters stuffing themselves with food at Perez's expense, squabbling and demanding money from their father, giving her sidelong glances as if wondering how much she and her mother were going to make out of him, Milagro felt no desire for the bedlam of normal family life. She would retreat to the peace of her own home with a feeling of relief: no screaming babies, quarrelling relatives or senile grandparents. And a bedroom of her own with a comfortable bed, a bed she did not have to share with anyone else.

How hard it was to be young, she would often think. When she had children of her own, she would make sure she loved them, she would hug and kiss them, not treat them with scorn and contempt.

Her mother's unfeeling ways were not her biggest worry all the time, though; it was more being told every Sunday that she was a sinner. She did not feel particularly sinful and how could she have committed so many sins so young? When she went to confession, she had to think hard what she ought to confess. Stealing an orange from the kitchen in her own home, was that going to send her to Hell? She was told repeatedly to repent impure thoughts but she was not at all sure what they were. The priest's exhortations were confusing more than anything else, and the dutiful repetition of a dozen Hail Marys, into a void as it were, did not seem to be the answer to anything. She did not know, then, that the original sin, the one that was the initial step on the downward path, was one she would not recognise as such until it was too late.

*

It was Felipe's fault. He was the one who changed everything. She was grudgingly sweeping the chaff and dust out of the grain store one morning, daydreaming as usual. A shadow fell across the floor and she looked up to see a young man standing at the door which led into the street. He was tall, oddly dressed, and he smelt of fish. His long hair, tied roughly back from his face, was fair, his lips broad, his skin pale, much paler than her own. He wore a curiously cut shirt, apparently his only article of clothing, which reached down well below his knees, halfway down to his bare and dusty feet. He had a kind of leather sack over his shoulder and carried a bag made of reeds, from which came the smell of fish. He had a long pole too, taller than he was himself, which he leant on as he regarded her unblinkingly from eyes strangely blue in colour, not brown like everyone else's, quite alien. His steady gaze was unnerving and, overcome with shyness, she could not look him in the eye.

'I didn't know Teguise had such beautiful women.'

This made it worse and she felt herself blushing hotly, though not for the usual reason. The young man's compliment was not a tiresome platitude, like those of her stepfather, or the fool that her mother had singled out as a good catch for her—the son of a cabinet-maker even better off than Señor Perez but unmarried at twenty-six, a sure sign that he was not a good catch in everyone else's opinion. She had by now worked out what Perez intended when his arm lingered round her waist as he ushered her out of the door, what the pock-marked cabinet-maker's son wanted when he breathed sweatily in her ear after church.

The young man before her now was undoubtedly having similar thoughts, but her confusion was due to her own feelings. Not to feel revulsion but to be suddenly unable to breathe properly, to have an inexplicable sensation of excitement deep inside her—this was something entirely new.

'My name is Felipe.' He gave her a dazzling smile. 'I've walked all the way up from Arrecife to sell my fish here. We had such a good catch yesterday, no one else down there wanted any more fish. I've been walking since dawn.'

He set his reed bag down on the ground. She did not know it was made of reeds, there were none in Lanzarote; she only knew it was as outlandish as the man himself.

Felipe held up a heavy, meaty-looking fish for her inspection.

'A tuna,' he told her. 'It's good eating, you can feed a whole family on just the one fish. I don't want money, I want to trade the fish for corn and fruit, perhaps some wine too. Is your husband at home?'

He continued to stare intently at her; if her husband was away, he thought, he might be able to prolong the encounter until it could take on a more physical aspect. Women held a fatal fascination for him: he could not see or speak to one without wanting to touch her, to caress her hair, her breasts, to feel her body pressed against him in irresistible passion.

Milagro blushed again, fidgeting from foot to foot, momentarily lost for words.

'I'm not married,' she stammered out at last, 'I'll call my mother.'

'What's your name?' The mother was bound to interrupt them at any moment.

'Milagro. They named me that because my mother thought she was past child-bearing age when she had me.'

She wanted to ask him questions—where did he come from, why was he so strange, with his fair skin and blue eyes, the long pole he carried, the odd word he had used for corn, *gofio*, a word she had only heard used by one of their maids, long dead now—but she turned away to call her mother, to break the spell he seemed to be putting on her. She did not notice the surprise and gleam of anticipation in Felipe's eyes. He had not come up to Teguise to look for a girl, there were plenty in Arrecife, after all, and he wanted to trade the fish. But coming upon an unmarried one, and a beautiful one at that, was too good a chance to miss.

Then the mother was upon them and Milagro was sent back inside. Doña Constancia treated Felipe and his fish to the same suspicious stare, but she had to admit that fish would make a welcome change from eggs and stewed kid or chicken. She haggled briefly over the exchange, though Felipe would virtually have given her the fish in the hopes of getting another look at her daughter.

Doña Constancia must have been a striking woman too when she was young, reflected Felipe as he stowed ears of corn and fruit away in his leather sack—the same wide dark eyes and hooked though shapely nose, not to mention the ample breasts which had most caught his eye. The mother was corseted and stiff where the daughter was soft and round, but the family resemblance was there.

He soon disposed of the other fish, though the ladies down the street had no daughters to compare with Milagro, and came back to lurk near her door. It was firmly closed now but, undaunted, he sat down to wait, sucking on one of the oranges he had obtained in exchange for the fish. His patience was rewarded not half an hour later when she emerged and began to walk in his direction. She was carrying a basket and seemed lost in thought. He leapt to his feet as she drew level with him, startling her considerably.

'I thought you would have gone.' She was blushing once more, and trembling into the bargain. She had made some excuse to leave on the pretext of visiting one of her friends; suffocated by all the new feelings flooding through her, she had felt she must escape for a while, though she had hardly hoped to see Felipe again so soon. She would not have dared to walk round the town looking for him.

'I can't be long, my mother will come looking for me. I shouldn't, I don't...' She was going to say, I shouldn't talk to strange men, but it was as if she knew him.

Felipe surveyed her with renewed appreciation. She was quite tall, not as tall as he was but not a squat little pudding like so many of the girls. Smooth skin unblemished by disease, tinged a delightful pink by her blushes, straight white teeth, perfect voluptuous figure. He halted his catalogue of her more obvious physical attractions—he was not buying a horse after all—and took her arm to walk her down the street, away from the house and any potential interruptions.

'Why do you look so different?' she dared to ask. She knew she should pull away from him, run home as fast as possible, but she was already in his power.

'I'm a Guanche.'

'A Guanche? One of the old people?'

'You've heard of them?'

'Well, Teguise is not a very big place and I know I'm very

ignorant but we had a Guanche maid once and she had hair the same colour as yours.'

'My family come from La Palma. My father came to Lanzarote when I was four. He wanted to go to Spain to make his fortune but he never got further than here. He had been a herdsman in La Palma and that's all he was here, up in Yaiza, and worse off than he had ever been in La Palma. The land is so dry here, he struggled and struggled but his animals kept on dying and so did he, when I was ten. That's why I decided to go fishing, you don't have to worry about it not raining, there are always fish in the sea.'

He slipped his arm down round her waist and Milagro could not bring herself to move away.

'Why didn't your family move back to La Palma when your father died?' She had barely heard of La Palma, the island furthest away from Lanzarote and as remote to her as Spain itself.

Felipe evaded the question. 'Why do you stay here?'

Why did she? She had no thoughts of actually leaving the island; her vague longing for adventure had not taken her imagination further than simply leaving Teguise. The other towns and villages on Lanzarote were foreign enough. She had once been taken down to Arrieta, on the coast, when she was a small child and she had spent the day on the rocks, fascinated by the flowing water, its endless splashing, the coming and going of the waves. It might be nice to live by the sea, she had thought that day, to have this restless, ever-changing pattern to watch. But leaving Lanzarote altogether, to live among people she did not know for the rest of her life, she could not envisage that. Besides, it was, in practice, out of the question.

'How could I leave here? Where would I go?'

Felipe smiled at her ignorance. 'I have my fishing boat, I go everywhere, I can go to Fuerteventura, to Gran Canaria, it's easy.'

'Easy for a man, perhaps.' Milagro was scornful. 'Not

for a woman on her own. A woman can't do as she wishes, she can't go off to another village just like that and move in with strangers.'

'Come with me, then.'

She stared at him in alarm. 'With you?'

'Why not?'

'Of course I can't.' How could she leave Teguise with a man she did not know, whom she had only just met? It was... unthinkable.

Or was it? She tried to suppress her sudden feeling of excitement, a feeling that here was an opportunity to change her life, that the freedom she longed for could become a reality. No, no, the dreams of escape and adventure were only dreams and Felipe just a smooth talker.

But the temptation refused to go away. He had a lot to say for himself, true, but he kept talking, thrilling her in a way she never had been before, telling her about all the other islands, about all the many sights she had never seen, giving her a glimpse of a different life.

'Have you been to Spain, too?' she asked him when he paused for breath.

'Spain? Not yet but I'm going soon, I'm looking for a berth on a trading ship to Cadiz. Then I'll come back for you and then... off to the Americas!'

'You're crazy. It takes weeks and weeks to cross the seas, doesn't it? You can easily get shipwrecked and drown in the middle of the ocean. What a fool I'd be to go with you, to leave my home. I can just see myself, dumped somewhere in a foreign town where no one even speaks Spanish, with you gone off across the sea again, perhaps never coming back.'

Not a bit abashed that she could see through him so easily, Felipe risked a kiss. 'I'm going to take you to Hispaniola, it's one of the most beautiful islands in the Indies—rain every day, trees, flowers, fruit everywhere. There's always work to be had, too.'

She summoned up the strength to pull away from him, frightened by the rapturous feeling his kiss aroused in her. 'I don't want to have to earn my living as a whore in a strange city.'

'Why would you be a whore? You'd be the most beautiful woman on the island and the wife of the wealthiest merchant in the Indies.'

'You're a bigger fool than I thought!' She could not keep the disappointment out of her voice. Kiss or no kiss, she had enough sense to know that dreams did not make vegetables grow or goats produce milk. 'I must go back now, before my mother comes looking for me.'

'Don't forget me, Milagro. You'll be seeing me again.' He took his long pole and used it to vault over the wall and off down the street in great leaps. She had to laugh at his antics and there was little chance of her forgetting him.

*

He did come back, not very often, about once a month or so, sometimes with fish to sell, sometimes with a few coins to buy grain. He would intercept her in the street, persuade her to come and sit with him in some secluded spot. He seduced her, with words at first, fantastical stories of storms at sea, encounters with whales, old Guanche legends of princesses in peril and kings fighting fierce battles with invaders. She did not know whether to believe him or not, but his stories worked their magic on her and she would sit for hours, watching his mouth as he talked, imagining his wide lips pressed against hers.

'Why do you carry that long pole?' she asked him one day. 'What do you use it for on the boat?'

He laughed. 'It's not for the boat. We use poles like that in La Palma when we are looking for lost animals; we can jump over gullies and rocks with it, rather than walk all the way around, and I suppose I've never got out of the habit of carrying it around. You must see La Palma one day, it's not far, just a couple of days at sea if the weather is right. Not like last month, we had a terrible storm when we were out off Fuerteventura. It was night, it had begun to blow a bit but we put the nets out anyway.

'Suddenly this squall hit us, the boat went right over on its side and there was water everywhere. The sail was torn and we were lucky not to lose the mast. We lost two men overboard, we couldn't find them and it took us all night to get the nets back. No fish that night, of course.'

Milagro shuddered; she would never want to leave the island if that was what she would have to go through.

Felipe put his arm around her. 'Doesn't your mother wonder why you stay so long at the market?'

Milagro leant her head on his shoulder and sighed. 'No, she doesn't seem to. Sometimes, I think I don't exist for her, I'm just a nuisance. She's always been like that, she never kissed or hugged me when I was little. All I ever got were slaps if I'd been naughty.'

'I'll make up for that.' Felipe caressed her luxuriant dark hair, pulling it free from its pins. 'You've got such beautiful hair, I've never seen anything like it.'

He buried his face in it and kissed the back of her neck, sending shivers down her spine. The arm round her waist tightened and, as he talked, his hand began gently, so gently, to stroke the curve of her breast. She was powerless to stop him.

Then he broke the spell, jumping to his feet, leaving her breathless.

'I have to go, I'll be back as soon as I can.' Before she could really take in what he had said, he had crossed the road and disappeared.

*

She was so overcome, she could hardly get to her feet. She did not associate the passion he aroused in her with the sinister descriptions of wrongdoing and the dire consequences of immorality she was accustomed to hearing about in church. It never occurred to her that something so wonderful could be wrong; despite all his menaces, the priest never made it clear that sinful sex was a physical pleasure it took great strength of character to resist. She had a vague idea that this was what was meant by impure thoughts, so now at least she had something to confess, but an additional twenty Hail Marys did nothing to quench the fire that Felipe had lit in her.

Felipe came back the next week, to press home his advantage. He had discovered an abandoned hut on the outskirts of the town and now he had little difficulty in persuading Milagro to enter it, so overjoyed was she to see him again so soon.

'There we are,' he said. There was a broken down bed covered with a piece of sacking, and he pulled her down on to it. 'It's much better with no prying eyes.'

He kissed her face, her neck, her breasts, and began to unlace her bodice. His mouth and his hands, and his body, felt hot and hard against her now naked flesh.

'No, no,' she protested feebly, 'you shouldn't be doing that.'

'Why not?' he murmured, his hands curling round her breasts and stroking her nipples until she could not think straight. 'Don't you like it?'

'Oh yes, yes.' She moaned and writhed as he kissed her and her nipples hardened almost painfully under his caressing hands. Then he was lifting her skirts. She was sure she should be telling him to stop but she was quite defenceless.

'I don't know what to do,' she whispered.

'Don't be afraid, let me do everything.'

She was succumbing to his soothing voice and when he put his hand between her legs, she began to tremble with fear, not that he would carry on but that he would stop, that her inexperience would put him off. What he was doing to her, what he wanted her to do, seemed so outlandish at first but then he was pushing inside her and her body was arching itself up to meet his of its own accord.

'What is happening to me?' she cried, and almost fainted from the tide of physical ecstasy which swept through her.

Then it was over and she lay panting on the rough bed, still unable to work out what had really happened. Beside her, Felipe seemed to be trying to catch his breath too, then he was on his feet, pulling down his long shirt.

'We can't stay here too long, someone might find us and tell your mother.' He gave her his hand and she stood up groggily. He helped her to tidy her clothes and the touch of his hands seemed to be setting fire to her once more.

Then he was gone.

She found her way home, dazed with emotion and aching all over, but so deliciously that she longed for it to happen all over again. The idea of granting such liberties to Señor Perez made her flesh creep, but Felipe was quite another matter. She did wonder dizzily how this could be, how it was that she had not wanted to stop Felipe. She stole up to her room, unobserved, to lie down, to try to recreate those incredible sensations. She found she could do it to herself, just rubbing and stroking herself in the right places and thinking of him. She lost track of time completely, until her mother hammered on the door to demand whether she was ill or whether she was going to help with dinner.

Doña Constancia guessed that something was going on when Milagro staggered downstairs looking pale and exhausted, but it did not occur to her that a man was the cause of such distraction. She was not too concerned, the girl was lazy and sulky, always moping around and neglecting her daily tasks, particularly when it came to that time of the month. Spending hours at the market and coming back with the wrong things or nothing at all was not new. The sooner she was married and off her mother's hands, the better.

*

For Milagro, from then on, her stepfather's house was like a prison. Perez was making his interest in her increasingly obvious, it was as if he could smell the sexual desire on her. He pressed himself against her when he passed her in the passage, he pinched her breasts at every opportunity, even when her mother was in the next room. His horrible touch disgusted her even more when she thought of how Felipe could arouse her. She no longer dared to wash or change her clothes unless she knew her mother was close by.

Doña Constancia herself was determined that Milagro should be married off as soon as possible and began serious negotiations with the cabinet-maker. Even before she met Felipe, Milagro had found the idea of marriage to someone she did not love, who had been chosen for her and not by her, distasteful, but now, in her desperate love for this foreigner, a Guanche, a man she hardly knew and hardly ever saw, she felt she would rather die than be forced to share some other man's bed.

If her mother had been more truly interested in her daughter's welfare, if perhaps her sisters had been still at home to talk things over with her, Milagro might have had a chance of saving herself, of finding a middle way between the dumb submission demanded of her and open rebellion. But she was alone. Her mother's coldness was such a barrier between them that she could not even think about revealing her feelings, and the only other women in the house, her mother's maid and a down-trodden kitchen girl, were hardly likely confidants either. She had never been sent to school and had been given servants' tasks from an early age—sewing and mending, making preserves—so sometimes she felt she was neither one nor the other, neither the daughter of the house nor a servant. In any case, she had no example to follow, no one to explain to her what pitfalls love and lust might put in her way.

*

Felipe. He would appear and disappear without warning. Dreamily stirring a pan of boiling fig jam, or mending a torn pillowcase, she would imagine him touching her and let the jam boil over or prick her finger, reducing herself to helpless tears. She would look for him every time she went to the market, heart beating faster if she glimpsed a stranger, going home again with dragging steps and stone cold despair. He invariably did turn up in the end, when she had almost given up hope, but he was so restless—leaping up as soon as they had made love to pace the floor of the shabby hut. She should have recognised such a warning sign, she thought later, but her ignorance let her down again.

'Why are you so restless?' she asked him one afternoon. 'Why are you always talking of going to Spain, to the Americas? Why can't you just stay here?'

'Here? In Lanzarote?' He spat out a date pit scornfully—she had stolen a handful of fruit for him. 'What's here? Nothing. No life, no adventure, nothing but black rocks. I don't intend to spend the rest of my life praying for rain or breaking my back over fishing nets, just to gain the privilege of owning a small stone house, having too many children and earning the right to be buried in the same churchyard as my father. His dreams ended here. I'm not going to let mine end here too.'

She had no answer to that and she was too frightened of losing him to ask if she had a place in his future. In her heart of hearts, she knew this was all fantasy, but she liked to picture herself crossing the sea with him, regardless of the consequences, to start a new life somewhere else, far from the nagging of her mother and the lascivious gaze of her stepfather.

*

Then it all went wrong. She did not bleed one month, or the next one either, her breasts started to swell uncomfortably and she soon realised in horror what was happening to her. She had small chance of concealing her state from her mother. Doña

Constancia found her being violently sick one morning and was not deceived.

'You wicked, wicked girl!' she screamed at her errant daughter, beating her about the head with her fists, tearing at her dress and kicking her in a fury. All that time she had wasted, dismissing the girl as useless.

'To think a daughter of mine has turned into a harlot! Who's going to want to marry you now, with some other man's child in your belly? Wait till Juan hears of this.'

Milagro, cowering on the floor, hands raised to ward off the blows, did not dare to point out to her enraged mother that Juan could well have been the one responsible for her condition, given a little encouragement. She had no choice now, she must run away and go to Felipe. She did not know the name of his boat or where he lived. She would have to escape, to walk down to Arrecife and hope to find him.

Her mother wearied of berating and belabouring her delinquent daughter at last and swept out in search of Señor Perez. Milagro wasted no time. She grabbed the largest basket she could carry and filled it with a few possessions. She had very little that seemed worth taking—her Sunday dress, a pair of extra shoes and some silver jewellery which had belonged to her grandmother. She could hear her mother in the distance screaming at Perez, and she risked sneaking into the larder to take a loaf of bread and a few dates. She had no idea how long it might take to walk to Arrecife. Felipe had said it was not far, just a few hours, but she did not know the way.

*

She left without allowing herself so much as a backward glance, anxious only to get away before Doña Constancia returned with her stepfather, and without encountering anyone who might prevent her from leaving was soon at the city gates. She could not let herself stop to think, to contemplate the boldness of the step she was taking. She knew nothing of Felipe;

she had let herself be seduced by his persuasive talk and irresistible hands and was now a victim of her own folly and weakness. That he might not be overjoyed to see her in her present condition, she dared not admit to herself.

The rugged landscape, its brown and grey rocks laid bare under the hot midday sun, the shadowless road with hardly a tree or even a cactus in sight, did not welcome her as she stepped out of the protection of the fortified walls. The sun struck brassily on her head; even under her big straw hat she winced as she hurried away from the gates, but she could not change her mind now and creep back home. Scorn and physical abuse were all that awaited her there. She set off boldly into the heat, down the dusty road into the unknown. Her life was her own, not her mother's, she told herself with a confidence she was far from feeling; it was up to her to take charge of it.

The elderly guard at the gate was sitting comfortably in the shade; he stared lecherously at her retreating back. He knew who she was, there were not so many people in Teguise after all, and he was curious to know where she was going. To meet that young Guanche, no doubt. It was too hot to do more than leer after her.

*

Only a few hours to Arrecife it might be, but Milagro did not know which way to go when she came to a fork in the road. If she made the wrong decision, she could well be wandering around until after sunset. She took the right-hand fork; it seemed a wider road, the other one being a mere track between arid brown fields. As luck would have it, she had not gone far before she came across a man ploughing, trudging wearily behind his camel, directing the wooden ploughshare as it bumped and lurched through the stony ground. He was old, at least he seemed old to her, his chin stubbled white, his head nearly bald and his face wizened by sun and hard work. He was also, it would seem, deaf, for she had to ask him three times for directions, but he did at last confirm that she was on the right road for Arrecife.

'Go down to the sea and follow the coast. You can't miss it.'

The camel turned its head towards her, curling its lip and revealing its set of unpleasant yellow teeth. It evidently disapproved of her. The farmer looked her up and down, unable to imagine what a young girl like her was doing walking down to Arrecife on her own. He reached into the pouch round his neck and produced a bruised prickly pear which he solemnly presented to her.

'You'll find it a thirsty walk, young lady.' He turned back to his plough, hissing at the camel to get it moving again.

Milagro thanked him for the fruit and hastened on. She glanced nervously behind her from time to time, fearful of seeing a cloud of dust containing an avenging Juan Perez pounding after her on his mule to take her back to retribution, but there was no one else on the road. She passed more arid fields, a few miserable huts round which grew some scrubby vines. The extreme poverty of those who lived outside Teguise had never struck her before, cushioned as she had been from real want by the comfortable position of her stepfather. What might be in store for her with Felipe? Was she going to end up like the poor women she saw, with ragged clothes and bare feet, bent double scratching at the infertile soil, building all those little stone walls to protect their meagre vegetable plots from the hostile sun? Would she too find herself living in a tumbledown camel shed with a broken roof? She almost turned back more than once.

By mid-afternoon, she had reached the sea and she could just make out some houses way down the coast to her right. The sea sparkled at her, the sun glinted dazzlingly off the water. She took off her shoes to cool her tired feet, sitting on the black sand and letting the waves wash over her up to her thighs. Her face was hot and dusty after the long walk and she splashed some sea water over it to get rid of the dust and heat. She had learned as a child not to drink the sea, that day at Arrieta she had tasted the water, spitting out the horrible briny stuff, but she was unpleasantly surprised when the water dried salty on her skin, making her face feel more uncomfortable than it had before. How ignorant I am, she thought as she attempted to remove the salt with a corner of her skirt. If I lived by the sea I would know all about salt water. If she was to survive away from the ease of her home, if Felipe was not in Arrecife, she would be obliged to find work. She would have to learn how to fend for herself very rapidly. She shivered. How could she have been so foolish? A young girl, pregnant and on her own, what chance would she have of surviving?

She ate some of her bread and the prickly pear the farmer had given her. The food gave her enough determination to continue and she trudged along the coast towards the houses she had seen in the distance. It must be Arrecife. It seemed to be quite a large town but so different from Teguise. Houses sprawled along the shore, not fortified in any way, poor-looking hovels built out of scraps of volcanic rock and roofed with palm fronds. However, she could see the tower of a large church above the roofs of some more substantial buildings further on.

It was not long before she came to the port, but she hesitated before going down on to the quays, shy at seeing so many strangers. The harbour was bustling—two fishing boats had just arrived and were berthing alongside several boats already tied to the quay. She assumed they were fishing boats; she had never seen one but, like the picture of the disciples fishing on the sea of Galilee which had pride of place in Señor Perez's best room, the boats had nets hanging up. Their blue and white paint was battered and peeling and the sails the crew were busy folding away were much patched. What Felipe's boat might look like she had no idea, she did not even know whether it was big or small, let alone what its name was. All the boats had their names painted on the side, but she hung back, frightened of interrupting one of the preoccupied sailors.

The ground trembled slightly beneath her feet and when she looked towards Timanfaya, she could see a plume of smoke arising, billowing out as it ascended, tinted pink by the setting sun. She must ask someone soon, it would not be long before dark. She walked timidly along the quay towards where a gang of men was warping a ship alongside with much jeering and cursing, a larger ship than the fishing boats, with dirty black topsides and a shabby unpainted mast ringed with rusty iron bands. She could not see Felipe anywhere.

The scene was totally new to her, fascinating yet alarming in its strangeness. The water of the harbour was bright blue, even though the harbour was now in shadow; little waves raised by the afternoon breeze slapped against the boats and the quay, the craft bobbed up and down making her feel slightly dizzy as she watched them. The ropes creaked and groaned as the men shouted and heaved on the capstans. It all seemed very noisy compared with the tranquillity of Teguise. Seagulls squawked overhead, raucous in a way that land birds never were; even the crows after the seeds in the fields did not make as much noise as the gulls.

The cobbles of the quay were smooth beneath her tired feet and shiny with fish scales. She picked her way carefully through the tangle of debris—nets, old rope and bits of wood, fish bones and scraps of torn canvas—and sat down on a bollard to watch, spellbound, the rhythmic actions of the sweating sailors. One of them happened to turn around and noticed her sitting there. His eyes lit up, as men's eyes always did when they saw her, and she shrank back in alarm as he ogled her. She had learnt to come to terms with that kind of reaction in Teguise, but here, with nowhere to retreat to, she was frankly terrified.

'Hey, lads,' the man called to the other seamen, 'Look what chance has washed up for us.'

He came towards her and she got to her feet, trying not to tremble too obviously.

'I'm looking for a fisherman called Felipe.' She spoke as firmly as she could, trying to face him down. The man was very close to her now and she could smell the sweat on his body. His teeth were broken, those that he had left, his beard matted and his ragged shirt revealed a raw wound on his forearm, which did not seem to have affected his ability to haul on a rope. He laughed, breathing heavily into her face, and tried to maul her breasts. She slapped his hand away with surprising success.

'You must be his little girl from Teguise. For once he wasn't lying, you're the prettiest thing I've seen in a year.'

He lunged at her again but she was ready for him and evaded his grasp once more.

'Please, which is Felipe's boat? Is it here?'

'Come with me, I'll show you where to find him.'

He seized her arm and drew her towards his companions who had all stopped work to watch. She could not get free this time and was terrified of what might happen if she were to be dragged into the group of eager men. More were coming along the quay, attracted by the disturbance, but one of them, she saw with infinite relief, was actually Felipe. When he realised, in some surprise, who was at the centre of the commotion, he wasted no time in disposing of the ruffian who had hold of Milagro with a well-aimed kick and escorted the distressed girl away from the crowd of sailors. They muttered in disappointment but let the couple pass.

*

Milagro was on the verge of collapse—the long walk, the strain of confronting the rough sailors, her pregnancy had all taken their toll; she had never before felt so fragile and Felipe had to hold her up. She did not know how to break the news to him either; all the way down from Teguise, she had fought shy of imagining what she was going to say, fearful of hearing his certain rejection of her. He would take to his heels, leaving her alone on the quayside, at the mercy of the loutish sailors.

Felipe's initial reaction to her appearance was one of delight; to have a girl friend like her readily available in Arrecife was definitely preferable to having to resort to the whorehouse as he normally did, or to the wives of absent fishermen, with the attendant risks that implied; but there had to be a catch. If she had come to seek him out, apparently on her own, there was something going on, something not quite right, and his agile brain ran rapidly through the possible reasons for her presence.

'What brings you to Arrecife? Is your mother here too?'

Milagro turned away from him before she told him, not wanting to see the scorn and derision in his eyes.

'I'm on my own, I've run away.' She had to get it out as quickly and plainly as she could before her courage evaporated altogether. 'I'm pregnant, I'm going to have your baby.'

There was no possible way round the truth.

Aahh. Why had he not seen this coming?

'You're pregnant? How...?' His first reaction was one of fright. He was going to say how can you be but of course he knew only too well. She was going to ask him to marry her, he was sure of it, and that was quite out of the question. It did not actually occur to him more than fleetingly to send her packing; he was not likely to admit it, even to himself, but he was in love with the girl. His long silence so unnerved Milagro that she began to cry.

'I'm so sorry.' She could not stop tears pouring down her cheeks. 'I shouldn't have come here, they always say men don't like to hear such things but I didn't know what else to do. My mother beat me and they would have married me off to some awful man, just to get rid of me. I had to take a chance and come to you, even though you don't want me any more.'

'Nonsense, my darling.' Felipe put his arm round her,

surprising himself by saying words he did not expect to say. 'Of course I still want you. It's such a surprise, that's all.'

He was trying to think. What *was* he to do with her? First of all, he would have to find some sort of lodgings; she could hardly be expected to sleep on the deck of the fishing boat and there was no question of her staying with one of the rough girls who normally frequented the harbour, who would be bound to tell her more about him than he preferred her to find out, at this stage at least.

No use asking the priest for guidance either. Don Miguel, a sour censorious man with little sympathy for the personal problems of his parishioners, had no time for those who did not obey God's laws and would merely lecture Felipe on the dire consequences of transgression, rather than coming up with some practical solution to the most immediate problem of where Milagro could lodge. Felipe's current landlady, a fisherman's widow, would probably take her in for the night, and allow her to share Felipe's bed, though she had hopes, only thinly disguised, of doing so herself on a permanent basis.

He led the girl away from the harbour, round the back of the harbour offices and customs buildings to where there was a patch of waste ground, plans for the future rushing through his head.

'I'm sure you can share my room for tonight. The house belongs to a widow and she needs the money.'

Milagro looked aghast, she had not thought of that. 'I've got no money.'

'I have,' Felipe reassured her, 'and tomorrow we can find somewhere else and get some work for you too. You can't mend nets, I suppose?'

Milagro's face fell. 'Of course I can't, I've never even seen one. I might be able to mend sails, though, I've always been good at needlework.'

'There's not much fancy embroidery on a sail, you know.'

The mockery in his voice brought her close to tears again,

but there was a gleam of hope; he had not turned her away, everything was not yet lost.

'We'll find you something, there's always work to be done and we'll get a place to live, just the two of us.' His imagination expanded into an idyllic picture. 'We'll have a house of our own, we'll grow vegetables, we'll have a goat. It'll all be fine, you'll see.'

He had recovered from the initial shock of her announcement; nothing could perturb him for long and he could see the future stretching out pleasantly before him: a woman, a little house, no more scratching around having to fend for himself every time he returned to Arrecife. They were some way from the harbour now and no one seemed to be in sight. He pulled her down on to the ground behind an outcrop of tufa, kissing her hard and squeezing her breasts till she cried out with pain and pleasure. As always, she could not resist him, as always she was instantly swept away by the rising tide of physical ecstasy he aroused in her. She felt the ground rough against her back, stones dug into her buttocks and shoulders as he pushed her skirts up round her waist but she did not care. Not a time for prayer, she thought hazily as she felt the wonderful sensations flooding through her, but the words came anyway: please, God, let him want me forever.

The fisherman's widow, a pale exhausted woman, worn out with childbearing and the struggle of existing without a husband, surveyed Milagro bitterly. She had no chance with Felipe now, not with such a girl, young and fresh, knowing nothing of the vicious treatment that life could hand out. She had five children herself and her situation had been on the verge of desperate even before her husband drowned. It showed in her face, in the dark circles under her eyes, her sagging figure, her hair grey before she was thirty. She swallowed her resentment and allowed Milagro to share Felipe's bed that night in exchange for the few extra coins which she sorely needed.

*

Milagro could not sleep at all that night. She had never shared her bed with anyone before, let alone a man, and their brief frenzied couplings in Teguise had been nothing like this night-long orgy of lovemaking. Felipe himself fell asleep at last but she lay awake, unable to come to terms with the strangeness of her circumstances, racked by feelings of guilt, amazed at her own rashness in leaving her comfortable home so precipitately. It was as if she was suddenly living someone else's life, hearing an unfamiliar story of which she did not yet know the end.

She could not share Felipe's airy confidence that all would be well. Finding work might not be so simple and she was beginning to realise what a privileged position she had given up; instead of being one whose family employed servants, she would most likely be one of the servants herself or, like the unfortunate widow, find herself mending nets far into the night by the light of one inadequate candle, just to pay for her children's food.

Children. During the last few hours she had deliberately put out of her mind her current predicament and her woeful ignorance. She had never had to look after a younger brother or sister, never been in a house when children were born, she had no idea at all of the problems of childbirth and raising children. All her experience had been second-hand and she was still a child herself in many ways. Her survival during the next few months had to depend on her own efforts to adapt to a new way of life; she sensed without anyone having to tell her that Felipe would be of little practical help and she had not the slightest idea how to start going about anything. She had no choice now, she thought, staring wakefully at the broken roof above her; she wanted a new life and now she had got it. There was no going back—she had to go on.

Chapter III – Her Life

The next weeks were the hardest she had ever known. Her impulsive decision to flee had not taken her further than finding Felipe and convincing him to let her stay in Arrecife despite her pregnant condition. Now life had changed overnight, she had her freedom but it was so bewildering that she had to force herself to get up in the morning in order to try and make sense of what she must do.

She did not know Felipe at all—she was living with a stranger, learning everything about him all at once, good points and bad, trying to adapt herself to someone else's life, one utterly alien to her own former existence. She had had so little idea of what a fisherman's life involved that she had not even known he would be away at sea for days, perhaps weeks on end. The boat was not his, she discovered very soon, and he could not come and go as he pleased. She was quite dumbfounded the first time he left her. She had known he was going but his airy goodbye, a brief kiss and a 'see you next week' took her totally by surprise. It was still dark when he left and she lay weeping helplessly till gone daylight, unable to contemplate even getting out of bed.

'What do I do now?' She had wanted a new life, now she had got it but she was completely at a loss. She would wake up, alone, with a sense of panic till, eventually, common sense took charge and she answered her own question—do what you will do every day till he comes back. Get up, get dressed, tidy the house, mend sails, mend nets or go down to the port to look for more work. She was used to work, but not to her sudden poverty—the lack of any of the comforts she had taken for granted in Teguise, the gruelling daily grind necessary for survival in a totally strange place. She had in fact little time for regret; nevertheless, at night in bed on her own, she would lie awake wondering what would become of her, and the child inside her, if she could really survive.

She had to overcome her shyness, force herself to walk the quays, asking strangers if they needed any sail repairs, any clothes made or mended, having to repel the overbold advances of the sailors—pregnant or not, she still attracted leering glances. Going to the market was, if anything, worse; she was one of the poor now and she saw how the better-off, beady-eyed matrons of the town scrutinised the poorer women, as if they had no right to be there amongst respectable folk.

Women like her mother. It puzzled her that her mother never came looking for her, that she had apparently been left to her fate. Days turned into weeks without any sign of pursuit or recrimination. She did not know whether to be glad or sorry; such a scene would ensue if she did appear, yet the thought that her mother no longer cared what happened to her daughter nagged at Milagro. She had been desperate to escape from her mother's domination but it was nevertheless something of a shock to find that Doña Constancia seemed to have abandoned her entirely. Hard work was the only answer and luckily there was plenty of that, leaving her little time to reflect on her own foolishness; though she shed not a few tears, sitting alone, spending long discouraging hours pushing a needle through stiff, unyielding sailcloth, so unlike the fine household linen of her former life in Teguise.

Felipe had found them a deserted hut, with rough walls fashioned out of lava and at least half a mendable roof; there were not a few on the outskirts of Arrecife, huts built by eager immigrants from Spain who soon found the life too hard and left for other, greener islands or simply died from discouragement.

Milagro spent many hours making it habitable, diligently levelling the rough floor and inexpertly rebuilding the fire-place, while Felipe repaired the roof with palm branches and made some primitive furniture. There was plenty of rain that autumn, but carrying the heavy buckets of water from the big cistern in the square to their own small one at the back of the hut, a task for men servants in Teguise, she more than once felt she had fallen as low as she could go. She could not manage a full bucket herself in the end, she was terribly afraid of harming the baby; Felipe would always help her if she asked him but he often forgot.

She was surprised to discover how fragile a man was. Felipe was physically strong, able to cope with the rigours of fishing life, and more than able to wheedle a favour out of some reluctant housewife; but he was oddly childish when things went wrong and if she did not press him to do some obviously necessary task, mending the roof or fetching water, he would wander off and she would discover him talking to a neighbour or in the tavern. He had even less idea than she did of the many tedious small details of everyday existence, of how many tiresome chores had to be got through to have enough to eat, to sleep comfortably, to avoid sliding down into total destitution.

Milagro had no servants to give orders to, she was both mistress and servant now, and realised how protected she had been from the more unpleasant aspects of life when she lived in Teguise. Her many reluctantly acquired, household skills were of little use in her present circumstances—she could mend and keep linen spotless but they had no linen, she could cook and make preserves, but what use was that when there was nothing to cook except fish and corn, no fruit except prickly pears and dates? The oranges and pineapples which Señor Perez always bought were completely beyond their means, the vegetables she was trying to grow in the hard soil outside their hut would not sprout for many months. Felipe sometimes brought home a loaf of fresh bread; one day he brought oranges, a whole sack of them—she did not dare to ask where he had got them. Otherwise it was fish, always fish because it was free.

She spent hours on her hands and knees in her so-called garden, picking stones out of what little soil there was, building them into the protecting walls needed to guard the feebly sprouting plants from the wind and keep in the moisture. The ever-present prickly pear grew in profusion nearby and she had transplanted a fig sapling which was showing every sign of flourishing but they could not expect it to bear fruit till next year. She was having to learn so many new things but at least she was free—though she had to work so much harder than she had had to in Teguise, she was answerable only to herself.

They were better off than many of the families around them, families with too many sickly children, women worn out by want and childbirth, men feckless and hopeless, living from hand to mouth. Felipe was feckless himself, a fanciful storyteller and a great womaniser (he had managed to conceal this from Milagro fairly successfully), but also a hard worker when he had to be, and a lucky fisherman.

*

Milagro was treated coolly at first by the fishermen's wives and the sluttish girls who saw to the unattached men; she had to prove that she was not just a fine lazy lady from Teguise. Her needlework was at least welcome when it came to mending sails and the married men came to be grateful to her: her presence kept Felipe from sniffing around their own wives and daughters.

She was just the girlfriend, though, the silly young thing who had got herself pregnant; she had been quite wrong in assuming that Felipe would ask her to marry him when they set up house together.

Living in sin, not going to church was the strangest part of her new life; her state of sin, unconfessed, soon to bear a child in sin as well, kept her awake at night, often wondering vaguely if lightning might strike her, if the ground, already murmuring and grumbling to itself, might open up and precipitate her straight into hell. She dared not confide these extravagant thoughts to Felipe and concealed her disappointment as best she could. The religion which had meant so little to her in Teguise suddenly took on a new importance.

She went to church the Sunday after Felipe left her for the first time, but it was not a comforting visit. The priest did not welcome her at all.

'Why do you pollute this holy place with your sinful presence?' were the first words he said to her as she hesitated at the cracked wooden door of the run-down church. It was nothing like as grand as the church in Teguise, but the priest, Don Miguel, was imposing and daunting in a way that the priest in Teguise had never been. Tall, gaunt, bearded, his flashing eyes seemed to see right through to her soul—her guilty soul.

'Your wickedness is as evident as your swollen belly. Repentance is the only way you will be allowed into God's holy presence and I can see little sign of that in you.'

Chastened, she crept away, though she did dare to return and hover outside the church from time to time when she was sure that Don Miguel was firmly inside.

She and Felipe were not the only ones on the fringes of the community. An odd-looking man passed by one day and paused to help her dig out a particularly well-embedded lump of rock in order to plant the fig sapling. El Moro, they called him, she found out, though he was not in fact a Moor but a Turk. His dress was much more peculiar than that of the Guanches, his flowing belted robe and big turban were so extraordinary that she stared at him, quite forgetting to thank him for his efforts. The turban was especially intriguing, she imagined him winding and winding it every morning, getting it just so. There must be more material in it than in her own skirt. His face was different too, dark eyes and darker skin, a heavy black moustache and a large hooked nose. A forbidding-looking man altogether and she could not think why he should have stopped to help her. And he had a limp, he walked in a curious screwed way, not with an effort, it was just that his leg seemed to be at the wrong angle. Few people spoke to him, she noticed later, and those that did would do so almost furtively. She asked Felipe about him.

'El Moro? No one knows where he came from or why he stays here. His story is that he was captured by pirates and they left him behind here because he had a broken leg, but most people think he was a pirate himself. He told me once he came from Turkey.'

'Turkey? I've never heard of such a place.'

Felipe did not like to admit his ignorance. 'I've never been that far myself; it's a long way away, full of pirates, men who aren't even Christian. He may be in league with the pirates himself, a lot of people think he is, he spies for them and tells them where to find children to take into slavery. They're always after children, you know. In return they bring him things from Africa, herbs for spells and suchlike.'

Milagro shuddered, thinking of her own child which would be born in a few weeks.

'I've got no quarrel with him,' went on Felipe casually, 'he seems agreeable enough. He's a doctor, at least he has many medicines, though not everyone's prepared to risk taking them.'

He did not think it necessary to tell Milagro that he himself had had recourse to El Moro, who had successfully cured him of an unfortunate infection, the result of an encounter with a girl on a German trading ship, passing through with a cargo of women on its way to spread the pox among the inhabitants of Hispaniola.

There were a number of things he did not think it necessary for Milagro to know. She had inevitably found out that the fishing boat was not his, that he was just one of the crew, but he had still been able to hint to her that he had a part share in it. He did not deceive her out of malice; he was by no means the only man around for whom truth and fiction were not too distinguishable and he really wanted Milagro to be happy with him, to believe in his prosperity and ability to provide for her.

[48]

Such a change had come over his life: a home to come back to, a beautiful smiling girl, a good meal and a comfortable bed. No more taking a chance in dilapidated lodgings or between the legs of one of the sluts around the port.

*

Milagro had worked so hard to make the little house welcoming for him; he appreciated her efforts though of course he neglected to tell her so. Over the months, she traded her skills as a seamstress for pots and pans, for a couple of hens; she begged a sagging mattress from the grocer's wife and re-stuffed it with some good straw, and she saved what little money she earned from mending sails till she could buy some cheap cotton material for a new shirt and breeches for him. He did not feel he was knowingly taking advantage of her, and she was happy living with him—she said so; she loved him to make love to her—she said that too.

Felipe was not much given to serious reflection or planning. In his view, things seemed to happen whether one made plans or not and worrying about the future ruined one's enjoyment of the present. A solution to most problems would always present itself in due course. The fact that this way of thinking had led him, at fifteen, into a disastrous marriage in his home village with a woman a number of years older than himself, and that he might very well be in the process of wrecking Milagro's life as well, did not occur to him.

Religion he had no time for and marriage was a meaningless ceremony. He had been forced to stand in church mumbling words he did not mean, making promises he never intended to keep, binding himself falsely to a woman he had never loved in the first place, and he had no intention of going through all that again, with Milagro or anyone else. He was never going to need to tell Milagro that he was already married, with any luck, and anyway Inés was miles away. He was easily able to dismiss her from his mind all the time he was in

Arrecife and there was no reason why Milagro should ever find out about her. The future was bound to take care of itself.

*

Milagro was impatient for the baby to be born, for her new life to be complete. As the weeks went by, free from her mother's restrictions, any feelings of doubt and dejection during Felipe's long absences at sea were short-lived, soon allayed by looking forward to his return. She knew he would return now, it was not like it had been in Teguise, agonising endlessly over whether she would ever see him again. He did not linger in the tavern when he came back either, like most of the other men, married or unmarried—as soon as the boat had docked, he would rush home to her, urge her to drop whatever she was doing and come to bed with him right away.

She was just as obsessed with him. She could never resist him, even during the last few weeks of her pregnancy; it made all the grinding toil and battle for survival worthwhile. Sometimes she would not go down to the port when the boats were expected in; she would tease him by hiding at home, waiting to hear his footsteps. He would fling open the door and seize her in his arms, kissing her lips, her neck, her breasts, dragging her down on the bed without bothering to undress, while she would tremble and cry out in delight as he pushed himself into her. She did not care that he usually smelt of fish, that his hands were rough from handling nets; her own hands were calloused enough now, hardly what they used to be when she lived in luxury in Teguise. Then she would shake the fish scales out of the bedding next morning, smiling to herself as she remembered how they got there.

It was true she wanted him less as she grew bigger, the weight of his body on hers becoming almost unbearable and diminishing her desire. He would make her lie on her side then, so that he could have her from behind, and she dared not refuse him, uncomfortable though she found this, lest he went elsewhere.

*

With a remarkable instinct for good timing, the baby made its appearance when Felipe was in Arrecife; a helpful and considerate Felipe (another surprise) who fetched the midwife and calmed her fright at the unexpected pain, who was over the moon to find he had a son. He had to leave a few days later, of course, though he swore he would be back for Christmas. Of course, again, he was not, but Milagro did not mind. She had her own family now, she need not regret her old one, she had her house, her son, her man. Not husband yet but surely that would come, Felipe was so delighted with his son. She was the mistress of her house and her life, answerable to no one except Felipe, and she had her baby, whom she loved and who loved her. It would not have been like that with the cabinet-maker's son; she would most likely have exchanged the cold indifference of her mother for the sharp criticisms of a mother-in-law.

Her baby. Named Felipe like his father, Pepito for short, though as yet unbaptised by the uncooperative priest. She lay in bed after Felipe had left, holding the baby tightly, her most precious possession, as the wind howled and wrenched at the branches on the roof. It was not entirely Felipe's fault that he did not return in time: the storm came in from the south-east, wrecking those boats already in harbour and covering the whole town with red sand from the desert over the water. Rain pelted down for two days; not an unmixed blessing this time, it was so loaded with dust and sand that it turned the streets into a quagmire and swamped her vegetable patch with sticky orange mud.

Milagro slipped into the church on Christmas Eve to pray for Felipe's safe return; she kept well to the back, hoping Don Miguel would not notice her and take her publicly to task for her sinful way of life. She could not stay long and Pepito began to wail; he was by no means the only noisy baby at midnight mass but she saw people staring at her, the unwed mother, the Guanche fisherman's woman, the one who had fallen from

[51]

grace. She felt she ought to ask the priest to hear her confession, but her courage failed her. Her prayers were still answered; the fishing boat came back on New Year's day, safe and sound, having sought refuge in Playa Blanca in the south during the storm.

Her scorching desire for Felipe rapidly returned after the baby's birth and she was soon pregnant again, and again a year later, two tiny feeble babies, a boy then a girl, neither surviving for more than a few weeks. They seemed to lack some vital spark, the instinct to cling to life was missing in them. As the second lifeless little body was buried by the scowling priest (he would have liked to deny them both Christian baptism and burial if he could) Milagro felt despair very close at hand. Her babies had inherited a family weakness, they were doomed like so many of her own dead siblings had been. She could not share Felipe's confidence, his perpetual optimism. The deaths upset him certainly, he wept for his dead children, but his grief was short-lived.

'We've got one healthy baby,' he would say in answer to Milagro's tears, throwing a chuckling Pepito into the air and catching him again, and he never failed to return loaded with little presents—a clay toy or a wooden ball—and presents for her too, a necklace or a curiously decorated pot, explaining that they had stopped in Fuerteventura for water and he had bought them off an old woman or traded some fish for them. She never thought to question why he should need to explain where they came from.

*

It was the summer of 1730, four years since her flight from Teguise, and Milagro found herself pregnant once more. Felipe was delighted as usual; Pepito ought to have a little brother or sister and he was sure this time the baby would survive, but Milagro could not rejoice. She dreaded burying yet another baby, hastily baptised as it lay dying so that it would not be a lost soul like its parents.

She longed to ask Felipe outright why he did not want to marry her, she wanted to feel free to go to church openly every Sunday instead of furtively while Felipe was off fishing, hiding to avoid the stern eye of the priest; she wanted Don Miguel to greet her in the street with a smile instead of a frown. He had relented to the extent that he would allow her to sit at the back by the door on a broken chair, and she forgot how empty all the ceremony and ritual had seemed to her before she left home, how pointless the routine confession and repentance had once been. The notion that her new way of life was immoral, that her children were dying because of this, passed through her head more than once, but it was only while Felipe was away that such thoughts had any chance of taking hold.

She could not work out Felipe's aversion for the church. It was not because he was a Guanche, that he was different from the other people in Arrecife; there were not a few Guanche families, living normal lives, not shunned by Don Miguel or their neighbours. They did not mix so much with their fellow-citizens, the ones of Spanish descent; they had their own customs and modes of dress and their speech contained many odd, old-fashioned words, but they were dutiful churchgoers, or so it seemed to Milagro. When she did go to Mass, she would always see them there, sitting in a row together, but strange, almost as strange as El Moro in a way, their different garments and features distinguishing them from the Spanish members of the congregation. They were different in a way that Felipe was not, and she came to understand why Felipe might feel he had little in common with them except ancient racial ties, why he avoided contact with them as much as he did with Don Miguel.

His Guanche past had more significance for her than it did for him. She wanted to be part of his life, really a part of it, and unless this included his Guanche origins she would still be the outsider. All the stories he had told her when they first met, the legends, the mysteries, the Guanche people's battle for survival, she had listened to them spellbound and they still fascinated her as much as ever, but now they were together on a permanent basis, he seemed to want to forget all that. To Felipe, the Guanche were hopelessly old-fashioned, their idiotic old habits drove him mad. That was one of the problems with Inés and all her brood, the old ways trapped him as much as marriage did, they bound him to something he didn't want. He had broken free by going off fishing and he was not going to go backwards, either back into the past or back into the suffocation of routine family life. He did not say any of this to Milagro.

Milagro made some friends, but not such friends as she had had in Teguise—girls she would not even have spoken to once, the girls from the tavern, the sort of girl she hoped she would never have to become herself. They were always hanging round the port and greeted her cheerfully when she came down to look for work; perhaps, she thought uneasily with that obscure nagging desire for respectability rising to the surface again, because they did consider her to be like them.

*

Lourdes, Isabel and Caterina—Lourdes and Isabel from Tenerife, Caterina black, dark ebony black with a skin that shone with a reddish bloom in the sun. She had been rescued by a fisherman after jumping overboard from a slave ship, she hardly spoke any Spanish and she had had little choice: whoring or starvation. Yet she was always cheerful, eyes and teeth flashing as she made the rounds of the port when a new boat was in. The other two were less light-hearted, Isabel particularly was frequently sick, and poxed, rumour had it. I am better off than them, Milagro would often think; if I had to sell myself every day just to eat, I would rather starve. With Felipe, even not married, she was saved from such a fate.

Respectability. If the choice was between respectability and love, when it came down to it, she would rather have love.

But love was not so simple. She loved Felipe, she was desolate when he went away and she could not come to terms with the extraordinary intensity of her sexual feelings for him. She would lie awake at night when he was not there, tossing and turning—the aching wetness between her legs, the hardening of her nipples each time she imagined his touch, tormented her so much that she frequently could not sleep. When he did come back to her, the physical relief was like an explosion, she would sometimes think she was turning into a sort of wild animal. She could not believe that respectable people acted like this.

She should have saved those nights and days with Felipe, stored up the memories, preserved them like the fruit she used to bottle in Teguise for later, darker days, but she did not know that then.

*

Respectability. One can't have everything, she mused one July day, happiness is what counts. This respectability was what she had originally fled from—respectability was marriage to a solid tradesman and solid everyday prosperity but lack of excitement, lack of love and passion too, all the things which her life with Felipe offered her. She was not so well that morning, she had woken with a fever and some kind of rash as well as the inevitable queasy morning stomach, but she ignored these, thinking only of Felipe's return in a few days. She sang to herself tunelessly as she hung out the washing—there had been a rainstorm during the night, a very unusual occurrence at that time of year, so she was taking advantage of the unexpected extra water supply. She was just draping the clothes carefully over the barer branches of the fig tree, now several metres high, so that they would not blow away before they dried, when her joyful mood was abruptly shattered. A voice sounded behind her.

'So this is how you've ended up. I hear that useless

Guanche fisherman has refused to marry you.'

Doña Constancia. Milagro was too amazed to speak; she held on to a branch, feeling she might faint, gaping at her mother. Doña Constancia had aged: her hair was very grey now under her broad straw hat and just four years had given her many more wrinkles than Milagro remembered, but she glared at her delinquent daughter with as much ferocity as ever. She held her fine linen skirt and petticoats fastidiously away from the muddy, sticky mess left by the rain, her shoes were already stained beyond redemption by the brown muck. She scrutinised her daughter—the tattered dress, the mean-looking hut, the sickly appearance of the girl herself.

'You've not made much of things, have you? Too proud to come home, I suppose. We could have found you a decent husband in spite of the child, if only you'd stayed. You were still pretty then.'

Milagro was dumbstruck. At her mother's words, she saw herself through her mother's eyes—an old worn-out faded dress, untidy hair tied back with a ragged ribbon. If Doña Constancia had aged then so had she; successive pregnancies had made her breasts droop, stretched her stomach. She had no looking glass now but she did not need one to know that the girlish bloom had gone from her face. She was so tired all the time, heavily pregnant, with a naughty toddler, that she would neglect her appearance when Felipe was not there to see her.

Pepito was wearing her out. Her only surviving baby, she loved him to desperation but this seemed to make him even more wilful and uncontrollable. He would run off and make himself a nuisance to the neighbours or find his way down to the harbour, whence he would be brought back by some short-tempered sailor. She could do nothing with him. When Felipe was home, he did not discipline the child; he was there for too short a time to do more than indulge him, ride him around on his shoulders down to the port to see the boats or to the market to waste money on some unnecessary trifle. Pepito became irritable with her, the one who said no all the time, the one who tried to make him behave. Already, though barely four, he was extraordinarily like his father and she sometimes got the impression that he was just as wayward, that he would refuse to obey her unless it suited him. She had few illusions about Felipe's character after their four years together, though she did not love him any the less.

Hearing an unfamiliar voice, the little boy appeared in the doorway of the hut, regarding Doña Constancia with curiosity and suspicion, sizing her up as friend or foe. Milagro was relieved to see that he was moderately clean, his feet were covered in mud but he had not been rolling in the ashes of the fireplace or digging up the floor again. She took his hand and drew him towards her.

'This is Pepito.' She recovered her voice and returned her mother's stare defiantly. 'Your grandson.'

'I've had enough of children.' Doña Constancia twitched her skirts out of reach of the child's clutching fingers. 'Don't think I came down here to see how you've added to the family. Juan had some business in Arrecife and I wanted to buy some cloth, otherwise I'd never have come.'

She looked pointedly at Milagro's stomach. 'You've another one on the way, I see.'

Nothing escaped her mother but Milagro refused to be brow-beaten; she straightened up, letting go of Pepito who instantly ran off to kick at a stray cat, and stared her mother down with a confidence only partly assumed.

'I'm managing perfectly well. I have my own life now, I'm not a child any more.'

'So I see.' Doña Constancia strode into the hut unasked and looked around her. She was almost disappointed: though the hut was small and very shabby, the floor was swept, the bed was made and the few pots and pans stacked in an orderly way. Poverty yes, but not the squalor she had been certain she would find.

She swung round to face her daughter who glared at her defiantly. 'You've hardly improved your position in the world though, have you? Still unwed, two children, it's surely only a matter of time before you end up on the streets.'

'And where would I have ended up if I had stayed in Teguise?' Rage gave Milagro more courage than she used to have when faced by her mother. 'Married, no, *traded* to a man of your choice after your husband had had his way with me?'

'No!' The accusation astonished Doña Constancia. 'No! Juan would never do that.'

'Oh yes he would. You never saw it, did you? You don't know him as well as you think you do.'

Doña Constancia flung a purse of money on the table and left without saying another word, considerably shaken by Milagro's revelations about Juan Perez. After some four years of exasperation and frustration at Milagro's bold escape from her sphere of influence, recent months of reluctant deliberation had caused curiosity to get the better of her. She should have stayed away.

Milagro watched her go. The expression on Doña Constancia's face boded very ill for her stepfather, and a feeling of small triumph took the sting out of her fury. Her mother's cold and contemptuous behaviour, unchanged with the passing of time, made her come within an inch of hurling the purse after her but, weighing it in her hand, she managed to swallow her pride. She needed it; it meant new clothes, more seeds, perhaps even a kid. If they had a goat, they would have their own milk and cheese. She had to keep it; better that than obvious charity, begging and bargaining in the marketplace, pleading for small favours.

*

It was even more annoying to discover how much her mother's disdainful visit had given her new energy. She would not let herself be caught out in such disorder again. Above all, she swore to herself, she would never sell her body. Doña Constancia's prediction that she would end up on the streets had rankled the most. She had been prepared to sell her daughter, for what was an advantageous marriage if not a sale? Milagro's good looks and presumed ability to provide a man with an heir in exchange for material comforts—a good bargain in her mother's opinion though an unacceptable one for her. After her years with Felipe, sharing her bed with a man she did not love, some lecherous old fool like Juan Perez for example, who would paw her breasts with podgy hands and force himself into her with or without her consent, was even more terrible to think about than it had been when she was fifteen.

She counted the money: more than Felipe could earn in a month. She ignored her queasy stomach and feverish head and set about tidying herself up, spending the next few days sewing and mending without stopping. She also gave Pepito a couple of well-deserved slaps, which surprised him so much he actually behaved himself for a while; at least he did not pester his mother or make such a nuisance of himself as he usually did.

It was ten days before Felipe returned and she did not tell him of her mother's visit; he never bothered to enquire what she had been doing during his absences, not that she had much to tell him generally, in any case, and he took the appearance of a young goat, hobbled resentfully close to the house but well away from the young fig tree, to be a matter of course. Milagro determined to keep her humiliation by her mother to herself.

*

It was the hottest time of the year and water was very short now; the product of the recent rain shower had evaporated in a few hours from the parched ground. The spring at Famara in the north, the only one worth bothering with in the whole of the island, had practically dried up, though no one guessed why except possibly El Moro. Just another scheme on the part of the island to make life hard for its inhabitants, everyone thought.

The ground stirred and grumbled; in Timanfaya, a field of corn suddenly caught fire when flames spurted out of the ground, but no one gave that too much thought either.

Milagro and Felipe lay together naked on the hard bed the night he returned, soaked in sweat after making love for several hours. She had quite recovered from her fever and responded passionately to his demands, insisting that he make love to her over and over again, despite the tenderness of her breasts and her swollen belly. She had a premonition that their love would not last, that the constant rumbling under the earth signalled some appalling disaster, that Felipe was tiring of her.

Why, she could not say; perhaps because she realised that her youth was fading fast and he would look for someone younger if she could not keep his affections alive. She knew very well now how to provoke and excite him, how to inflame him to the point of delirium, but this might not always be enough.

Exhausted at last, they lay holding hands. It was too hot to do more.

'The old man in the market who sells prickly pears says flames are going to come out of the ground and set the mountains on fire.' She had not believed him. How could rocks burn, she had asked. Felipe was equally sceptical.

'There can't be a fire under the island,' he observed practically. 'Can you imagine how hot the ground would be? It would be like sitting on top of a burning stove all the time. He's never been right in the head, that man. He came from Tenerife years ago, he was a fisherman too once and both his sons were lost at sea. He's been crazy ever since.'

He pulled her on top of him, despite the sticky heat. 'I could catch fire again if you do the right things to me.'

The bed trembled and the whole house shook this time but they were too absorbed in each other to notice.

As he was in such an ardent mood, she risked hinting at the subject of marriage once more.

'I went to the market this morning.' She prodded him in case he was falling asleep. 'No one talks to me still, all the women stare at me, they think I'm not respectable enough for them. Don Miguel scolded me again as well. He said it was a good thing I don't go to church much, it would be deceitful of me as I live in a state of sin.'

Felipe laughed, refusing to take the bait.

'Why do you take any notice of that pack of old gossips? They're jealous because you're so much more beautiful than they are, because you've got a man who's a better lover than their fat husbands. As for Don Miguel, forget him. He wouldn't be happy unless you were on your knees all day and half the night. I can pray just as well on the deck of my boat as I can in his church.'

He pinched her bottom so hard that she shrieked, waking Pepito and ending the conversation for that night at least.

*

Felipe was home for nearly a month, longer than usual; the fishing boat had sprung some planks in the last storm and needed to be hauled out of the water for some extensive repairs. Milagro did her best to bring up the subject again as often as possible, though her courage failed her when it came to asking him outright why they could not get married and her oblique references to their lack of social standing fell on deaf ears.

Felipe had no more time for the niceties of society than he had for Don Miguel; nevertheless, he understood only too well what Milagro's seemingly innocent remarks intended to convey. Very much to his own surprise, she had become the one he could not do without, even though marriage was out of the question. She had given him a son while Inés had only produced girls, and he adored the child. He would frequently take him down to the boat, where Pepito could bang away at a tiny block of wood while his father hammered caulking in between the new planks, and he took him to the tavern on the way home, where the girls cooed over him, exclaiming how like his father he was.

Felipe was not unfaithful to Milagro, not in Arrecife at least, another surprising detail. He did find it odd that he had lost his taste for womanising but it did not trouble him that much. In the four years they had been together, Milagro had not lost her attraction for him and an approximation to fidelity did not dampen his ardour.

*

The nagging of the priest he was able to ignore too, though he came close to confronting the man one day. Preaching to an already fearful population whose dread of hell fire was increased daily by the constant subterranean rumblings, not to mention the puffs of smoke arising ever more frequently in the region of Timanfaya, Don Miguel singled out the sinners in his community by name, insinuating that catastrophe could be averted by their instant repentance. Milagro was deeply distressed by this indictment, some helpful neighbour having wasted no time in repeating the priest's words to her, and she had difficulty in restraining Felipe from going and having it out with Don Miguel on the spot. It was one of the few times they quarrelled.

'Why should he blame us? We're not the only couple living in sin. What about the whorehouse, the men who go there? Some of them are married. At least (mentally crossing himself at the lie) I have only one woman.'

'Felipe, he's right. What we do is a sin, I feel it is, I know it is.'

'A sin you're very happy to commit. It's not troubled you before, I've never noticed you praying for divine guidance before we make love.'

'Felipe, don't blaspheme. It wouldn't be a sin if we were married.'

'Damn you, why do you want to force me into church? I'll do it when I'm good and ready. I'm the one to decide that.'

He was shouting at her, his face red with anger; she had never seen him so furious, certainly not with her. Pepito began to wail with fright and Felipe bent down to comfort him, his rage subsiding.

'I'll pray on the boat when I need to, without some whining cleric on my back. Come on, Pepito, let's go down to the port. We're leaving tomorrow morning and I want to make sure everything's ready to go.'

Milagro collapsed in tears when they left. Now he would never marry her, he might not even come back from his next trip. What a stupid girl she was, she had only made matters much worse for herself. Felipe returned many hours later, after dark, deposited a sleeping child in its cot and began to stow his few belongings in his sea bag.

'How long will you be gone this time?' She hardly had the courage to ask. He turned towards her; she could not see his face in the dim light of the one candle and his breath smelt of wine.

'I don't know.' He pushed her on to the bed, dragging at her clothes. She let him do as he pleased, though she did not feel like it. For once, his touch did not inflame her as it had in the past but she dared not resist him. How much nicer it was when I didn't worry about it being sinful, she thought miserably, pretending an enthusiasm she did not feel, listening to him grunting and snorting on top of her. Suddenly, the whole act seemed ridiculous and degrading and she was glad he did not take long over it.

He rolled off her without a word and was asleep in minutes. She fell asleep too, despite her wretchedness, waking drowsily as he got up to leave before dawn. He did kiss her briefly before he went.

*

'Don't worry about the townspeople. Words can't hurt, you know.'

Easy for him to say, he was not the one who was staying behind. He had forgotten the bitterness of their quarrel but she had not, and she burst into tears again after he had gone. Alone and forsaken, the butt of everyone's scorn, one child born out of wedlock and another about to make its appearance, what hope had she for the future? And it's my own fault, she thought, the priest is right. Respectability doesn't come into it, my life is evil and I am evil too. I care more for Felipe than I do for Pepito, I love Pepito only because I see Felipe in him. I would grieve over Felipe's death more than I ever did for my dead babies.

She could not sleep any more, she got up and went outside to pick some figs and prickly pears for Pepito when he woke. She caressed the thick leaves of the fig tree; they felt rough but warm to her touch. Like Felipe's arms, she decided in a moment of unaccustomed fantasy. The moon had set but the sky was growing light, restoring what little colour there was to the street; the walls warmed to their monotonous daytime ochre and the green of the leaves became less muted.

The new day would not change anything for her. She seemed to be caught in a trap, one of her own making, her physical feelings overwhelming her floundering ideas of what was right. The sun came up jauntily in front of her but at the back of the town, behind the hills, smoke billowed up and the ground continued to shake.

Chapter IV – The Eruption

The dawn that broke on September 2nd, following that first night of fire and terror, was no dawn at all. The frightened people of Arrecife, emerging from the church as some sort of light began to spread across the town, beheld a daybreak more awful than the darkness. The sun peered dimly through the smoke that filled the whole sky. In the west, massive sombre clouds loomed up over the hills, shot with bolts of fire, and the ground shook beneath their feet. The throbbing of the earth could be felt even through the heavy flagstones which paved the church, while the bell in the tower tolled incessantly of its own accord, its already cracked note adding a further element of lamentation.

It's the end of the world. Milagro was not the only one to think that, as she made her way down to the harbour once more, a fretful Pepito trailing behind her, complaining that he was hungry, he was thirsty, he wanted papa to come and take them away in his boat. Milagro had no reason for hoping otherwise but the sight of the still empty harbour made her break down altogether. She sat on the quay sobbing, holding an uncomprehending Pepito tightly in her arms. The whole island had caught fire, they would all be burned to death and she would never see Felipe again, in this world or the next.

Could it be her fault, she asked herself? Did Don Miguel's harsh condemnation of her way of life really have some justification? Ever since her flight from Teguise to Felipe's arms, she had struggled hard to convince herself that what she had done was the only choice she had, that her happiness depended on her making that choice and in the end she had come to believe it. She was so happy with Felipe. Joyful days far outweighed the gloomy ones and she knew that resigning herself to the sort of existence her mother had mapped out for her would have been merely an even course of moderate despair. But now, all chance of future happiness had vanished, blown away by the

[65]

explosions, totally obscured by the smoke and flames which covered the island. She managed to choke back her tears, as much for Pepito's sake as anything—the sight of his mother's anguish would only increase his terror and bewilderment.

She strained her eyes, staring vainly over the sea wall to catch a glimpse of a sail, but there was nothing to be seen, just a haze of cloud and smoke. There were not a few despondent observers of the deserted horizon that morning; other fisher-men's wives had gathered at the harbour, hopefully gazing out to sea or glancing apprehensively at the flaming hills, then looking away hurriedly from a spectacle too awful to contemplate for very long.

The wind began to rise, as it often did towards the end of the morning, a touch of normality in an unreal day. The smoke rolled away from the town and back towards Timanfaya, allowing the sunshine to penetrate as far as the outskirts of Arrecife, but not diminishing in any way the real drama of the scene: the backdrop of smoke and flame in the distance which seemed to rise higher and higher, the grey haze of falling ash which obscured the nearer hills and the town itself, silent, apparently as yet untouched by the catastrophe but waiting for disaster to strike. The sun shone with a muted yellow glow, distorting the colours of the sea, giving it a dull brownish tinge, muddying its usual brilliant appearance. The small waves raised by the breeze seemed dingy and sluggish, the harbour had lost its sparkle and, empty of its normal complement of busy crews and ships, it too appeared dismayed by the calamity which had befallen the island

The air was oppressive, laden with evil-smelling fumes even after the smoke had dispersed, and at dusk the wind dropped and the reeking clouds rolled over the town once more. Unwillingly, as darkness fell, after a fruitless day of staring at an empty skyline, the watchers on the sea wall abandoned their posts and made their way home. Pepito cried and shrank back as they left the harbour area: it seemed as if they were walking towards a fiery furnace. As it grew darker, the fires in the hills burned brighter and seemed ever nearer.

'We must go home.' Milagro dragged the whimpering child through the streets, hiding her own reluctance. It was as pointless to return home as to stay down by the water.

'We'll have something to eat and Papa will come back tomorrow.'

She did not think so. Her heart was leaden, the future had ceased to exist for her; she could not see how she could survive without Felipe.

No one knew what to expect. That the hills had blown up was clear, the mad fisherman's prophesy had come true, but why? What would happen now? Would there be further explosions, perhaps in the very centre of Arrecife itself? The clouds dispersed gradually during the next few days, helped by the daily breeze, but the earth continued to tremble and the people with it. Nothing happened in Arrecife, no gouts of flame started up in the streets, the houses remained standing, and the people plucked up their courage and began to go about their business once more. It soon became obvious that they and those in the north eastern villages on the coast were the fortunate ones. A few survivors from the centre of the island trickled into town, telling dreadful tales.

On the fifth morning, such a group arrived from Masdache, one of the villages up in the hills. A woman, her legs bound with rags, rode on a camel whose flanks were scorched and raw; three dust-covered children clung to her skirts, while two men limped alongside them. The refugees stumbled down the main street and stopped in front of the church, too numb with fatigue and terror at first to give any coherent account of their ordeal to the curious townspeople who surrounded them. Their village, which lay just east of Timanfaya had, it seemed, ceased to exist.

'There was a terrible noise in the middle of the night.' The man holding the camel's bridle stammered out a few words. 'A mountain of fire in the middle of my field, in the corn, there was. It got bigger and bigger every minute. Then it spread to the village.'

His face was blistered, as were his hands, and there were marks of singeing all over his clothes. 'My wife...'

He sat down abruptly on the ground and started to cry, great hiccuping, heartbroken sobs.

'A river of burning rock came out of the mountain and she was burned up in it.' The other man seemed less shocked than his companion, though his legs and arms were covered with raw burned patches and he had no shirt. His hair was singed too and his eyebrows completely burned away, huge weeping blisters covering his forehead.

'But what happened?' asked one of the old men of the town. 'How can a mountain catch fire? How can rocks burn?'

'God has sent Hell to earth.' Don Miguel appeared from the church, grimly triumphant that the wrath of God had proved his point. 'Man's wickedness is now being punished.'

He turned away from the fugitives, beckoning his population into church once more with an imperious wave of his arm. One or two of them remained to help the stricken little group. Someone induced the camel to kneel and the woman and children were helped from its back. The woman appeared dazed, her eyes vacant and unseeing. She screamed as she was lowered to the ground and Milagro noticed with horror that she had no feet. The rags which bound her legs fell away to reveal two blackened stumps. Someone went for a pitcher of water but the woman continued to scream hoarsely, unable to swallow even a mouthful. One of the men took the pitcher.

'She's my sister,' he said unsteadily. His hand shook as he drank. 'Those aren't her children, all hers are dead. In the fields. The fire caught them.'

Milagro hovered on the edge of the group, uncertain what to do to help. She felt a hand on her arm, El Moro had been standing, watching too.

'Do you want to survive?' His tone was severe. 'Don't try to save others, save yourself. Be sparing with your food and water, keep it for yourself and Pepito only.'

Milagro looked helplessly at the exhausted fugitives. A woman, the baker's wife, had returned with food—fruit and bread—and was trying to coax the children to eat but, like their aunt, they were too stunned to do anything. They crouched on the dusty ground, staring at nothing, while the woman with no feet continued to cry and groan.

El Moro pulled Milagro aside from the crowd. 'Come with me, I'll show you what to do.' He led the way back to her hut, where he inspected her small cistern. There was a scum of ash floating on top of the water and he frowned.

'You must keep this cistern covered,' he told her, 'especially if it rains. And filter the water through a cloth before you drink it.'

She looked blankly at him.

'You see all the clouds up there? They're full of ash from the eruption. When it rains, all that ash will come down and the rain will be like mud.'

'I still don't understand.'

She could not grasp the nature of the disaster which had overtaken the island and she was more and more inclined to believe Don Miguel: God had sent hell fire to punish them, her in particular. Was it really possible that her small sins would have caused God to punish the whole island so brutally, that other people were being made to suffer so that she would never see Felipe again?

El Moro seemed to have divined something of what she was thinking.

'A volcanic eruption is a natural disaster, it has nothing to do with the wrath of God. It's been coming for some time. All the tremors we've been feeling during the summer were a sure sign that something was wrong. I went up to Timanfaya a month ago and there were already cracks in the ground. The earth was too hot to walk on in many places.'

'Is Don Miguel wrong, then?'

El Moro sighed. 'In that all is the will of Allah I suppose you could say he is right, but I can assure you the misdeeds of Lanzarote, of such as you and I according to Don Miguel, are far too insignificant to warrant so much of his attention.'

His cynical and irreverent pronouncements only served to confuse Milagro further. 'But the river of fire the man talked of, will it come to Arrecife? Will we all be burned in it too?'

'I don't think so, I think it will all flow away down the other side of the island. There are hills between us and the main site of the eruption. Let me show you...'

He was interrupted by shouts in the distance. Someone came running up the path towards them.

'There's a fishing boat coming in.'

Milagro scooped up Pepito and ran, stumbling over the uneven ground in her haste and arriving completely out of breath at the harbour. The sea wall was crowded with people and she stood among them panting, hardly daring to hope that Felipe might be on board. The sun and wind had swept away the menacing clouds and the sea had taken on its former aspect, blue and sparkling in the fresh breeze. Only the drifts of ash beneath the feet of the anxious people crowding the quay reminded them of what had happened. Over towards Timanfaya the sky had cleared too; there was still a light haze lingering in the air but the red glow beneath it was hardly visible in the bright sunlight.

The fishing boat tacked laboriously in through the harbour entrance, its mast just a short stump from which a ragged sail flapped inadequately. There seemed to be more men on deck than the crew of just one boat and it was hard to make out their faces from a distance.

'Only one boat,' someone muttered. 'Where are the rest?'

A woman who had been unable to see her husband anywhere amongst the men visible burst into tears. It was not

Felipe's boat, that much was certain, but as it neared the quay and the useless sail was lowered, Milagro could see with infinite relief that Felipe was one of those manning the big sweeps amidships as the boat manoeuvred alongside. The blue paint on the hull was blistered and flaking off near the waterline; great patches of blackened wood were everywhere and the men on deck all showed traces of a fiery ordeal—singed hair, charred and blistered skin, hands and arms burned raw. Their garments were in shreds, some of them in no more than grimy rags, and they barely had enough strength to handle the lines. Men lay on deck too, some moving, some not.

Milagro sobbed as Felipe climbed over the gunwale into her arms. He himself was shaking, his face and hands were so raw with blisters he could not bear her to touch them and he stammered incoherently as he tried to tell her what they had been through.

'We were on the other side of the straits.' He stammered so much she could barely make out what he was saying. 'We were rowing up to Graciosa when... when we saw a huge explosion over the island. There were flames, going miles up into the air. Then, later, I think, we saw the fire coming down into the sea and it began to boil. There were other boats near us, five or six, but most of them disappeared. We never saw them again, or the men.'

He coughed and wheezed as he spoke, he was on the verge of collapse. 'Burning rocks fell from the sky, that's what sank all the boats. Let's go home, Milagro. No, no, take some fish first. The sea was full of dead fish.'

He climbed painfully back on board, to take some of the fish heaped up in the well deck, wincing as he picked them up. They were an odd grey colour and Felipe smiled faintly as Pepito stooped to examine one which had fallen on to the dock. The little boy sniffed it suspiciously.

'They're cooked already, boiled in the sea.'

Milagro helped him walk slowly away from the dock and

up the track towards their hut. Most of the men were in the same state as he was, coughing and spitting repeatedly, incoherent with fatigue and shock, hardly able to believe that they had actually made it back to port. Felipe was staggering and Milagro had to support him up the last few yards.

'Home, home,' he muttered, but his knees were buckling under him and Milagro had to put his arm across her shoulders and drag him across the threshold. She was so relieved to have him back safe, if not sound, that she did not question him further. Once in the hut, he fell like a log on to the bed and she could not wake him to undress him. He muttered in his sleep as she pulled his singed clothing gently off him, but even this did not rouse him and she sat down to mend and patch the many holes in his shirt and breeches as best she could.

Pepito, oblivious of his father's exhausted condition, tried to wake him up too. He wanted to play and began to whimper when Felipe would not stir.

'Papa is too tired.' Milagro tried to explain things to him. 'He was in that great fire we saw but now he has come home. We must be happy that he's back and let him rest.'

She fed Pepito some of the fish but he refused to eat more than a mouthful, and in irritation she bundled him outside to play. She tried some of the fish herself and she could hardly blame him for not eating it. It was not actually bad, at least it did not have the foul smell of bad fish. As Felipe had said, it was if it had been cooked already in the boiling sea, but it had an odd bitter taste.

Some time during the night Felipe woke. Milagro, watching anxiously over him, had almost dozed off herself and she leapt up in fright when he cried out. He was sitting up, shouting about burning water and men on fire. She put her arms around him but he continued to cry out. He was still asleep she realised; he suddenly stopped and fell back on the bed again without really waking.

She did sleep herself, safe now that Felipe was home, and

when she woke it was light. She went outside to look up in the direction of Timanfaya. The earth no longer trembled so much, no more than a slight quiver from time to time; she could see an ominous cloud of black smoke still looming up in the distance but less, much less than before. Her heart grew lighter; with Felipe back all would be well again.

She heard voices in the hut. Felipe was awake at last and playing a game with Pepito. Haggard and unshaven but revived after his long sleep, some of his habitual optimism had returned. He flinched as he caught the ball Pepito threw to him, though—the blisters on his hands had burst and his palms were bleeding.

Milagro bound them up with some clean rag, sacrificing Felipe's second-best shirt, and set out bread and dates on the table. He could manage the dates but she had to cut up the bread, his hands too painful to handle the knife.

'You were lucky here in Arrecife,' he told her through a mouthful of food. 'Many people were killed in Timanfaya. They told us in Playa Blanca some villages just disappeared.'

His face became sombre again. 'A huge river of fire came out of the ground and swallowed everything up. We saw all the flames from the boat, the sea was bubbling like water in a saucepan and there were dead fish everywhere.'

'Are the fish all right to eat? I didn't like to eat very much, they tasted so funny.'

Felipe laughed shortly. 'We've been eating them for three days ourselves and we're still alive.'

He got up. 'I must go down to the boat, there's work to be done. Come with me and bring your sewing things, the sail's in very bad shape.'

They spent the day on board; Milagro did what she could with the sail, though it was more patches than whole cloth when she had finished. Showers of red-hot stones had hit the boat, one of the men told her, and many of them had been burned and injured trying to get the incandescent rocks over the side before they set light to the deck or burned their way through the hull.

She was glad to be busy again; the inaction of the past few days, waiting, waiting, waiting, wondering if she would ever see Felipe again, wondering what new form disaster would take, had nearly driven her mad. Sewing steadily away at the tattered sail she could relax, she did not have to worry about what the future could bring. He was back, he was here with her now and she could watch Pepito playing cheerfully for once with the other fishermen's children, sorting through the pieces of volcanic debris still lying around, calling to his father to see the stones floating away in the water rather than sinking.

The men did not talk much; they wrapped their injured hands in rags and, solemn-faced, set about repairing what needed repairing, making good the damage as far as they could. It was not so much a conspiracy of silence, it was more that they did not want to relive the all too recent horrors in order to satisfy the curiosity of the townspeople. They worked as if in a trance, busying themselves to stop remembering the terrible events of the past few days.

That evening, lying in bed, Felipe began to tell her some of what had happened.

'We weren't far off the coast. There were five or six fishing boats together, all of us going up towards Graciosa. When the wind drops at night, you can row up the coast quite easily with two men to each oar. In the daytime the wind's too strong but it was calm that night, the moon was up and we could see the coast very clearly. We were off the salt pans, you could see them white in the moonlight. There was no warning, nothing to show that anything was amiss, just a terrific explosion above Yaiza. We saw a huge fire, flames roaring into the air, higher and higher. All I could think was, that's where the fields are, how can there be such a big fire there? Under the fire we could see a mountain growing as we watched: red then black, then it would crumble away again in streams of fire running down towards the sea. There was this noise all the time, a roaring noise and a hot wind coming off the land. We'd stopped rowing and the wind blew us out to sea. The water began to boil and bubble, it was as if we were being tossed about in a cooking pot like lumps of stewed meat.

'We weren't safe out at sea either. We saw balls of fire hurled into the air with a great whistling sound, we could see flames bursting from the ground round the salt pans wherever they hit. Then it got worse: we thought it was a rain squall though the sky seemed to be clear. A pattering noise, a hissing, then a clattering. Stones started falling on our decks and they were red hot, glowing lumps of rock, too hot to touch. What could we do? We were cowering in the bottom of the boat, trying to protect ourselves but our clothes began to catch fire. It lasted only a few minutes but it cost most of us our ships.'

He broke off, shuddering, the images of all the men and boats lost were too harrowing. Milagro stared at him in horror, she could not find any words to comfort him. Eventually she touched his arm but he would say no more and turned his back on her. He seemed to be crying, which shocked her even more than his horrific recital of his ordeal. At last he fell into a heavy sleep but there was no sleep for her; she lay awake most of the night seeing visions of hell, while Felipe muttered and moaned beside her.

More refugees arrived from Timanfaya that day; some had relatives who took them in, others were obliged to sleep on the floor of the church. It was hard for those in Arrecife to understand how these people could have lost everything, how they could not even have had time to seize so much as a crust of bread before the fiery flood destroyed their homes and their lands.

The woman with no feet had been given a room in the tavern by the waterside; she screamed and moaned continuously, making Milagro shudder as she sat on deck sewing. Towards evening, the woman died and more than one person sighed inwardly with relief. There had been something so grisly and horrible about the incessant cries. El Moro had offered to give the woman a sleeping draught but Don Miguel had already established himself at her bedside and refused to hear of any diabolical potions being administered, thus forcing the wretched woman to spend her last hours in agony. There was no Christian doctor in Arrecife, had not been for many years, and the old woman who acted as midwife, though competent where childbirth was concerned, as Milagro had reason to know, was totally ignorant of any other medical procedures.

*

One of the fishermen died too, one who had been badly injured by a falling rock, which had struck him like a cannon ball. Felipe appealed to El Moro to do something for the other crew members, some of whose burns were turning septic. El Moro refused.

'How can I treat so many men?' he said scornfully to Felipe. 'You're in no danger of dying of anything other than ignorance, as far as I can see. Keep your wounds clean and they'll heal without wasting valuable salves on them. Go away.'

Felipe was not put off by the Turk's cold and unhelpful attitude. He was one of the few men to whom El Moro was normally civil and he stayed where he was, lounging in the doorway of the hut. It was in better repair than his own and better appointed. The walls were whitewashed, there were rugs on the floor of an intricate red and blue design, a curtain at the window and brass pots round the fireplace. The bed was covered with a curiously patterned cloth and had a shelf next to it containing many books.

There were rumours—but then rumours about El Moro were too numerous to be counted—there were rumours that he kept a small store of gold buried under the floor. No one had ever been brave enough to attempt to verify this, even when the

Moor was absent. It was certain that he would have used magic to guard his property.

'What do you want now?' El Moro was brusque. He did not, being (as he himself reasoned) an educated and rational man though fallen on hard times, need casual friendships, certainly not with the likes of the average inhabitant of Arrecife; but he was not averse to conversing with anyone who was prepared to speak to him and not reproach him for being a foreigner and an infidel.

'I need your advice.'

'My advice to you would be to take Milagro and Pepito to Gran Canaria as soon as you can. Life has never been easy here and it will soon become impossible.'

Felipe looked uneasy.

'You mean the mountain might explode again? Surely the whole island can't go up in flames.'

El Moro began to explain to Felipe as much as he thought the fisherman might understand of the principles of vulcanology. He was not sure himself exactly what might happen but he had witnessed an eruption in Sicily during his active pirate days and he knew the consequences had been disastrous for men, crops and livestock on a fertile island. What would happen on a barren rock like Lanzarote was bound to be a thousand times worse.

'The volcano will almost certainly erupt again. We probably will not get rivers of molten rock in Arrecife, they will more than likely flow towards the western shores, but we could have clouds of poisonous gases over here, and when it rains, if it does rain this winter which is not at all a foregone conclusion, the water will be full of ash and undrinkable. You saw what happened the other night, it could be worse next time.'

'I thought we had gone to hell,' muttered Felipe. He began to tell El Moro what he had told Milagro the night before, what they had gone through. He could barely get the words out at first, the nightmare memories were all too vivid, but then as if he was in the confessional, somewhere he had not been since he was fifteen, he felt lighter in spirit when he had shared the burden. Why he was able to tell a stranger, he did not know; he felt perhaps that El Moro, being a man, could withstand the dreadful details of his story better than Milagro might and he was able to tell him the whole ghastly story.

*

Felipe had been one of the first to realise the extreme danger they were in. His clothes were smouldering where the stones had struck him but that was of little importance. Where they had struck the deck, the wood had begun to catch fire. Impregnated over the years with pitch and fish oil, the deck was smoking and little tongues of flame were already licking up from the pile of nets in the well. Felipe went to pick up a handful of the smaller rocks but dropped them again with a yell. They were still red hot. He and the mate stamped out the flames in the nets as best they could but it was only too obvious that the shower of incandescent stones would soon set fire to the whole boat. In desperation, trying to ignore the pain, they forced themselves to pick up the stones and throw them overboard. They sizzled as they hit the water.

One of the other fishing boats was in a worse plight than they were, with flames already taking hold of the sails and mast. It soon sank, the fire dying down as it settled lower in the water. Felipe could hear the frantic cries of the crew striving to keep afloat; like himself, like most fishermen, they could not swim. The oarsmen swung their own boat towards where the stricken vessel had gone down, but by the time they reached the spot, despite the continuing flashes of light from the fires of the eruption, they could see no survivors

They were taking on water too fast themselves; so many of the rocks had lodged in the tangle of nets and fallen down into the bilge that they had not been able to put out the fire in time. The hull must have been holed, but they were luckier than their colleagues and managed, by constant bailing, to keep themselves afloat till dawn.

El Moro began to write down the details of Felipe's description with a ghoulish relish. His nature, already cynical and calculating, had been further soured by his own misfortunes—wounded and dumped on a virtually barren island by his crew—and he had developed a morbid interest in the misfortunes of others.

'I don't know how we got through the night.' Felipe found tears coming to his eyes but he was ashamed to cry in front of El Moro as he had with Milagro and, after some gulping, he forced himself to go on.

'We bailed in turn with two men resting at a time. Every time I could rest and close my eyes, I would hope that when I opened them again the fires would have gone, but it was all still there: the wreck, the mountain blazing on land, my friends struggling to keep alive. When the sun came up, we could see the shore was black instead of sandy, no green fields any more, just a mountain of fire. And a red stream, coming down into the sea. The water was boiling and hissing and I could see one wreck. Only one out of all the boats I knew should be there. There were some men swimming and holding on to bits of wood but they all had burns.

'So many men were lost. Maybe thirty or more. Most of them were from Playa Blanca but quite a few from here too. We got everyone left onto our boat and put into Playa Blanca on the way back, but it was horrible, the sky full of smoke and a dreadful smell of rotting eggs. We were all choking, nothing could get the taste out of our mouths. There were plenty of dead fish in the water but they tasted pretty bad too. We had to eat them, there was nothing else.'

El Moro nodded. 'The sea was probably full of poisons from the lava flows, sulphur and so forth.'

Felipe grabbed him by the shoulder, despite his painful hands.

'Swear you will tell no one what I'm about to tell you. I have another family, a wife and children in a village near Yaiza. Only Francisco knows, the captain of the fishing boat who rescued us; his girl friend is my wife's cousin.'

El Moro frowned.

'You've made your life very complicated, young man.'

'It wasn't my fault. My family made me marry Inés when I was only fifteen. She was much older than me and she was my first woman. I was just a boy, I didn't know anything about women, about life. Well, I knew what boys and girls did, of course, and she got pregnant, four months pregnant by the time they made us get married. But I didn't love her. I refused to be a farmer, I hated ploughing, walking behind some stupid camel day after day. I was sure there was something much more exciting to do than that. I used to run off down to the port and I talked one of the fishing boats into taking me on. I was terribly sick the first time I went to sea but anything was better than going back to the land.'

El Moro smiled wryly; at least Felipe had a little more imagination than many of the inhabitants of Lanzarote, though he did not seem able to use it to any profitable end.

'I had an excuse not to go home then,' Felipe went on. 'I would stay on the fishing boat and Inés never knew where I was. I did go home sometimes and you know how it is, babies always come along whether you want them to or not. Three or four, only girls, I can't remember how many of them died either, one or two at least. Inés' sisters live with her and I could never be sure which were my children and which were not.'

'Why are you telling me all this? Why should I be interested in your affairs?'

'I have to tell someone, it's weighing on me too much. Besides, who can I tell? Milagro? She would throw me out. Don Miguel? He would tie me up with prayers for the rest of my life and make me give up everything that makes my life worth living. Inés? Her family would kill me.'

'I don't see how I can help you, all I can do is listen.' Despite his apparent indifference, El Moro was getting considerable satisfaction from listening to Felipe's tale of infidelity, death and destruction; it was far more interesting than the usual everyday saga of woes.

'I just need to talk. So then I met Milagro and she gave me a son and Inés was nothing. I hardly ever go home now, to Yaiza that is, except to see my eldest daughter. Rosa, she's nearly ten now and she's always glad to see me. All Inés does is complain. I can't explain to Milagro why I can't marry her, can I? I must go back soon, I don't know what's happened to my mother and brothers. They live in Los Rodeos, right where the fire started, and I could get no news of them at all when we stopped in Playa Blanca. Milagro and Pepito mean much more to me but I must make sure everyone's safe at least. Things are very bad down there. You can hardly breathe for all the horrible smoke and fumes and so many of the cisterns cracked when the ground moved there's hardly any water left.'

Felipe's voice began to tremble. 'There were some people who got away from Uga and they said many of the villagers had been burned to death. The rocks melted and flowed everywhere, those who couldn't run fast enough died. I didn't believe them at first but they all told the same story. I didn't know rocks could melt and burn, it doesn't seem possible.'

'Only too likely in the circumstances,' commented El Moro. 'You can't imagine the temperature inside a volcano. I saw an eruption once in Italy and just such a thing happened. No one knows why, but it's nothing new and nothing to do with divine retribution either.'

'I never thought it was. I've always avoided Don Miguel because of, well, because of my wife, but that's not the reason I don't believe we're all damned. I do my best to keep two families happy, is that so bad? I think Don Miguel would prefer everyone to burn, to prove the people of Lanzarote are not worthy of being saved. I wasn't so sure myself the other night,

I think hell must look just like what we saw then.'

El Moro said nothing. His religion was just as fanciful and condemnatory in its way as the more extreme aspects of Christianity, but he preferred not to think about it.

'We'll be off again as soon as the boat's repaired. Francisco wants me to crew for him. Many of the men don't want to leave their families alone now, but we must fish if we're going to eat and I have to go back to find out about my family. I suppose that's why I want to tell you all this—could you, I'm really worried about Milagro and Pepito, could you look out for them, see they're all right?'

'So you have two wives. If you convert to Islam you can marry both of them. Islam allows a man to have four, though I've always thought one is too much trouble.'

'Four? All at once?'

Felipe scratched his chin thoughtfully; he could not decide whether such a prospect would be a delight or a disaster and he failed to notice that El Moro had not replied to his request.

'I can't choose between them, I can't choose between Pepito and Rosa, that's what it boils down to. If it wasn't for the volcano, everything would still be so simple. If we have to leave the island, we'll all have to leave together. Inés will do as I say of course, but Milagro…'

He began to pace up and down in great agitation while El Moro laughed.

'You must learn to control your women, and yourself too for that matter. Then you won't make so many wrong choices.'

'It's too late. I love Milagro, you may laugh but I do. If I'd met her years ago, before I married Inés, things would have been different. Now I'm twenty-five, half my life is over and I'm doubly trapped. I can't abandon Inés and Rosa, not now when they must really need me, and my mother, well I haven't seen her for years but I can't just leave Lanzarote without making sure she's safe.'

'You'd be better off without all your fine feelings of

loyalty and devotion.'

'How can you be so callous? Don't you have any feeling for other people? You must have some family somewhere. I know many people here treat you harshly, like they do me, but that's no reason to despise them.'

'I don't despise them, I have no feelings about them at all. They're not the same as me, not the same race, they don't believe in the same God and that's an end to it.'

'You believe in God? I wouldn't have thought it. You're not exactly full of Christian charity, you're worse than Don Miguel.'

'I'm not a Christian.' El Moro turned away dismissively and took a book from the shelf by his bed, one bound elaborately in red leather with a brass clasp. He sat down and opened it, ignoring Felipe.

'What are all those books?' inquired Felipe curiously. He peered over El Moro's shoulder at the pages; they were covered with patterns which did not look like any writing he had ever seen. 'Are they all about magic? Is that why you know about the volcano?'

'Don't talk nonsense. Go away and leave me in peace.'

There did not seem to be much point in staying and Felipe wandered off. He should go back to the boat, there was still much to be done before they left. He did not relish the thought of leaving Arrecife and returning to Playa Blanca; his conscience, such as it was, was pricking him unpleasantly about Inés and the rest of his family and Francisco wanted to go as soon as possible. It was fish or starve in any case. The volcano had quietened down somewhat, it still rumbled and spat out gouts of flame while smoke billowed up continuously from Timanfaya, but there had been no spectacular display of blazing fury for some days. Perhaps El Moro was wrong.

Chapter V – Survival

It was late morning. The sun shone in a sky free of smoke and the harbour, bustling with activity once again, was its old colourful self. The people had taken on new heart with the freshness of the air. Though the fishermen's families were sad to see their men leaving, most of them attempted at least to conceal their distress. Two boats were preparing to depart, Francisco's, newly repaired, and one which had stopped in from Orzola up in the north to pick up some new crew. A trading schooner had put in from Spain, knowing nothing of the catastrophe; it evidently did not intend to stay a moment longer than was necessary, the sailors were not even unloading its cargo and the few passengers on board had refused to disembark. Hurried negotiations were being carried out for their continued passage to a more prosperous port.

Milagro stood on the quay, watching the men make their final preparations. Dragged down physically by the weight of her pregnancy, she had to sit on a bollard for a little and put her head between her knees in case she fainted. Felipe, as usual had noticed nothing. They had had an argument about his departure the night before but that was, well, the night before. He piled nets into the hold, shouting cheerfully to the other sailors as if he had already forgotten her existence.

When she felt well enough to get to her feet again, she could not at first see Pepito; her heart sank; surely he could not have fallen in the water during the short time she had not been looking out for him. Then she glimpsed a small head with a blue and green handkerchief tied over it, visible above the gunwale where Felipe was working. The men began singling up the lines.

Felipe lifted Pepito over the rail into Milagro's arms, but he was so big and heavy now that she had to let him slide to the ground. Belatedly, Felipe noticed her wretchedness.

'Don't worry, we came back last time, didn't we? The

worst is over, there's nothing to fear.'

The words were hardly out of his mouth when they were proved wrong. There was a dim rumbling in the distance, more prolonged than thunder; it increased to a roar and the ground began to shake as it had on the night of the first eruption. Everyone turned towards Timanfaya as fire blazed up once more over the hills. An immense black cloud shot with fire began to form and fountains of sparks spurted up, seemingly miles into the air. Milagro screamed and flung her arms round Felipe's neck, nearly pulling him over the rail into the water between the boat and the quay.

Felipe stared aghast at the spectacle, no less appalling by day than it had been by night. Oblivious of the hysterical girl and the frantic toddler snatching at his mother's skirts, he gaped at the menacing cloud boiling up into the morning sky, imagining he felt the searing hot breath of the explosion as he had last time. He could not leave, could not abandon Milagro and Pepito, but he could not stay. His wife, his lawful wife and his daughters, particularly his beloved little Rosa, as dear to him as were Milagro and Pepito, would be watching the same awful display bursting out of the raging ground, and might be in mortal danger from it, down where they were. He was being torn in pieces.

Men cried out curses, children screamed in terror and despair, the women and not a few of the men fell to their knees fruitlessly, not even knowing what they were saying. It had seemed that the disaster was over, that life would be able to return to its normal pattern, but the mountain seethed and roared and the terrible clouds of smoke and ash rose again to blot out the sun.

Felipe was not the only man in a dilemma. Francisco himself was anxious to have news of a girl in Playa Blanca, but he could not give the order to cast off if his family in Arrecife was in peril. What to do? Where to go? There was no way of fleeing except on the fishing boats. Francisco contemplated briefly embarking his wife and children, but he would have to take those of his crew as well. Common sense told him this was impossible, there were too many of them for his small boat to carry: more practically, the women would become even more hysterical than they were already and the children would be seasick. Besides, it was a night and a day to Gran Canaria and they would need more food and water.

One of his sailors was already helping a woman over the rail. 'We must get everyone on board and go now,' he cried to Francisco, 'we'll all be burned to death if we stay.'

His action caused a rush of frantic women and children onto the fishing boat, which began to tilt drastically as so many people crowded onto one side, helping others over the gunwale. Milagro was pushed roughly aside and almost fell into the harbour, dragging Pepito with her. She scrambled to safety and stood helpless, watching the struggling mass of people.

'Keep them off!' shouted Francisco to Felipe. He stamped on the arm of a man who was trying to cast off and re-secured the line. The man, gibbering with fear, fell to the deck and lay there groaning while his wife clawed vainly at Francisco, screeching hysterically. Felipe called to Milagro to stay clear and not let go of Pepito; stunned, she did as she was told, staring in disbelief and shock as Felipe went to Francisco's aid. He pulled the woman off him and slapped her face hard. She too fell to the deck and lay howling on top of her husband.

The two men were the only ones with the presence of mind to recognise the more immediate danger to their boat if they did not control the panicking crowd. The other fishing boat had already cast off, dangerously overladen with distraught men and women, while their own boat was with considerable difficulty resisting the onslaught of those who had not been able to scramble on board the first one.

Francisco seized two belaying pins and handed one to Felipe. They stood firm but they were obliged to crack a number of heads and shout themselves hoarse before they managed to get the attention of the mob besieging them. Those already on board, feeling themselves safer at once, quietened down, whilst those on the quay did not dare to try to climb over the rail for fear of being knocked into the water. Francisco addressed them.

'We're not leaving yet,' he announced. 'We'll wait till evening to see what happens. You were safe here last time, much safer than those in the west. Perhaps you'll still be all right. If the fires start to come too close, we can be away in a few minutes.'

'We may not be any safer at sea,' interjected Felipe. 'What if we meet with pirates?'

The idea had only just occurred to him and it had the desired effect on his listeners. The thought of ending up in a Moorish prison was even more ghastly than that of dying in the fires of Lanzarote and by degrees the crowd began to disperse. It was by no means certain that they would be safe in Arrecife but the fires were still far off, as they had been last time.

They came no closer; the ground shivered and shook, the hills belched out their flames but the town was not imminently threatened. Ash began to settle, insistently, silently, covering everything and everyone with a whitish-grey powder. The houses, the trees, all was in mourning, shrouded in a pall of grey. Whatever colour the houses and streets had once had, and it was not much—shades of brown and sand daubed here and there with whitewash—all had gone, obliterated by a winding-sheet of ash. In a few hours the town had grown old and the people with it: grey hair, grey faces, grey clothes. The people stared at their transformed surroundings, their feet scuffed up clouds of choking dust and they coughed as the insidious powder entered their lungs.

The wind eventually swept the darkly menacing clouds away but the ash remained. By evening it seemed to be clear that the volcano had done its worst and the women and children stood aside, resigned, to let the men cast off.

'We must go.' Felipe picked up Pepito and hugged him. 'If we don't fish, we'll all starve. Ask El Moro for help if you need anything.'

Faces streaked with ash and tears watched the fishing boats hoist sail and make their way towards the harbour entrance. It was dark before the sails disappeared over the horizon and the people drifted away. The town was lit by the red glow from the eruption and the earth quaked anew under Milagro's feet as she carried an exhausted Pepito home. Worn out by the day's events, he had mercifully fallen asleep before the boats had even passed the harbour wall and he did not wake when she put him to bed.

She could not get to sleep herself even though she was as weary as her son. Every new rumble of the earth, every flash of crimson lightning brought her to the door of the hut to peer fearfully at the sky. She felt she should be on her knees like most of the other townspeople, praying for deliverance from the evil which hovered over them, for Felipe's safe return, but she could not find the words. Fear disordered her thoughts and choked her feeble efforts to appeal to heaven. She had never felt more alone and deserted than she did at that moment, the inevitable sensation of despair at Felipe's departure increased beyond measure by the terrible circumstances.

*

Many people left Lanzarote during the next few weeks, as the hills continued to vent their anger. The port was in continual confusion as the wealthier citizens of Teguise and Arrecife thronged the quays, seeking to get passage any way possible for Gran Canaria.

Not everyone wanted to leave; there were pirates out there, lurking just over the horizon. An occasional lateen sail would even appear brazenly in view only a few miles offshore. Felipe's pronouncement was borne out when a small trading vessel was towed back in with two men on board, dead from ugly sword wounds. It had left not many days before with at least a dozen townspeople on board with all their possessions. There were no survivors and the ship had been stripped of everything moveable.

Felipe did not return. When the fishing boat came back in without him, Milagro's first thought was that he had met with an accident and Francisco's halting explanations did not convince her otherwise.

Eventually, his incoherent mumbled remarks about Felipe having to see to his family began to make sense and, unconsciously saving herself much grief for the time being at least, she came to the wrong conclusions.

'Does he still have family in the south? I suppose it's not so odd, though he's never spoken of them. He is coming back, isn't he, Francisco?'

Francisco seemed to be embarrassed to be talking to her. There must be some mystery about Felipe's absence, but surely if he was dead or badly injured Francisco would tell her.

'Of course. He still had family near Yaiza and some of them made it to Playa Blanca.' He seized thankfully on her misunderstanding of the situation. 'He'll be back soon. Maybe on the next trip.'

But Felipe did not come back. Time dragged on, smoke-filled, ash-covered. The baby moved feebly inside her now, it seemed barely alive. It will be born dead, thought Milagro sadly as she felt the faint stirrings within her, less noticeable than the shuddering of her little house each time the volcanoes exploded into action.

*

There were many terrible days when the sky was so dark with ash and cloud that it was almost like night. People coughed and gasped for breath when they ventured out. Most stayed fearfully at home, not daring to do more than creep tremulously into church to pray for salvation and deliverance. Don Miguel was in his element, his firmly entrenched belief in the imminence of hell and damnation proved without a doubt by the terrible eruptions. He would stride through Arrecife, eyes blazing, ragged dusty robes billowing out behind him, a wailing mob of penitents straggling in his wake as he bellowed out his dire warnings about the manifestations of God's wrath. Milagro would run and hide if she heard him coming, and she could certainly hear him from many streets away. He caught up with her in the end, at the town cistern, where she was waiting in line for her pitiful weekly supply of water.

'Repent, repent,' he shouted at her seizing her arm in a vice-like grip. 'You can see the fires of hell waiting for you, up there, in the hills. Prayer will not save you from hell on earth but it may give you fewer years in Purgatory. Repent, repent, down on your knees!'

The ragged, attendant crowd shrieked and wailed behind him, grovelling in the dust, shrinking back as he turned to glare at them in their turn. Milagro quailed and fell to the ground in her turn when he released her. Don Miguel was far more terrifying than the fiery furnace in the mountains.

El Moro was one of the few who was afraid of neither, though he avoided any kind of confrontation with the priest. Don Miguel would sometimes pause in his peregrinations outside the infidel dwelling to demand that heretics be punished even more severely by divine retribution, but El Moro never bothered to reply. He was kind to Milagro; he had no obligation to comply with Felipe's request to keep an eye on her but he did make sure she covered up her water supply and advised her to hold a damp rag over her nose and mouth if she had to go outside when ash was falling.

The ever-present thirst was the hardest to bear. Even though the people of Lanzarote had long been used to conserving water, there had always been enough if one was careful. Not any more: it was not just their scanty crops which were threatened, they themselves were faced with the prospect of dying of thirst. Water was strictly rationed, the big communal cisterns put under armed guard; however, it was nobody's fault when one of them cracked of its own accord one night, spilling all its precious contents. A string of camels had to be dispatched to the spring at Famara with as many water containers as they could carry. They returned with water tainted with sulphur and even more brackish than usual. The spring had slowed to a trickle, the camel drivers reported.

'Drink as little water as possible,' El Moro advised Milagro. 'Make it last, it may not rain for months.'

For once he was wrong. Towards the end of November, it rained heavily all one morning, but it rained wet ash, leaving the houses streaked with dirt, the streets sticky with a horrible black sludge which clogged the feet and clothes of those who were foolish enough to risk leaving the shelter of their homes. Most of the animals died that day too.

Milagro found her goat lying on its side, motionless, its white fur clotted with mud and its yellow eyes staring sightlessly up at the ragged remains of her prickly pear. She had ventured out into what had once been her vegetable garden when the black deluge ceased. The vegetables had completely disappeared into the mud. The hens were ominously silent, though they had not laid since the night of the first eruption, and she found them dead too, lying on their backs, legs sticking ridiculously up out of the mounds of grimy feathers. There was a horrible smell in the air which caught at her throat and made her feel sick. In a panic, she ran to fetch El Moro.

'I've never seen anything like that before.'

He stood perplexed, his words muffled by the damp cloth he held over his nose and mouth. Normally clean and tidy, particularly by contrast with the other townspeople, even his face was streaked with black and the hem of his gown was caked with the disgusting muck of the street. He had given up his turban in favour of a less imposing conical cap. He poked at one of the dirty black lumps with a mud-encrusted slipper.

'Quite dead. It must be something to do with the smell of sulphur, though it only seems to have affected the smaller animals. We're still alive and the camels don't seem to have suffered. If I were you, I would eat the hens, don't waste them. Rinse the mud well off in the sea before you pluck them and clean them out properly. The flesh should be all right if you do it now.'

He turned on his heel, as if he had more important matters to attend to than the problems of a foolish girl, and she stared after him in bewilderment. She had not understood more than what to do with the hens, why sulphur should have killed them was beyond her. She and Pepito took the dead birds down to the seashore, picking their way through the wet black sludge in the streets. They were both even dirtier when they got there and it was an unpalatable task, cleaning and plucking the filthy corpses. Pepito splashed around in the little waves and they played games, dowsing each other with water just as if life had returned to normal. At least they were clean for once when they finished, though salty.

The birds smelled peculiar when she cooked them and they tasted worse, like the fish boiled in the sea which Felipe had brought back at the beginning of the disaster, but they made a welcome change from vegetables and dates. Whether she had eaten too much or whether there was really something wrong with the meat, she felt very ill that night. Pepito did not seem to be sick, though he had eaten as much as she had. At least, he was sound asleep. By morning she realised that her stomach pains were not being caused by indigestion at all. She was going into labour, far too early.

By the time she had correctly identified the cause of her griping pains, they were so bad that she could hardly move, much worse than with the birth of any of her previous children. She felt her waters go and she had to call out and wake Pepito so that he could go for the midwife. He got up reluctantly, grumbling that it was only just light, and it seemed hours before he came back. He was eating a handful of dates and he reported sulkily that the midwife was not in her hut and no one knew where she was. Milagro groaned in despair. She was sure he had done no more than wander around outside till he found someone he could beg something to eat from. In between contractions, she was forced to drag herself to the door of the hut and call for help.

She could not believe that the baby, hitherto so feeble, should cause her so much trouble and pain in its efforts to be born. The midwife arrived at last but there was little she could do except wait, feeling Milagro's distended stomach at intervals and muttering discouraging comments.

Please be born, please, whispered Milagro desperately to the unwilling baby, please don't make me suffer like this. It was not until late evening that the agonising contractions suddenly gave way to a feeling of blessed relief as the baby at last slid out of her tortured body. She could hear the midwife mumbling to herself anew but there was no sound from the baby. She opened her eyes and tried, without success, to sit up. The old woman was slapping and shaking the tiny body, still covered in slime and blood, holding the poor little thing up by its heels in an attempt to get it to breathe. It was a girl. The midwife's efforts were at last rewarded by a faint wail, but when Milagro took the baby in her arm she had the impression she was barely alive. She did not move except to gasp for breath and her eyes rolled unseeingly in her head.

The midwife shrugged when Milagro appealed to her for help and advice, continuing her ritual cleaning and tidying up after the birth with no more than a sarcastic comment or two about children born out of wedlock being doomed to an early death—a piece of superstition dredged up from nowhere and calculated to plunge Milagro into the depths of despair.

She felt that night as if she was struggling to stay alive too, her body hot with fever, torn and exhausted after so many hours of difficult labour, her throat dry and raw after so much screaming in pain. She held the unfortunate little girl close and tried to get her to suck, but she did not seem to have the energy to do even that. Towards dawn, she had some kind of convulsion and stopped breathing for a moment but by some miracle she recovered. Mother and daughter lay together gasping for breath, but when the light came they were both still alive. The tiny wizened body lay like a rag doll in Milagro's arms. She willed her to live, at least till Felipe should return.

*

More than six weeks passed. The fishing boats came and went twice, bringing her only some fish and a vague message that Felipe would not be long. There was something about someone who was very ill, who needed nursing so Francisco said, but Milagro received this piece of news with decided scepticism. Felipe was the sort of man who would avoid an invalid at all costs.

He had deserted her for good. Either that or he was dead. Francisco would not tell her the truth and she had no time to interrogate him, for all her energies were devoted to keeping her baby alive. She neglected Pepito too, spending all her waking hours talking to the baby incessantly, stroking the scanty black hair, imploring her not to give up, to wait for Papa at least, but the baby did not respond.

Pepito would stand sullenly, watching the tiny infant as Milagro cradled her in her arms; he resisted all Milagro's efforts to draw him to her, to make him hold the baby.

'She's your baby sister,' she told him with such a note of desperation in her voice that he backed away all the sooner. 'She's very ill but if we both love her enough she'll live. When Papa comes back he'll be so happy to see her.'

But she felt her words were hollow, she did not believe what she was saying and Pepito would pull away and run outside. The baby seemed to take only enough milk to survive. She did not put on any weight and what little milk she did swallow would be vomited up again more often than not. She had convulsions too, the only time she moved her limbs was when she went into a fit, flopping back afterwards totally motionless, so still that Milagro had to feel her skinny chest to see if she was breathing or not. The midwife was no more help than she had been when the baby was born: it would certainly die and that was that. El Moro was hardly more encouraging when Milagro appealed to him.

'She's blind, I think, probably deaf as well.'

He pronounced the sentence in his usual unemotional way, but he did agree to give the unfortunate baby a soothing syrup to stop the convulsions. From then on, for the last few days of its pathetic little life, it lay in a torpor, its breathing so shallow and slow that Milagro gave up all hope.

She went to see Don Miguel. After debating endlessly, wringing her hands over her daughter's tiny gasps for breath, she dared to brave his wrath; she had to give her baby a name, she could not let her die unbaptised. She was harshly received.

'Impious girl', bellowed the priest when she crept into the church, her dying baby in her arms. 'How dare you appear in God's presence when you have declared yourself in league with the devil? You have betrayed your God and your people, you have sided with the forces of evil, you have brought down this punishment on the island through your wickedness. You permitted the evil one to lay his hands on this innocent baby.' Nothing seemed to escape his notice.

She could only acknowledge her faults dumbly, head bowed under the storm of invective.

'If you want me to baptise your child, you must make your own confession,' he went on, running out of abusive phrases. 'God will not forgive you easily but you must ask for his forgiveness all the same.'

She made some sort of stumbling incoherent confession, hardly knowing what she was saying, and the priest consented to sprinkle the baby with holy water, naming her Milagro like herself, though no miracle took place. The baby lay silent throughout the brief ceremony and did not stir as the drops of water fell on her forehead. Don Miguel seemed slightly surprised, as if he had expected the baby to shrivel up or cry out at the very least, being so obviously the devil's spawn. Milagro realised, with a sinking heart, that her little daughter had died during the ceremony, her frail life coming to an end unnoticed. She wept bitterly over the motionless bundle, huddled on the ground in front of the font.

Don Miguel's attitude softened somewhat; perhaps she was genuinely penitent.

'Tears are not enough, only good actions are proof of true repentance,' he intoned, but he did not reprimand her further.

Milagro's mind was in turmoil. Distraught with grief after her daughter's death, she was repentant, truly repentant, she would really go and sin no more, but Felipe was not there and what was she to do when he returned? Send him away again? She knew she would not have enough strength to resist temptation. She tried her best for Pepito, or thought she did, and it was not her fault that Felipe did not want to marry her. God had punished her by taking her baby away from her, but many women who went to church regularly had babies who died too. If they were punished for nothing, where did that leave her? She dared not put this question to Don Miguel, it would have brought down even more wrath on her head.

One thing she could do to please the priest was to avoid El Moro, though she was loath to do so. He was the only one who ever had a kind word for her these days, who ever offered help. He was not a Christian and he indulged in all sorts of heathen practices but it was an odd kind of devil who had time to think about helping a poor woman. Was the devil so desperate for souls that he would go to such lengths to entrap hers? She could not believe she was so important.

She avoided going to the market for a while, as it meant passing in front of his house. There really was no market any more in any case, there was so little to sell and so few people who could afford to buy anything. The price of grain had doubled, then tripled. The townspeople took to trading amongst themselves and those who still had money were those who were also able to pay to leave the island.

Like Doña Constancia and Señor Perez. They chartered a trading schooner, one of the few which still made a regular run from Cadiz and thought it worthwhile calling in at Lanzarote on the way to or from Gran Canaria. Milagro went down to the port nearly every day, to scan the horizon for returning sails, to see which boats had come in overnight, in the hope that Felipe might be on one of them. She had to look for work too, there could be the odd net to be mended, a torn sail that needed patching.

*

She was idly watching the activity on the quay one morning. A ship was being loaded with an important cargo of household goods and a carriage swept down the quay towards it, nearly running her over. A familiar figure alighted—Doña Constancia. Her fine linen gown, with its stiffly corseted bodice and volu-minous red skirts, contrasted strikingly with the drab and ragged sailors on the ship and Milagro looked guiltily down at her own shabby skirts. Not quite as ragged as last time; she made sure her hair was neatly tied back, and straightened her own bodice before she made her way through the busy throng of seamen and would-be passengers. Doña Constancia saw her coming but her expression did not change.

'We're leaving for Gran Canaria.'

She did not seem to think it necessary to volunteer any more information and turned away to give some instructions to her maid, who was struggling to unload several small boxes from the carriage. Milagro did not know the girl; when she had left home, Doña Constancia had had a fiercely competent mid-dle-aged woman to wait on her, not this downtrodden, timid village girl.

Señor Perez was already on board; he had emerged on deck on hearing the carriage and he scowled when he saw Milagro. He beckoned to his wife and they exchanged a few remarks out of Milagro's hearing, but it was perfectly obvious what he was saying: he had no intention of being saddled with his step-daughter and her illegitimate family.

Milagro had not even thought of asking her mother to allow them to accompany her; she could not possibly leave Arrecife till Felipe came back, in any case . She was not all that surprised by her stepfather's hostile attitude. He seemed to bear a grudge against her and she assumed that he must think of her as a business transaction which had gone wrong, an article of merchandise which he had not been able to exploit for his own ends. Or perhaps, more likely, it had cost him a great deal to make his peace with Doña Constancia when she learned of his attempts to seduce her daughter.

Doña Constancia stared pointedly at Milagro's now flat stomach, taking in the little boy at her side but the absence of any baby in her arms. It was as if she already knew what had happened. Milagro bit her lip and would not speak; her mother's accusing expression revived all her feelings of grief at the little girl's transitory existence. She was afraid of bursting into tears if she said anything at all and she would not cry in front of her mother, though it now occurred to her that she might never see her again.

To a casual observer, they were so obviously mother and daughter: the same height, the same features, the same stance as the haughty older woman confronted the defiant girl. Then Doña Constancia's expression softened imperceptibly, despite herself, as if she too realised that this might be their last meeting. She took off one of her gold bracelets, one of the thinner ones, and handed it to Milagro.

'Goodbye,' she said. 'You'll be able to sell that for a good price. I can see you still need money.'

Milagro took the bracelet, so surprised that she could

hardly stammer out a farewell herself. Doña Constancia gathered her skirts, lifting them disdainfully clear of the filth on the quay, and went towards the gangplank, heels clicking on the cobbles. The sailors hauled it in after her and cast off the last lines. The ship swung out from the quay. As the men hoisted the main sail ash showered down on to the deck, but the wind was brisk and it soon dispersed; murky clouds still hung over the town itself but the boats in the harbour showed up white and red and blue again. The sea could not free itself of its pall of ash, though, and the water slapped dully against the bright paint of the hulls.

The schooner quickly made the harbour entrance. Milagro gazed after it, not taking her eyes off the stiff, scarlet-clad figure clearly visible on the poop deck. She did cry at last, though she could not say why; for her dead children, her own lost youth, for her mother who was still her mother, whatever had passed between them.

She was distracted by a howl from Pepito who had got into a fight with a boy much bigger than himself. Milagro comforted him guiltily. His behaviour had become much worse over the last few weeks and she knew she was to blame. Wrapped up in her own grief at the baby's death and her increasing despair at Felipe's continued absence, she had shown little interest in the only being who needed and wanted her love.

*

The volcanoes continued to spout their fire and wretched refugees continued to trail into Arrecife, so many with those terrible untreatable burns, from which they soon died. They would squat in the streets or in houses deserted by those who had fled the island, the lucky ones. For there were frequent fights over the few berths available on departing boats. The governor had attempted to halt the exodus but with little success, and some opportunist captains had taken to charging an exorbitant price for the passage to Gran Canaria—actions bitterly resented by those who did not have the means to pay. Sailors armed with clubs became a common sight after several ugly incidents, when departing ships were the object of fierce attacks by disappointed would-be passengers.

Milagro did not like to go down to the port any more; ogled and threatened constantly by all sorts of rough and desperate characters, she saw the lawlessness spread to the citizens of Arrecife themselves, everyone clutching at fragile means of survival. She barred her door at night, something she had never needed to do before, only leaving the house to go to church. She attended regularly now, spending many hours in repentant prayer. Perhaps God would forgive her, though what she longed for most was still what was most forbidden.

She found herself living in total isolation, like many of the inhabitants of the town; friends proving unreliable, neighbours fleeing without waiting to say goodbye. Even if she did go down to the port, there was no one she knew there. Lourdes and Isabel had gone and Caterina was dead; already ill with some wasting disease which caused her to cough continuously, she had not survived the most recent fall of ash. There was no praise from Don Miguel for returning to the fold and it was not a time for renewing or making friendships. The townspeople regarded each other with deep suspicion, jealously checking the amount of water each was allowed to draw from the communal cistern, watching fiercely anyone who might approach their scanty vegetable plots or date palms too closely.

Her efforts to involve herself with the Guanche community met with a chilly reception; she might be associating with a Guanche but it was made quite clear that she was not one of them. 'We know who you are' was the only response she got when she smiled and greeted one of the women coming out of church one day. She began to realise that her solitary existence might very well continue for months—Pepito's life, her own life, her sanity, would depend on her efforts and hers alone. She no longer dared to hope for Felipe's return, El Moro destroyed any illusions she had on that subject.

On returning from Mass the week after Christmas, another bleak, cheerless festival for her, she unexpectedly came face to face with him. She wanted to turn away but it seemed impolite to do so. She stood nervously before him, unable to avoid his gaze. He had never seemed menacing or threatening to her before; though many people were afraid of him, he had never given her any cause to shun him. But now, because she had done so without giving him any reason for breaking off their acquaintance so abruptly, she wanted to flee. She believed she read scorn in his expression, as if he knew only too well why she had kept away from him and despised her for being a weak, easily-led woman. But he only said,

'How are you, Milagro? I hear Felipe has still not returned. Are you finding life very difficult without him?'

'No.' In her embarrassment, she answered more curtly than she had meant to. He seemed to be mocking her too. 'I can manage very well on my own.'

'Don't you wonder why Felipe hasn't come back?'

She stared at him, realisation dawning. El Moro knew more about Felipe than she did, there was some terrible mystery about his continued absence which he could clarify—if he chose to. His face was impassive, he was waiting for her to ask. She had never really looked at him before, never considered how strange and alien he was, his dark robe of fine linen with its elaborately plaited sash making him a far more impressive figure than Don Miguel. There was something devilish, truly, about his dark eyes and hooked nose and she had a sudden terrified thought that the tall cap he had adopted in place of his turban was there to conceal his horns. She should have feared him always, should have cringed before his penetrating regard, have crossed the street when she saw him coming like all sensible people did, but she had left it too late. 'What do you know about him?' Her desire to learn the truth overcame her dread.

El Moro weighed up the advantages of telling her, or so it seemed. He stood silent for so long that she could not bear it.

'Why won't you tell me?'

She put out her hand to grasp the front of his robe but drew it back. She did not dare to touch him. His face was grave, he was reluctant to tell her the bad news.

'I don't know what has happened down in the south but Felipe has a wife and daughters in a village near Yaiza. He has been married to this woman, a Guanche like him, for ten years. He was obliged to go and find out if they were safe; he will return for you and Pepito as soon as he can.'

Whatever Milagro had been preparing herself to hear, it was certainly not that.

'It's not possible.'

Her voice was so faint that El Moro could hardly hear her.

'Why should it not be possible?'

'Because...' Milagro fell silent. There was no reason at all why it should not be possible. She knew nothing of Felipe's past other than what he had told her; in the four years they had been together, he had rarely spoken of his family and her assumption that he had no close relatives left was completely without foundation. She had not pressed him on the subject. The break with her own family having been so dramatic and abrupt, she had been glad that Felipe seemed to have no family ties himself, that she could create a family for him, for them both. Now what did she have to show for it? One son, three dead babies and a husband who was no such thing and never would be.

'I don't believe you.'

She fled down the street to the shelter of her small hut, Pepito trailing after her complaining as usual, and collapsed on the bed, weeping bitterly. How could Felipe have deceived her so and for so long?

What a fool she had been to believe him. She should have known right from the start, should have seen through his smooth talk and facile explanations of his prolonged absences. She had been so naïve in those days.

Her tears were of anger as much as grief, anger at herself, anger at her faithless lover. She had no claim on him except that of affection, which seemed to have vanished, for surely he would have come back by now. A foolish girl with an illegitimate child, that was all she was. She could no longer believe that he would return, he had been gone for too long.

She lay in a stupor of misery; she could not decide what she should do, if there was any way out. She could stay in Arrecife and starve, waiting for him to come back, waiting forever perhaps, or she could leave for Gran Canaria, beg a place on a boat she could not pay for, be obliged in lieu of payment to share the bunk of some lecherous, callous seaman who would abandon her once they reached port. Then she would be completely destitute, becoming a whore the only way of providing for herself and Pepito. She shuddered; she could not do so. Other girls seemed to find it so easy, Lourdes had told her over and over again that there was nothing to it, easy money, always customers, no need even to think about it. Not yet, not yet, maybe it would never be necessary, maybe Felipe would come back after all.

She could hear Pepito outside, quarrelling with the son of some refugees who had lodged themselves in a dilapidated abandoned hut nearby. Pepito. He was her greatest problem: he idolised Felipe and he at least believed his father would come back. He would refuse to go to sleep at night, demanding a promise that his father would be there in the morning, bursting into tears when he woke to find his father still absent. He would have nightmares too, screaming in the night that he had seen his father disappearing into the fire.

He was greedy and aggressive with other children, stealing food or toys, snatching whatever he wanted and, when reproached, turning on his accusers such a glance of put-upon innocence that many did not like to scold him. It horrified her to think that at such a young age he could manipulate people like Felipe could. He would do the same with her: a crying fit if she wanted him to sit down and eat or put on clean clothes would suddenly, when she was quite exhausted and her patience at an end, change into total capitulation and he would turn on her blue eyes full of reproof, Felipe's eyes, saying,

'Why do you shout at me so, I was just going to do it.'

It was her fault, she knew that, for neglecting him but she could not reach out to him and give him the love he needed, she was too confused herself, fighting for her own survival. Lately, he had become convinced that she had sent Felipe away on purpose and it was in vain that she explained to him that he had had to go, that he was only away for a little while, that he was really and truly coming back any day now. Then they would all go to Gran Canaria, she assured him, far out of reach of the volcanoes, to a place where the sky was not full of smoke and ash, where they could breathe freely and live happily. Pepito refused to believe her; she did not believe it herself any more but she had to make herself pretend that it was still possible, that some kind of future less bleak than the present was not out of the question.

Chapter VI – 1756 – The Ruined Island

The trading schooner Concepción limps at last into the port of Arrecife one afternoon in late September. Any changes to the port since the time Milagro watched her mother depart have been for the worse. Collapsing quays, rocks thrust up by the power of the eruptions, the devastation caused is still only too evident. The ship scrapes its keel briefly on one of these rocks; Bartolomé, the captain, winces and yells at the man on the bow with the lead line, but he is far too tired to make a big issue out of it. A graze on the keel is nothing to what the trading schooner has just been through. The island of Lanzarote is cursed, there is no question about it. It looks like the backside of Hades, with its black and brown countryside and its still smoking peaks, and every voyage he makes, either down from Cadiz or back up again, is the same—a gale coming or going. Sometimes both ways. Lanzarote's only advantage is that it provides the first safe harbour in the Canaries before sailing on to some more profitable destination, like Tenerife or Gran Canaria.

The captain signals wearily to the man on the capstan to let go the starboard anchor and to the sailors at the foot of the mainmast to lower sail. The gaff, on its much-frayed halyard, creaks slowly down and the ship swings gradually round head to wind, as the anchor bites into the sandy bottom of the harbour. The men gather up the unwieldy bundle of sailcloth. It is not their big mainsail, it is a much smaller, heavily patched square sail, the only usable piece of canvas they have left, jury-rigged to get them into port when the southerly gale at last subsided.

Bartolomé glances up at the rig, or what is left of it. The forward topmast has gone altogether, its stays clacking uselessly against the rest of the mast in the stiff breeze which still blows, though from the north east now. The yardarm, broken in three pieces, is lashed inside the bulwarks starboard of the poop deck, across the yawning gap through which their solitary cannon had battered its way to freedom and a watery grave. The bowsprit has miraculously survived; though several planks have opened up round the stem owing to the ceaseless pounding of the monstrous seas, the bobstay has held firm and prevented the bowsprit from being wrenched out of its socket. If that had happened, it would probably have taken the stem with it and they would have sunk.

Bartolomé shudders. They have survived and reached port, thanks to... luck? God? St. Christopher? After the cannon went over the side, sweeping one of the deck crew along with it and leaving another with a broken arm, even he had been tempted to offer up a few prayers to some appropriate saint.

He wonders what chance there will be of doing any repairs in Lanzarote. Spars they cannot hope for; there are no trees on the island apart from palm trees and the Concepción will have to stagger as far as Gran Canaria on what she has left before they can think about any work on the mast and yardarm.

Still, it should be a downwind run now the gale has passed, and if he can scrounge a few coils of rope and a small quantity of canvas the sailing master should be able to improve their jury rig enough for them to make Gran Canaria in not more than twenty-four hours. They have been lucky to have enough tackle left to erect any kind of rig at all.

The bosun appears from below decks to report: they have shipped a good deal of water and everything—hold and cabins alike—has been swamped, but there is little actual structural damage. He hands Bartolomé a pewter mug of dubious-looking Xeres, his dripping moustache revealing that he has sampled it himself on the way up from the hold.

'Quartermaster says it's undrinkable. It's got salt water in it.'

Bartolomé seizes the mug and boots the man down the deck.

'That's for me to say, not you. What about the rest of the cargo?'

The hold contains, besides forty kegs of the afore-mentioned sherry, quantities of bundles of hides and bolts of cloth for the merchants of Gran Canaria and several chests of assorted weaponry—swords, daggers and pistols of an ornamental variety, totally useless, in Bartolomé's opinion, for any practical hand to hand fighting. The bosun picks himself up, cursing.

'All wet.'

'Too bad.' Bartolomé shrugs. It is not the first time he has arrived in the islands with a sodden cargo. The merchants will pay anyway; they have to, they need the goods, damaged or not. His eyes are burning with ten days' accumulation of salt and he rubs them with his claw-like left hand. It is missing two fingers. A Turkish pirate had slashed them off in a close-fought duel, or so he tells impressionable whores, but the truth is more prosaic. He lost them through dropping a hatch cover on to his hand when he came back on board one night dead drunk. He is going to get drunk tonight too, with any luck. There seems to be little sign of life ashore at present but he knows where the tavern is. And the whorehouse. He scratches his crotch, itchy after ten days in the same salt-encrusted garments, and it swells hopefully at the thought

'Gómez!' he yells. The cabin boy comes running. 'Tell our esteemed passenger we've arrived.'

*

Bartolomé dislikes taking passengers, even ones who have paid as much as Don Rodrigo has, but sometimes it is a financial necessity. Passengers are invariably trouble: demanding to know how long it will be before they reach land, why the wind is blowing, why it is not blowing, being sick over the wind-ward rail, wanting food and drink during a sail change. The list of their crimes is endless.

Don Rodrigo has, as a matter of fact, been little trouble. He remarked that they were suddenly heading straight out to sea but he accepted Bartolomé's explanation that it was better to get some sea room before the impending gale struck, rather than risk being blown onto the inhospitable African shore with its reefs and sandbars. He retired to his cabin on the second day of the gale and stayed there, sick and terrified no doubt, but out of the way. In an uncharacteristic moment of compassion, Bartolomé did send Gómez to knock on his door at one point, in case the noble lord had died or something. Gómez reported hearing groans so Bartolomé let him be. Both storm jibs chose that moment to part company with their respective halyards so there were other things to think about than moribund passengers.

Gómez taps on the door of the so-called best cabin, one that is in theory reserved for passengers rather than crew. After a long pause, the door opens and a haggard, whiskery face peers through the aperture. The face is accompanied by a disgusting smell of stale air, vomit and excrement. Even worse than the foc'sle.

'Señor, we've arrived in Lanzarote.'

'I guessed that.' Rodrigo's temper has been considerably soured by his enforced confinement. 'Get me some wine and something to eat, anything. And some water.'

He hands the lad a small copper coin and closes the door again.

Gómez retreats from the stench. It is quite beyond his comprehension why such a one as Don Rodrigo should, from choice, wish to undertake such a voyage, why he should want to pay to risk his life. Gómez himself is black and blue with bruises, his throat sore from praying and swallowing salt water.

Even more to the point, why would Don Rodrigo want to visit such a bleak and miserable island as Lanzarote. He must be crazy. However, Gómez ties the coin carefully into the ragged tail of his shirt; crazy or not, the man's money is perfectly good. He scuttles off in the direction of the galley to see if there is anything left to eat.

Rodrigo contemplates the shambles the storm has made of the cabin. He has heard the anchor chain run out and, correctly, assumed that they have arrived in Arrecife. The sea was much calmer during the last twenty-four hours but, shamefully, he was too exhausted and weak from the buffeting of the storm to do anything but lie on his bunk. With some difficulty, he now opens the porthole and attempts to unlatch the deadlight which protects the precious glass from the pounding of the waves. It is not till he manages to get both of them open that he realises how foul the cabin had become. He takes several deep breaths of fresh air before turning to apply himself to the muddle on the cabin floor.

The stout iron-bound trunk which holds his geological equipment and notebooks, though wet outside, is intact inside, fortunately, since it also holds his pistols and ammunition, but every time the ship rolled it was sent sliding across the cabin and has succeeded in demolishing a chair and a stool and splitting open his smallest box, the one which contains more fashionable items such as his wigs and hair powder. He picks out one limp bedraggled object, dark with sea water, and hurls it with disgust into the corner, where it lands with a splash in the puddle formed under the leak from the poop deck.

The box of powder is in no better shape, caked solid by the damp air. He might as well abandon any hope of appearing properly dressed in Lanzarote: it is pointless to wear silk breeches and a brocade coat without a wig or powdered hair at the very least. Perhaps he should plait his hair with tar like the sailors do and not bother to trim his beard, grown impossibly bushy after ten days of neglect. On no account. He is certain to find the island somewhat primitive and lacking in amenities but this does not mean he is obliged to dress like a peasant himself.

A knock on the door announces the return of the boy bearing a jug of water, another of sherry and a basket containing a hard knob of bread and an even harder knob of cheese, together with two uninviting-looking oranges.

'Señor, the captain wants to know if you're going ashore now.'

'Certainly not,' retorts Rodrigo tetchily. 'Can't you see what a mess there is to sort out?'

He pushes the lad out again and closes the door on him. He is ravenous. Nothing he has eaten for the last ten days has stayed in his stomach long enough to do any good and even the unappetising choice of victuals on offer looks appealing. The sherry has gone sour and tastes brackish into the bargain but he drinks some, feeling the alcohol rush to his head. Thus fortified, he addresses the difficult task of selecting something wearable from his third trunk, the largest one, battered but still sound.

He is battered too. He aches all over; he has been thrown out of his bunk onto the floor more times than he can remember and the clothes he has on, the same ones in which he left Cadiz, are unspeakably disgusting, stinking with vomit and piss. He strips them off, hurling them into the corner after his wig. He picks out his plainest breeches and a shirt made of cotton rather than silk with not too many touches of embroidery at collar and cuff. A cursory glance out of the porthole tells him that there are hardly likely to be any notable dignitaries waiting on the quay to receive him. His rough riding boots and oldest coat will do.

No. He is still looking far too much like one of the crew of the Concepción. He combs the tangles, and a few lice, out of his filthy hair and ties it neatly back. He selects a smarter, better-cut coat, one which does not smack too much of the exaggerated styles of Madrid nevertheless, and puts on his best riding boots. The sort of clothes he would normally wear in the country.

Not only is Lanzarote not the place for silver buckles but, more practically, his best clothes are dreadfully creased, beyond even Fernando's help. He sighs; perhaps he should have insisted on Fernando accompanying him after all. At least it would be up to him to sort out the mess. But then he would probably have died of fright during the gale and Rodrigo would have been looking after him rather than the other way around. On the way back from the Lipari Islands to Naples, the man lay moaning in his bunk the whole time and the Atlantic has been ten times worse.

Rodrigo's stomach heaves anew at the recollection. The first few days were good: with the brisk trade winds behind them, they sped down towards the African coast. Then, on the third evening, there was an ominous calm. Rodrigo was on deck and observed Bartolomé anxiously scanning the horizon. The sails flapped uselessly in the failing breeze and, even to a landlubber like Rodrigo, it was clear that the dark clouds massing round the setting sun boded no good. When questioned, the captain was laconically pessimistic.

'Don't expect to see land for a few days,' he informed his alarmed passenger. He turned the head of the ship out to sea and barked an assortment of commands at his unsavoury looking crew.

A repellent bunch, the men who were scurrying up and down the deck, making fast all the moveable objects and reducing the size of the mainsail to a mere pocket hand-kerchief. Twenty-three of them in all, mostly Spanish or French, plus three blacks and a cook who spoke no known language. To a man they resembled the type of villain one would hope never to encounter in a dark alley late at night, but they were competent enough and, despite their lawless appearance, they generally obeyed orders without question. Rodrigo, though no seaman himself, had travelled enough to know how to pick out a well-found ship with a professional and reasonably honest captain, who would employ a capable crew. He came to learn, too, that looks are not everything. Ragged breeches, an unkempt beard and uncouth manners do not necessarily mean that a man is incompetent or that he lacks the instinct for self-preservation which is necessary for communal survival, the instinct which compels one to do what one has to for the safety of the ship, disregarding one's own fear and the foulness of the weather.

*

He did not linger long on deck once the storm had fairly got under way. The violence, the scream of the wind, the constant deluge of salt water as waves broke over the deck itself, the rolling and pitching of the ship as she tossed and tumbled in the grip of the relentless sea soon drove him down below to lie miserably in his bunk or, more often than not, on the floor. Not only was he sick, he was angry and ashamed at himself, such a seasoned traveller and soldier, for being so frightened. His blood ran cold as it never did in battle, hearing the noise of the cannon thundering from one side of the deck to the other, then the howls of the injured man and the even more terrible shriek of the sailor who was swept overboard with the gun.

He does not want to think about it. He takes another mouthful of vinegary sherry and gnaws at the cheese; it was once a good viejo manchego and is still edible. He dips the bread, which is not, into the sherry and eats it all the same.

Then he attacks his beard. It takes him a little while to trim it to his satisfaction; he can see nothing in the dim light of the cabin and when he takes the tarnished silver mirror over to the porthole, it proves to be so speckled with salt that he can barely make out his reflection in any case. As he splashes water over his face, he hears feet running on deck and the creaking of the ship's gig being lowered. He takes another glance out of the porthole. Weapons? Shouldn't be necessary; on the other hand, poverty and lawless desperation often go together. He buckles on his sword belt and sticks his dagger through it before going up on deck.

*

The Concepción is anchored in a harbour which, though sheltered, is strewn with reefs. Bartolomé must be very familiar with it to pick his way through the rocks, even though they are quite visible in the bright afternoon sun—Rodrigo had not noticed the slight bump as they nudged one of them just before the anchor was dropped. The natural curve of the land has been extended by a breakwater on which sits a castle of sorts, more of a large tower, shabby and crumbling, built of sandstone and lava, inadequately daubed with whitewash. The prospect is not inviting. There are few other craft in the harbour: a trading schooner even more mauled than the Concepción is anchored off too, and a couple of bedraggled fishing boats are tied up alongside a broken-down quay. Small houses line the wharves, some built in the same style as the fortress, some whitewashed, while a tumbledown row of hovels sneaks away along the shore as if ashamed of its mean appearance. The town does not seem to be large and appears to be still partly in ruins, missing roofs and dilapidated, half-repaired walls being commonplace. A church tower rises above the houses and Rodrigo is relieved to see one or two more imposing edifices and a number of warehouses at the town end of the breakwater, evidence that Arrecife has once had some pretensions to prosperity. He is not expecting too much. In Cadiz, he heard all the horror stories about the devastation caused by the six years of volcanic eruption, which is why he has come after all, but he has been assuming that by now, twenty years later, there would be a few more indications of, if not affluence, at least a relatively thriving town with some signs of a reviving agriculture.

Not so. The hills visible at the back of the narrow coastal plain on which the town sits are bare and bleak, black and brown and grey, innocent of any vegetation. Along the shore, a line of date palms and the odd straggling fig tree present a brave green face to their grim surroundings but that is all: desolation is the order of the day. A small boat is being rowed across the harbour towards the Concepción and the water is the most colourful part of the scene, bright turquoise and dark blue, glittering in the afternoon sun like a stained glass window.

'Why are we not alongside the quay?', Rodrigo demands of Bartolomé, who is watching the approach of the boat with a scowl on his face. He has not realised that he will be marooned on board a ship at anchor, at the mercy of the ship's crew who may not wish to take him ashore unless suitably tipped.

'It's too shallow.' Bartolomé is short with him. He too would prefer to be tied up to the quay. It is less perilous, coming back drunk late at night, to step simply onto the deck rather than to have to attempt rowing across the harbour. On the other hand, if he finds a willing girl, he need not be back till morning. With this pleasing prospect before him, he unbends sufficiently to give his passenger a more detailed explanation.

'The quays were built before the eruptions and the harbour was deeper then. They don't have the money to build another quay in deeper water or to do some dredging. In fact, they don't have the money for anything much here.'

The rowing boat has reached the Concepción. It contains two ragged and villainous oarsmen, and a fat official and a thin official, both clad in threadbare approximations of official uniforms. Bartolomé watches them climb laboriously on board. He does not order any of his men to give them a hand over the bulwarks and does not volunteer the ship's manifest until asked for it. Officials, like passengers, are high on his list of expend-able personnel. Rodrigo's presence arouses their interest but he has no intention of embarking on a long and tedious explana-tion of why such a one as Don Rodrigo should wish to visit their poverty-stricken land. He shares Gómez's sentiments on the subject.

Rodrigo wanders away up to the bow for a further inspec-tion of the island he has been so eager to visit. The sand on the beach by the causeway is black, volcanic; he has seen sand like that before in Stromboli, it is a common feature of a volcanic landscape, but it gives Lanzarote a dismal funereal air, unre-lieved by the verdure of other places he has visited. He ought to have realised. He has heard that the island has little natural rainfall and few springs but he has not really thought it would be this barren.

His musings are interrupted by a shout from Bartolomé.

'Señor, you can lodge with the schoolteacher. These men will send him to meet you on the quay.'

A schoolteacher. The first sign that Lanzarote might have something approaching a normal life, despite its initial appearance of wretchedness and poverty. A few children are splashing in the water at the end of the causeway, but he has not thought of them as being sufficiently civilised to warrant the presence of a schoolteacher on the island. The Canaries are not far from Spain, they are part of Spain, he must remember that; these people are Spaniards and Christians, not Turks or black savages, however savage their environment may appear. He hastens back down to his cabin to repack his trunks, a lengthy procedure accompanied by much discarding of water-logged items (he bestows the box of ruined wigs on a bemused Gómez). The officials have not waited for him and he is left to haggle with the bosun and the gig crew.

When he steps from the gig onto dry land, for the first time in a fortnight, his legs give way. The dock seems to sway and he almost falls over. The crew snigger. Rodrigo counts out a few coins then ostentatiously puts some of them back in his purse before tipping the bosun.

Chapter VII – Flight

Milagro stayed indoors most of the day now, a hostage to misery and despair, letting Pepito run riot and hardly caring what mischief he got up to. The birth, and death, of her baby had not affected her so deeply while there was still some hope in prospect, but now her distress took on a physical aspect. When she began to bleed again, it did not stop after the usual few days and she felt weak, despairingly weak. She found it an effort now even to rise from her bed, to creep across to the fireplace to make some food. Not that there was much left: the grain was almost finished and she had not been able to dig out much from the vegetable patch after the deluge of ash and sludge. There was part of a cheese, made before the goat's untimely death, but someone stole nearly all the fruit off the fig tree one night.

She was going to die, she was convinced of that and worse, she did not really care. There seemed to be nothing left to make life attractive. Pepito was not sufficient reason for her to want to hold on and her inability to love her son as she should increased her depression. She was truly a lost soul now, abandoned by man, by God, by human feeling.

One morning, she physically could not get out of bed. When she moved, she felt the wetness as blood trickled out from between her thighs. Her skin was burning hot and as she reached out for the table to pull herself up, it rippled and blurred in front of her. On the floor, too feeble to get back into bed, she felt waves of heat flow through her. She thought for a moment that the eruption had at last reached Arrecife and set fire to the town, then she realised it was her own fever.

Pepito stood watching her, aghast, tears running down his face. His father had gone, now something was happening to his mother. He knelt down and touched her hand; it was so hot that he drew back in terror, sure that she was about to catch fire, expecting to see flames licking up from her skirts, to see her skin begin to blister like the fugitives who had fled the eruptions.

He had seen so many of them with scorched clothing and burned flesh; now it was happening to his mother, too.

'Mama, Mama, get up, get up, please, Mama,' Milagro could hear him crying, but when she opened her eyes she could not see him clearly. The small figure was indistinct, one minute close to, the next far away. She tried to focus on him but the effort was too much, she tried to ask him to get help but the sounds that came from her mouth in no way resembled the words she meant to say. It's no use, she thought. The roof of the hut seemed to be closing in, pressing her down, the criss-cross pattern of its palm branches a cage from which she would not escape except by dying.

Some time later, it must have been later for it seemed to be dark, she woke with her mouth full of bitter liquid. She tried to spit it out but someone was holding her mouth closed, forcing her to swallow it. She was far too weak to resist. Voices, faintly familiar, penetrated the ringing in her ears.

'How did you find her?'

'I heard the little boy...' The ringing noise took over the whole of her head, drowning the next few words.

'If the fever abates with what I've given her, she may live.' That was El Moro's voice. 'I don't know about the bleeding, I've got nothing to stop that.'

*

She must have lost more time after that because the room was light again. The ringing in her ears had subsided to an indistinct buzz and she could see, more or less clearly, a woman sitting by her bed, a squat woman about her own age. A refugee. Her cheeks were hollow and marked with the scabs of barely-healed burns, her clothes ragged and her arms covered with sores. She sat there slumped, lost in her own dismal thoughts, but her face brightened when she realised that Milagro was conscious.

'The Moor told me to make you drink some of this.'

A clay beaker was tilted towards Milagro's lips and more of the same bitter brew touched her tongue. She gagged but most of it went down her throat. She lost consciousness again. This happened several times, the room now light, now dark when she came to; sometimes the woman sat beside her, once it was El Moro himself.

She came wearily back to life. The fever abated, the bleeding stopped but nothing else had changed. The woman, Nura, told her that the volcano was still wreaking its unjust vengeance on the island, in fact its explosions had become more frequent. And Felipe had still not returned.

Pepito would not leave his mother's side; he refused to go out and play, so afraid was he that if he let her out of his sight she might still catch fire and die while his back was turned. It was not until she was actually able to get up and walk across the room that he reluctantly went off to find his former friends.

Milagro improved slowly, her recovery little helped by Nura's account of her own tribulations . She was quite rational, or so it seemed at first, but a chance word would set her off. She was one of two survivors from a family which had been wealthy once, in land if not in possessions. Now, all they had formerly owned was buried under tons of smouldering cinders: land, animals, houses, parents and children, brothers and sisters. She would gaze at Milagro, not seeing her at all as she told her story, her hands constantly moving, picking at the sores on her arms, tearing at the hem of her skirt, already in tatters.

Milagro could not think how to comfort her, but she did not seem to demand comfort. She had a terrible compulsion to tell her tale over and over again to anyone who would listen. At least I am still sane, thought Milagro, as she listened to the awful narration for the third or fourth time.

'How did you find El Moro?' she asked her one day, in an effort to stem the tide of grim memories. Nura blinked, momentarily distracted.

'I heard your little boy crying,' she said after some thought. 'I came in to see if you were all right, I hadn't seen you that morning. There you were, lying on the floor, blood everywhere, I thought you'd had a miscarriage. Pepito was trying to make you stand up but all you did was moan. He's just the same age as my son, the younger one, the one who was inside our house when it happened.'

Her eyes glazed over as the tragedy played itself out before her yet again.

'We were all out in the fields, too far away to save him. We knew what the noise was, it was just like the first time and my husband ran and ran but the fire spread so quickly you couldn't believe it.'

Her voice was monotonous, repeating a speech she had learnt by heart, that her savaged mind would not allow her to stop rehearsing.

'We all ran, everyone tried to get to their houses and save something, but the fire moved too fast. The houses started to crumble away when the red stream reached them and the people ran in the other direction then, those that still could. It was like seeing people drown, you know, they waved their arms and screamed as they sank but then they started to burn up as well, their hair was on fire...'

'Nura! Nura!' Milagro shouted at her, shaking her arm and slapping her face to halt the dreadful recital. The woman blinked, gaping at Milagro as if wondering why she was making such a fuss.

'El Moro. How did he get here?'

Nura returned temporarily to the present. 'That was Pepito. I asked him where I could get help and he led me to El Moro. I don't know what the Moor gave you but it seems to have cured you, I thought you were dying. Tell me, can he really cast spells? Could he stop the volcano?'

It was Milagro's turn to gape. The thought that El Moro might have such powers had never occurred to her and the idea was terrifying. She imagined a hawk-nosed figure striding up into the hills, stabbing a long finger at the flames and commanding them to cease. If he could do that, he must be the devil. She felt faint and dizzy at the thought and bile rose in her throat, the taste like the bitter medicine he had made her drink. What if he had taken advantage of her weakness and given her some secret potion to make her his? She remembered vaguely one night, the night she had woken to see him sitting beside her, though it might not have been that night and it might have been a dream, hands touching her, loosening her clothing, flesh against her flesh, hot, even hotter than her own. Or had it just been her fever and nothing had happened at all? Her head began to ache and she gave up trying to remember.

Pepito had changed while she was ill. He clung to her nearly all the time, convinced that his mother was going to leave him too, his former unruly behaviour a thing of the past. Milagro could barely let him out of her sight either; she had to hold on to what she had left and not end up like Nura.

The miracle she had ceased to hope for took place one night. She was nearly well now, just a little weak if she tried to do too much, and she had resumed going to church. If she did not do so, she felt, she would fall totally under El Moro's domination, though she had no real reason for thinking this. He inquired politely after her health and would give her fruit for herself or Pepito from time to time, but apart from that he kept his distance. Her feelings of dread gave way to ones of embarrassment. She owed him her life and she was not at all grateful.

It was the end of February, and she had been on her own for almost four months when she heard a small noise outside, as if someone was trying to open the door. She froze in fear, it was the middle of the night and someone was attempting to break in to the hut. Then she heard a voice.

'What's going on? Why is the door barred?'

She rushed to the door, knocked up the bar which had kept it closed and flung it open. It was full moon and the sky was quite clear that night; she could see Felipe plainly in the moon-light, haggard and hollow-eyed like an old man. There was a long silence, an interminable space of time during which she began to think she had made a mistake, that it was not him, that she had forgotten what he looked like, that it was a stranger who stood before her. He spoke at last.

'I couldn't come.'

'It doesn't matter, it doesn't matter.' What El Moro had told her about his other wife and children quite forgotten, she dragged him over the threshold. She did not dare to let go of him in case he vanished, terrified, even feeling the solidity of his body against hers, that he might be a figment of her imagination, a hallucination like the ones she had had during her illness. He was rigid in her arms, unresponsive to her embrace and when she pulled him down on to the bed, he turned away from her. To her astonishment, she was unable to arouse him at all.

'What's wrong?' Her joy at his unlooked-for return was changed into despair. He put his hand over her mouth.

'I must get some sleep.'

And sleep he did, instantly, though she could not. Her suspicions and doubts had all night to fester. He had returned to her, but why, if he no longer wanted her? What of his other family? Did he now, at last, have a conscience about going straight from his wife's bed to hers? He had brought the woman to Arrecife with him, he must have. She lay awake the rest of the night in an agony of apprehension, the wonderful comfort of having his body next to hers physically in bed at last, completely ruined.

She could not ask him for the truth straight out next morning, not at first. Pepito was bubbling with delight at his father's return and Milagro could not bring herself to spoil his pleasure. Felipe was much altered. He played willingly enough with his son but he looked years older by daylight. Grey stubble on his chin, hair grey too and not just from the ash, dark circles under his eyes, eyes which had a defeated empty look—there was hardly a trace of his former spirit. He did not say a word to her, but when he proposed to go off down to the port with Pepito she had to break the intolerable silence.

'When did the boat get back in?' She asked the question as casually as she could. He would not look her in the eye.

'I didn't come back with Francisco, I came by land with some people from Playa Blanca.'

'Your wife and daughters, I suppose.'

'What?' He did not seem to understand what she had said for a moment. 'Some people who have a passage to Gran Canaria. I helped them with their belongings.'

'I know about your wife. Your real wife, the one you've been married to for ten years, your other children.'

She began to cry and Pepito burst into tears too, without knowing why. Felipe picked him up and went to leave the hut but Milagro stood in his way.

'Why? Why?' She was shouting and weeping, not knowing what question she was asking or what answer she wanted to hear. Felipe stopped, his back turned to her, saying nothing: responsibility had finally caught up with him, a burden he could neither shoulder nor shuck off, and for once he did not have an answer.

'I know I've no rights over you, I'm just the whore you keep in Arrecife. That's the way everyone treats me but I didn't know it was true before. You could have told me why you couldn't marry me, I would have accepted that. You're my whole life but I'm only a part of yours, aren't I, just a small corner of it.'

She ranted on like the kind of shrewish woman she had always detested. Felipe turned to face her, still speechless, and reached out his hand to caress her hair, but she shook his hand away. She did not want futile gestures.

'That's all I am to you, a convenient whore, a foolish woman who didn't have the sense to say no to you.'

Pepito wailed in Felipe's arms, looking desperately from one to the other of his parents.

'Your son, your bastard son, what about him? What will happen to him?' cried Milagro. Seeing the two of them together, so alike in feature, they seemed to form an alliance which excluded her. She had a sudden dreadful thought: Felipe had not come back for her, he had come to take Pepito away, leaving her behind. She was stunned into silence.

Felipe spoke at last. So preoccupied had he been with his own predicament that he had not noticed one important detail. He had totally lost track of time.

'Where's the baby?'

'She died like all the others.' The harsh words almost choked her. 'Except unlike all the others, she never saw her father. It's just as well she did die, she would only have been another mouth to feed. We're almost starving here as it is. What did you think we were going to live on while you were gone?'

'I don't know.' He had not thought about it; he had not forgotten them but he had been sucked into the vortex of ruin and despair that was the south and west of Lanzarote. He had pushed the memory of Milagro and Pepito to the back of his mind, hoping only that they could survive with El Moro's help. Now he was forced to look at them, their faces and hair caked with ash like his own, Pepito's skinny arms and legs, Milagro's hollow cheeks. The scanty food on the shelves told the same story—a few wizened dates, a handful of root vegetables, a very small hunk of dried-up cheese. That was all they had left.

She saw him glance at her empty shelves. 'There's no work here now, you know. I was lucky last week, I mended a net and got two small fish for my efforts.'

'We can't stay here in Lanzarote, I know that. We're going to Gran Canaria. That's why I've come back, to get you and Pepito.'

'Go? How can we go? It costs a fortune to get a passage

[123]

on a boat. What are you going to pay with?'

The way he had phrased his sentence suddenly struck her.

'Who's we? You and your wife, or you and your whore? Or were you thinking of taking us both together, so you can pick and choose?'

'Milagro, will you listen to me?'

The acute misery of his expression made her pay attention.

'It's true, I've been married to Inés for more than ten years.'

Milagro let out a great sigh, a groan of distress. If he had denied it she would still have half believed him, but now she could not ignore the truth.

Felipe set Pepito down on the floor. 'I had a family, a wife, two daughters, brothers and sisters, all of them lived in Los Rodeos, near Yaiza. Most of them are dead now, burned to death and Inés is dying.' His voice was dull and expressionless. 'She was terribly burned and I don't know how long she will live. My younger daughter died last week so there's only Rosa left, the elder girl, and I promised her I would soon come back for her and take her to Gran Canaria.'

Inés. Her rival had a name.

'So it's not a wife you want, it's a nurse, is it? I'd rather choke to death here.'

'Please, Milagro.' She was aghast to see he had tears in his eyes, he had never pleaded with her before.

'You can't stay here, you know that, and Playa Blanca's much worse. Think of Pepito too, do you want to see him starve and cough himself to death, choking on all the poisons in the air? Please, come with me, we'll get a boat, pick up Rosa and find somewhere safe on Gran Canaria or Tenerife. I know the islands, it's easy living there even if we have nothing at all.'

Milagro had no answer to that. It was true, they could not survive in Lanzarote. She looked at Pepito, saw how thin and sickly he looked. He no longer complained about being hungry but he coughed repeatedly, his legs were like sticks, his eyes huge in his sallow face. She must look the same. They had to go with Felipe, however appalling the idea of sharing him with another woman, even one who might be dying; but how could she bear to listen to him say to a stranger the things he ought to be saying to her, how could she take on another woman's daughter when hers had died? He was asking her to sacrifice her life for him and Pepito and she did not think she was capable of doing so.

Whatever she did, though, she had lost him. He no longer wanted to make love to her, she could no longer excite him. She could let him take Pepito and go without her, doubling her loss, or she could go with them and nurse Inés. What if the woman was not as sick as Felipe made out? She could not trust him to tell the truth, he had told her too many lies in the past. Inés could survive for months, years even; she could see herself caring for a hated invalid while Felipe came and went with his usual disregard for anyone's feelings but his own.

'How can we go without a boat?'

There was no choice; if she wanted them to survive, they would have to go with Felipe, but the practical obstacles to their departure seemed insurmountable and she no longer believed she could rely on him. Her former blind confidence in him had gone and he was reduced in her eyes, diminished by the dismal truths she had just learnt.

'What are you going to do?'

'I have to get some ointment from El Moro for Inés. Make everything ready tonight, no more than you can carry by yourself and what food and water we've got left. Make sure you don't let anyone know we're preparing to leave. I'm going to steal a boat.'

He strode out, followed by a Pepito overjoyed that his parents were no longer quarrelling.

Milagro was bemused. Everything had changed. She had waited so long for the joyful moment of Felipe's return, it had been her only means of clinging to life all through the lonely months; but now he was here she felt nothing, no overwhelming feeling of relief and hope for the future, no surge of love, nothing but the lethargy of before. A flatness, a greyness like the town under its covering of ash. Her love for him had been stifled.

*

She began to sort vaguely through their belongings; the thought of starting all over again confused her and she could not think how to begin to prepare. Food obviously, what they had left, and water, but how long was it going to take them to reach Playa Blanca? One day, two days? It took only a few hours to walk to Teguise, perhaps it would be only a few hours to sail to Playa Blanca. She felt foolish and stupid not knowing.

She looked around the little house, the hut she had once been so proud of, though with little enough reason. Its rough unpainted walls and bare earth floor, its primitive furniture she now saw once again with the eyes of the young girl who has come down from Teguise. There was nothing there she would regret leaving behind. She still had the gold bangle her mother had given her but everything else, anything even possibly saleable, she had sold long ago. Felipe's nets had gone but he had not even noticed the bare wall where they had once hung. There was one small net left; she had thought it beyond repair but now that it was all they had she would have to do something with it. She began to work on the torn mesh, her hands pushing the bobbin of twine mechanically back and forth, her thoughts elsewhere.

Inés. A Guanche like Felipe, with the same round features and fair skin, a Guanche like Pepito. Much older than Milagro and not so pretty, she must have lost her looks by now. She pulled herself up; she was thinking of the time before the eruptions, before childbirth and poverty had faded her own looks and drawn lines on her face. She was no longer the pretty young girl who had first taken the Guanche fisherman's fancy; her hands were those of an old woman, gaunt with months of deprivation and scarred with manual labour, nails broken and black. She touched her face, feeling the dry, scaly cheeks. At nineteen, she was already old herself.

Tears trickled down her face. It did not matter whether Inés was older or less attractive, she was Felipe's wife and Milagro was not. Her only advantage over her rival was Pepito. She had given him a son and Inés had not and Felipe loved him, more than he loved her or Inés, more than she herself loved either of them. She did not seem to be able to feel anything for anyone any more, she was a husk empty of any hope or feeling, dried out, aged and grey with ash, all emotion leached out of her during the long months of waiting. She could do no more to the net, it would not last long enough to ensnare even a small fish. It was as fragile as her life. She picked up some of Pepito's toys, a wooden ball, a clay horse with a broken leg, some wooden blocks with curious carvings on them which Felipe said had come from Africa. Those she should take and the ragged remains of their clothes, so little that she could carry the bundle herself. Her mother's bracelet she hung on a string round her neck; she could sell that in Gran Canaria. Gran Canaria: the promised land, where the trees were green, where there was water, food to eat, no ash, no smoke, where the ground did not tremble. She would soon find out for herself whether all this was true.

Felipe returned with Pepito, who was carrying a loaf of bread and a meagre bag of dates. Stolen surely; she did not dare to ask. Felipe had a small box tied up in a cloth.

'Keep it away from the food, it smells. Be ready tonight, I'll be back with a boat as soon as I can.'

He set the child down on the bed, where he fell asleep almost at once, much to Milagro's relief, and Felipe was able to slip away without an exhausting scene.

She watched him go off down the dusty track, wondering

whether he really would return that night. She was afraid, afraid of going off into the unknown, and she could no longer rely on him, but she was even more afraid of being left behind in Arrecife, reduced to making a living in the only way possible for a woman on her own. Her trust in Felipe had evaporated to such an extent that she almost believed him capable of obliging her to do such a thing.

She put the dates and bread into a basket, together with the pitiful remains of her cheese, and filled the two water bottles Felipe had brought back with him last summer. They were not a common item in Arrecife, these pouches of goatskin with a drawstring at the top. Guanche work. Perhaps they had belonged to Inés. She dropped one of them, feeling the hands of her rival in the leatherwork.

Fool, fool. She had spilled some of the water and now she would have to try to scoop up more from the dregs in the cistern behind the house, filtering it many times to make it drinkable. The idea that her efforts were only hastening her towards an encounter she dreaded dominated all her thinking. It could be that Inés was really dying, in great pain, like the woman whose feet had been burned away; perhaps she was truly deserving of pity, a victim of circumstances as much as Milagro was herself. She examined the box of salve curiously, it did smell very strong, a smell like sweet, herbal camel dung. She wrapped it up again hastily but the smell seemed to linger on her hands.

Pepito woke drowsily, demanding to know when papa would be back. Soon, she told him, feeling she was lying to him as she so often did even though this time it was the truth. What was she to tell him? That they were going to another island where they would have enough to eat, where there were no fires in the sky, if his father managed to steal a boat, if they escaped the pirates on the way. That papa had another family who would be going with them.

What about the pirates, though? She had not thought about

them before but once the idea had entered her head she could not get rid of it. By the time Felipe came to get them, she was in a state of hysteria.

He tried to reason with her in exasperation.

'They don't come to Lanzarote any more, they know only too well there's nothing for them to come for.'

He dismissed her account of the boat which had been towed in with two dead men on board. 'Pirates look for big ships with plenty of cargo, they won't be interested in a small fishing boat. We must go now, Milagro, we want to be out of sight of land before it gets light.'

He picked up the bundle of belongings and the basket of food. 'Can you carry Pepito?'

She hung on to Felipe's arm, crying hysterically, and he hit her hard across the face. She was so horrified that she could not make another sound; he had never hit her before and his eyes were blazing with rage. He seemed to be losing control of himself, which frightened her even more than the unexpected blow. He pinched out the candle on the rough wooden table and put it into the food basket.

'Bring Pepito now, or stay here by yourself.'

Dumbly, she picked up the little boy and followed him. She could hardly see her way outside. The moon was up but obscured by smoke and falling ash and she stumbled repeatedly as she followed Felipe's indistinct figure down to the sea. He did not take the usual track to the harbour but turned south out of the town to where there was a rocky beach, a little way down the coast from the fortress. It had a large outcrop of ancient black lava, a token of previous eruptions hundreds of years before, and the boat Felipe had stolen was pulled up on the stones there out of sight of any prying eyes. It was very small, not much bigger than the tender to a large fishing smack, with a short mast, a tiny sail and two oars. Milagro opened her mouth to protest but Felipe put his hand over it.

'Make no sound. Do you want me to go to prison for

theft? What would you do then? Help me push it into the water.'

He stowed their scanty possessions under the seat amidships and sat Pepito down on the bottom boards. Milagro felt dizzy with doubt and anxiety, her legs almost giving way under her as they pushed the inadequate craft over the sharp stones into the sea. Felipe helped her over the gunwale and sat down beside her, handing her one of the oars.

'Now row.'

She did know how to row, she had on occasion borrowed a little dinghy to row out to a ship anchored off to ask for work, but this was different. The oar was much bigger and heavier and after only a few minutes her arms and shoulders began to ache. Felipe would not let her stop and it seemed to take forever before the shoreline began to recede and he let her rest. It was growing light and a small offshore breeze was getting up; he set the sail and they lay back exhausted in the bottom of the boat.

Above the hills behind Arrecife, Milagro could see the monstrous eruption quite clearly, as the volcanoes demonstrated their power. Flaming boulders were launched high into the air and the massive clouds of smoke showed red and orange behind the furnaces which had burst forth where the cornfields had once been, a strange and terrible crop. New-formed hills rose continuously, only to crumble away again before their eyes in scarlet streams of lava. The grim clouds turned the sea a dark leaden brown with a sheen on it like pewter and the wind blew the lowering mass towards them. Out at sea, the sun was rising, an orange ball emerging from the more natural grey and white early morning clouds banked on the horizon, where there was still a narrow strip of blue between the fleece of the dawn and the smoke billowing out from the land.

The boat rocked gently as the wind filled the skimpy sail and Milagro found herself dozing off. She had had little or no sleep the night before through worry and apprehension and she was worn out with the physical effort of rowing. Pepito was asleep, curled awkwardly on top of the bundle of clothing in the bottom of the boat; he had not stirred since they left the beach and she let herself slide thankfully down beside him. Felipe sat in the stern, his hand on the tiller, watching the set of the sail intently.

When she awoke some time later, it was to a scene blank and featureless as a wall. The sky and sea had melted into each other, a brown uniform haze. There was no sign of the island at all. Pepito was fishing, at least he had a hand line trailing over the stern and Felipe himself had his eyes closed, though he still sat at the tiller.

'Where's Lanzarote?' She tried to scramble to her feet but fright and the sudden movement made her feel quite queasy and she fell forward, gasping over the gunwale, her stomach heaving. She was not really sick, there was little enough in her stomach to start with, and after a few moments of futile retching the ghastly feeling subsided. Felipe made no move to help her but he said,

'Don't worry about being sick, it happens to most people the first time at sea.'

Milagro found that she felt better if she lay back and closed her eyes, but the boat bobbed and jerked, waves slapped at its sides as they moved through the water. If indeed they were making any progress. The sameness of the sea and the sky was unnerving, they had lost sight of the island and she could not imagine how Felipe could know where they were.

'Are we lost?' Her voice trembled. 'Where's the island? How can we find it?'

'The wind's taken us out to sea; just as well really because we'll avoid most of the smoke along the coast and only come inshore for the last few miles.'

He was worn out, hollow-eyed, his face sallow in the evil light, his voice barely audible.

'When it gets dark, we'll be able to see the fires. The wind nearly always drops at night, so we'll row back in to the coast and find out how far we've gone.'

'How will you be able to tell?' She could not tell herself whether they were going towards the land or away from it; never having been at sea before, she did not know how to read the signs or indeed that there were signs to look for.

Felipe smiled at her ignorance, the first time he had smiled since his return.

'Don't you think I know the coast well enough by now? I've spent more than ten years going up and down it, I know what the wind does, I know every rock and stone on the shore. We won't get lost.'

Milagro was not convinced. The terrible confinement of the small craft, the invisible land so far away, or so it seemed because she could not see it, the oppressive sky above them, the ordeal was almost unbearable. The waiting during her solitary months in Arrecife had been nothing to this. She had no idea whether they were going north, south, east or west, or even whether they were moving at all. Felipe persuaded her to look over the side at their wake but seeing the movement of the water made her sick again.

*

Their surroundings never altered all day long—the sullen sky, the boat lurching through dun-coloured waves, hour after hour after hour. Pepito fished, in ecstasies when he, or rather Felipe, hooked two tuna one after the other, but the smell of fish made Milagro sick yet again. The boat rocked alarmingly as Felipe hauled the struggling fish aboard and clubbed them to death.

Later on, though it was hard tell when it was, as the sun did not manage to break through the clouds at all and they were in a uniform twilight most of the day, the breeze began to blow quite strongly. The wind had gone round to the north-east, Felipe told her, and was blowing them back towards the coast, to Playa Blanca. As the twilight gave way to real darkness, the wind dropped and she could see, just as Felipe said she would, the glow of the eruptions in the sky.

Felipe lowered the sail and reshipped the oars. They began to row slowly and painfully towards the faint crimson in the distance. It was as if the sun had set but never quite managed to disappear altogether.

They made little progress. Felipe kept falling asleep and Milagro herself was so enfeebled by this time that she could barely make a show of moving the big sweep back and forth. Their efforts were so futile that Felipe eventually gave up.

'We'd be better off trying to get some sleep.'

He put his arm round her, the first time he had voluntarily touched her, and she felt her spirits lighten. This nightmare journey behind them, when they reached Gran Canaria a new life might really begin. Weak as she was, she fell asleep almost instantly, not caring for the hard boards and cramped surroundings.

They were woken by the sun. It had already risen above the morning clouds on the horizon and the pall of smoke was far away, back over the island.

'There's Lanzarote!' Felipe seized the oars and they both set to, rowing vigorously in the right direction over the now blue and sparkling sea towards the distant land. Too distant still; the wind soon got up and blew them out to sea again.

Felipe's face darkened. He quickly hoisted the ragged sail and handed her the end of a rope.

'Hold that sheet and pull it tight. Pull on it, damn you? Trim the sail, don't let it flap like that.'

'I don't know what you mean, I've never done it before.' She hauled and hauled on the stiff rope with hands already sore from the rowing.

'Harder, harder!'

'I am pulling, it's too heavy, there's too much wind'.

All of a sudden he snatched it out of her hands and dropped the sail altogether. It fell over them, smothering her and Pepito with its folds of grimy canvas. The child immediately began to wail and struggle but Felipe silenced him with a clip round the head.

'Pirates!'

Felipe crouched down in the bottom of the boat himself, just his head above the gunwale. Tremblingly, Milagro peered over the side herself. Not so far away, silhouetted on the horizon, was a sail. A large triangular sail on a long slanting boom. They could not see the hull of the craft yet, just the disembodied sail drifting eerily across the skyline, coming slowly but surely closer. They cowered under the canvas, defenceless, their only hope being that the pirates would think their frail craft deserted and not worth their attention.

Hope fading yet again, Milagro prayed. Silently, so as not to antagonise Felipe, imploring a God she was beginning to lose faith in herself to turn aside this new peril, to let her have a glimpse of a more certain future. She promised to care for Inés, come what may, but all the while the fear still nagged her: her sin, this unforgivable sin of living with a man who was not her husband in the eyes of the church, this was what continuously brought down the wrath of God on her head.

She had no idea how long they lay there hidden under the sail. The box of ointment El Moro had given Felipe smelled very strong; perhaps its magic was drawing the pirate ship towards them. She expected to hear the harsh cries of foreign voices any minute, but there was nothing but the slap of the waves against the hull. The light began to fade, smoke and ash were once more obscuring the sky. There was a dull booming noise, far away, then another. More explosions in the distant hills. Felipe raised his head.

'That's a cannon!'

He risked a glance above the gunwale.

'We're safe!' He pulled Milagro to her feet and pointed. The lateen sail was still there, indeed the pirate ship was now so close to them that they could see the hull clearly and almost make out the men on deck. Not more than two miles behind her was a large trading ship, square sails all set, bearing rapidly down on the pirates. The cannon shots had come from her.

'Thank God.' Felipe had nothing against religious fervour in the right circumstances.

'She must be one of the ships bound for the Indies. She's big, going straight to Gran Canaria, I expect.'

Some of his old enthusiasm returned. 'We'll go too, we don't have to stay in Gran Canaria. We'll find a ship, just like I promised you. When Inés...'

He could not finish the sentence, he could not say those words, 'when she's dead', but Milagro understood what he meant. Her rival would soon be gone and Felipe would be free, hers alone. The way to her future happiness lay through the misery and probably the death of someone else and she did not want to dwell on such a thought. Felipe hoisted the sail and they bowled briskly along till the breeze began to go down with the sun. He thrust an oar into her hands yet again.

'Now we row towards the sun. See where it's setting? No matter how far we've drifted, the sun always sets behind Playa Blanca.'

They rowed with more energy this time. The round globe of the sun was just visible through the smoke and haze and by the time it was gone the false sunset of the volcanic eruptions had taken its place. Then the land itself came into view, low hills outlined against the ever-brighter fires of Timanfaya, and they rested, drifting half-asleep till dawn.

'We're almost there.' Felipe rubbed his bleary eyes, peering at the shoreline. 'See the white beach? That's why the village is called Playa Blanca.'

They floated in with the tide towards the high breakwater which protected the little harbour from the rough seas which often built up in the channel between Lanzarote and Fuerteventura, Felipe sculling with one oar to keep them moving in the right direction. Milagro could no longer row. She had never been so tired in all her life. Three nights of disturbed sleep, sea-sickness, terror, the rude physical effort of all that rowing, had left her in a state of collapse. Her shoulders and arms felt as if she had been racked, her feet were blistered after so many hours of bracing herself to pull on the cumbersome oar, and she sat slumped in the bow, gazing at but hardly seeing the village on the shore.

It was a small village, a very small village, just a hamlet with a few houses of stone and a couple of shacks made out of palm branches. The houses, no doubt once whitewashed as those in Arrecife had been, were drab and mean with walls grey and streaked with ash, their roofs covered in the same filthy mantle. A couple of skeletal children played listlessly on the beach beneath the houses, their feet kicking up choking clouds every time they moved. The air was heavy and oppressive, much more so than in Arrecife, foul with the smell of sulphur. Flakes of ash floated down slowly, adding themselves to the already deep drifts round the doors of the buildings. Milagro's heart sank.

Felipe rowed them towards a small slipway. A track led up from it behind the houses, a track up which someone had recently walked. Footprints could still be seen in the grey powder which covered it. Part of a small boat had been abandoned half-way up, bare ribs and a few charred planks all that remained.

Pepito burst into tears and refused to look at the dark desolation in front of them. Milagro roused herself to help Felipe haul the boat clear of the water and she felt the ground move beneath her feet, the unfamiliar solidity of land after the days at sea unbalancing her.

A tall, stern-faced man had appeared between the houses, a little girl at his side. They watched the couple struggling with the boat in silence.

Chapter VIII – Disaster

Milagro stared at them, the motionless hostile man, the sullen child, both smeared with ash. Then the little girl pulled her hand free and ran down to the water.

'Papa, Papa!'

Rosa. Milagro's thoughts turned to vinegar as Felipe hugged the child, his face transformed with joy. He had not greeted her like that the other night.

The man was making his way slowly down towards them, brushing ash from his long shirt. He looked ill, he paused to cough and spit and catch his breath, his movements were slow and difficult, his skin yellow under its daubs of ash. He surveyed Milagro coldly with bloodshot eyes; he knew who she was and she had no place in Playa Blanca. The little girl ignored her, clinging desperately to her father.

Felipe knelt down and gently unwound her arms from his neck. He lifted Pepito out of the boat and set him down next to Rosa, making the two children join hands. Pepito gazed at her, his grimy face puzzled.

'This is your little brother, Pepito.'

The child snatched her hand back, shaking her head.

'I don't have a brother.'

'Yes, you do. I told you, he was living in Arrecife and now I've brought him here.'

'No.' Tears gathered in her eyes but she said defiantly, 'I did have a sister but she's dead and Mama's dying. I haven't got a brother.'

She turned a look full of hatred on Milagro, who felt pity overwhelm her, despite herself. Why should Rosa think otherwise? It was Felipe who was at fault. She reached out to embrace Rosa but the girl recoiled, hiding behind Felipe.

'Rosa,' his voice was stern, 'Pepito is your brother and you must make him welcome.'

The two children eyed each other in mutual suspicion,

unwilling to accept the machinations of the adult world.

'This is Milagro.' Felipe forced Rosa to face the other unwelcome intruder. 'She will look after you much better than I can.'

'Mama looks after me.' She would not look at Milagro.

'You know Mama is very ill. Milagro will look after all of us.'

So I'm to be the servant. Milagro's fears were justified, but she had no energy left to protest. All she wanted at that moment was somewhere to lie down and sleep.

'You've come back, then.' The man put his hand on Rosa's shoulder, his glance even more hostile than hers.

'How is Inés?'

'No better. What did you expect, a miracle?'

Felipe turned to Milagro, his face as forbidding as the other man's. 'Bentor, my father-in-law.'

Milagro refused to show any fear in front of this grim and hostile man; she was repelled by his harshness but she could understand it only too well. She was the intruder, the unwanted guest, the home-breaker. Trapped by Felipe into another act of folly.

'Come.'

Bentor led the way up the track which stopped in a patch of wasteland behind the houses. Felipe picked up the fish and the remains of their food, while Milagro trailed reluctantly after them, her meagre bundle of belongings in one hand and Pepito's unwilling little paw in the other.

A few shacks built out of palm branches and covered in the inevitable ash stood on a rocky platform; people were gathered in front of them, mostly women and children, not more than eight or nine all told. Guanches. The only other man apart from Bentor wore a tall Guanche hat and a long shirt, the women were in garments of goatskin, their dirty grey hair plaited with wisps of straw.

They sat on the ground, evidently about to eat, round a

cloth which might once have been white but was now streaked filthy grey. The meal was hardly a meal—flat bread, a few dates and a clay pot of milk. A woman was carving up a large chunk of cheese and depositing the pieces on a rough wooden platter.

Bentor called out as they approached and the people turned to face them, cold eyes for the strangers and pleased smiles for Felipe who broke into speech, a dialect so odd that Milagro could not make out the sense of what he was saying. He held up the fish and the woman with the cheese put down her knife to leap up and take them from him.

These people are savages, such was Milagro's first reaction, they sit on the ground to eat, they do not even speak Spanish. Felipe seemed to have become one of them, she had little chance here of being anything other than what she had always felt herself to be in Arrecife, an outcast.

As she listened to their speech, she realised that they did indeed speak a sort of Spanish but a Spanish larded with so many odd words that it seemed a different language altogether. She would not let them get the better of her, she would show them that she was superior to their primitive ways. They might well consider her an outsider, the loose woman who had ensnared one of their people—indeed from their angry looks one might think that there were some outward signs of immorality engraved on her face—but they could not be worse than the disapproving matrons of Arrecife. If she had exchanged one outcast existence for another, so be it.

*

She swayed on her feet. If she had been among more welcoming people, she would have asked if there was a place where she could lie down; she had to sit, waves of weariness and discouragement made her legs too weak to hold her up. She had not eaten since they left Arrecife, two days with just a sip or two of water and a hunk of bread last night when they sighted land. The ringing in her ears was like when she had been ill after her baby died and she could not focus on anything. She found herself lying on the ground with everything whirling around her and a buzz of incomprehensible voices.

The jumble of ill-defined sensations gave way to some kind of clarity. Felipe was bending over her and a strange harsh voice repeated a word she did not understand.

'Ahemon, ahemon.'

'What's that?' She was still half unconscious.

'Water.' Felipe helped her to sit up and held a clay beaker for her to drink. The jagged edge of the primitive beaker cut her lip and the water was full of ash. She choked on it and had to lie down again, her head still spinning. Her exhaustion transformed her feebleness into a deep sleep and she woke some hours later, her face covered with ash, her body stiff and sore from lying on the bare ground.

What a barbarous people. In Arrecife, if someone fainted, the person would have been made comfortable, covered with a blanket perhaps, even carried inside a hut, not just left on the ground.

Animals were treated better than that. She managed to sit up, brushing the ash from her face and hair, and looked around her. She was alone.

No effort had been made to clear away the remains of the scanty meal. The ragged palm mats round the dirty cloth were still there, the cloth itself scattered with crumbs amongst the used beakers and platters.

Beside her was her bundle of belongings and the basket of food. Ravenously, she ate the remains of the hard bread and drank deeply from the still half-full water bottle. Back in Arrecife it had been almost undrinkable but here it seemed like the best spring water.

She got to her feet and made her way cautiously towards the nearest hut. She could hear voices inside and a sudden sharp cry of pain, and she hesitated before entering. Timidity would solve nothing, she decided, and went boldly in.

Several people were gathered round a woman who was lying on an ill-stuffed mattress. She was groaning and crying and Milagro could not at first see her face, just her legs. Her skirt was pulled up to reveal them—covered with suppurating burns, blackened skin and flesh rotted away right to the bone in places.

The man standing between her and the bed moved aside and she saw Felipe crouched by the woman's feet, the box of salve in his hand. He reached out to smooth some of it over her ankle but she screamed in agony. There was a dreadful stench of rotting flesh, more powerful, even than El Moro's ointment.

Inés. Milagro moved closer so that she could see her rival's face. Her feelings of jealousy and animosity gave way to pity, now she was confronted with the suffering woman. It was impossible to tell what Inés really looked like, her hair was tangled and matted with ash and sweat, her face pale and streaked with dirt, distorted with pain under its mask of grey.

The man standing by the bed, Bentor, turned and noticed Milagro.

'This is not your place.'

She found herself being pushed unceremoniously out of the hut. Bentor barred the doorway and watched her retreat. She could not contain her rage at such treatment; crying and shouting, she picked up a stone and hurled it at him. It bounced off his arm but he did not flinch. She took a step towards him, but his expression was so menacing that she did not dare pick up another stone, much though she longed to.

Pepito had not been in the hut, she realised. 'Where's my son?'

Bentor sneered at her. 'Your bastard son? Drowned, I hope.' He turned away back into the hut, where Inés' cries had increased to screams of agony.

Milagro was reminded of the woman with no feet who had died in Arrecife and shuddered. Where was Pepito? She ran down the track to the beach, the man's brutal words still sounding in her ears; she could hear children's voices and when she arrived within sight of the water there was Pepito, sitting on the boat. Three or four children were playing on the sand, one of them Rosa. Pepito sat watching them wistfully, not daring to join in. She scooped him up and hugged him in relief.

'I'll tell you a story,' she suggested. It would be a distraction for her as much as him. 'Which one would you like?'

Pepito thought for a moment, huddling closer to her and away from the Guanche children. He coughed and spat out ash, gasping for breath in between the coughs. He had never been that bad in Arrecife; here the air was truly choking, full of fumes and the revolting smell of sulphur.

'Tell me the one about the princess in the cave.'

A Guanche story, one Felipe used to tell him. Even her son had gone over to the enemy.

'Are you sure you wouldn't like to hear the one about the fisherman and the pirates.'

'No, I want the one about the princess.' Pirates were a too recent memory.

Milagro sighed and began.

'It was a long time ago, when Lanzarote wasn't even called Lanzarote and there was a king here, King Maseguay. He lived in a fortress up in the hills, they were all green then with no volcanoes at all. The fortress was called Teguise.'

'Have I been there, Mama?'

'No, Pepito. We saw it in the distance once when we borrowed a camel to get some corn but you were very small. I don't expect you remember.'

Pepito frowned in an effort to remember what they had done that day. He coughed again. 'I remember the camel.'

'I showed you where it was, I told you I was born there.'

'Oh. Was I born there too?'

'No, you were born in Arrecife.' It was some time since she had thought about Teguise and she lost the thread of the story.

Pepito pulled at her sleeve. 'Mama, go on, you haven't got to the princess yet.'

Milagro sighed again. Her throat was already sore with the sulphur fumes but she swallowed hard and continued hoarsely. One of the children had come over to them and was listening too.

'Well, the king was a good king and when a ship from Spain had to come into port one day during a dreadful storm, he invited one of the men on board, Don Martín, to come and stay with him. The king had a beautiful wife and Don Martín became very friendly with her.'

'Was she the queen? What was she called?' It was the Guanche child who asked.

'Yes, she was the queen and her name was Queen Fayna. Don Martín didn't stay very long, he found Lanzarote very boring and he wanted to go back to Spain.'

'What's boring?' enquired Pepito.

'Boring is when you've got nothing to do, like when you tell me you want some new toys because you've played with all yours too often.' Like when you tire of your mistress and find her boring—she felt her eyes filling with tears and had trouble going on.

'Anyway,' her voice choked, 'anyway, after a while, when the weather was fine once more, he left and it was not long after he left that the queen gave birth to a baby, a girl called Ico.'

'Why have they all got funny names, Mama?'

'I can't help it, that's what they were called then. I told you, it was a long time ago. The queen was getting old and she was very glad to have a little girl.'

'Why was she getting old?'

'Pepito, if you keep interrupting me, you'll never hear the end of the story. Everyone gets old, just like you get bigger every year.'

Pepito looked sceptical, he was not very satisfied with her

explanation and the Guanche child giggled. However, he did not interrupt again and Milagro went on with the tale.

'The king was old too and eventually he died, so Ico's brother Iguafaya was made king, but it wasn't long before more Spanish came to Lanzarote. They weren't so friendly as Don Martín, they captured Iguafaya and took him away to Spain. So Lanzarote had no king, no one to rule except Ico. Poor Ico. People began to spread rumours: Don Martín must have been her father and she had no right to be queen, she looked too Spanish to be the old king's daughter.'

'Very often, you look just like Papa.'

'Oh.' Pepito was nonplussed; he put his hand up to his face as if to feel whether his features were really like those of Felipe. Far too like Felipe, thought Milagro sadly. His features were still unformed but there was no doubt whose son he was. They could say what they liked here, Pepito was Felipe's son, his only son.

There was a tug at her skirt. Several of the children had gathered round her—gaunt, ash-covered faces, skinny arms protruding from ragged shirts.

'Please, what happened to Ico?'

'The people wanted her to undergo a trial to prove she really was the king's daughter, the Trial of Smoke. The judges of Teguise took her, with three old women who were just peasants and didn't matter, to a cave. They lit a fire in the cave and when it was full of smoke, they shut them all in. It must have been horrible, like it is here now but even worse. At last, when they opened the cave again, the old women were all dead but the princess was still alive.'

'Did she cough all the time, like we do?'

'I expect so. But she had a secret. An old sorceress who believed she was of royal blood had told her what to do. She secretly gave the princess a wet sponge and advised her to hold it in her mouth while she was in the cave and breathe through it when the smoke got very bad. We were doing that in Arrecife the day the animals died, remember, Pepito? So the princess lived, everyone saw she was really of royal blood and she was made queen of Lanzarote.'

'That's one of our stories.' Rosa had come over to listen, the last of the children to do so, resentful that Milagro was telling a Guanche tale.

She too resembled Felipe but, Milagro decided as she studied the sullen little face, the likeness was as much racial as anything. She was a Guanche, Felipe was a Guanche, so was Pepito: light-coloured eyes, broad lips, fair skin, they were all the same. Milagro was the odd one out.

'Do you know any other stories?'

Another girl, smaller than Rosa, was standing at her knee, her left arm a mass of raw sore patches to which the falling ash had clung in a putrid crust. The little girl held her arm away from her body so that it did not touch her ragged shirt, her only article of clothing. Most of the children had burns, some healed in rough scar tissue, some still festering. Milagro realised that she had one reason to be grateful, she and Pepito had at least been in Arrecife and not here or in the west when the volcanoes exploded.

'I'll tell you another one tomorrow, it's getting late now. See, the sun is setting.'

An eerie light had begun to spread across the village. The clouds of ash and smoke were tinged with red and orange; out at sea, the sun was competing bravely but uselessly with the filth spewing out from the eruptions. The afternoon breeze had blown the showers of ash clear from the village but none of the children had bothered to brush the grey residue out of their hair or off their faces.

Rosa was already making her way back up the path and the other children trailed after her. Milagro sat alone on the beach, trying to summon up enough courage to follow them, to go in search of Felipe and brave Bentor's wrath once more. It was getting quite dark now, the sky was turning brown, shot with only a few residual streaks of red. Pepito threw a few stones into the sea, his face dejected. He kicked at the little waves which broke on the beach and Milagro watched him anxiously. He had not ventured to follow the other children, not because he thought she might not let him but because he too felt he did not belong here. Milagro could not explain anything to him, he was too young to understand.

'Mama, let's go back home, I don't like it here at all.'

Before Milagro could think of some suitable reply, steps sounded on the pebbles behind her. It was Felipe.

'Inés is very bad, she may die tonight. The ointment hasn't done any good at all.'

He sat wearily down beside her, defeated and downcast. She knew without having to say it that things had changed irrevocably between them. It was no use thinking that when Inés died Felipe would be hers and hers alone; the present disaster and the influence of his own people had created a rift which would not be healed.

'What are you going to do?' There might still be a chance; with Inés gone and one set of family ties broken, Felipe might still want to cling to what he had left.

'We'll go to La Palma.'

We. She waited to hear who was included in that 'we'.

'I promised to take the children and Inés' sister. You and she can look after them when we get there, we'll have water, food, green grass, green trees, I can't even remember what they look like any more. Lanzarote is an island of ghosts and dead people.'

He gestured at the miserable huts, desolate in their shrouds of ash, the few people around ghostlike indeed as they went about their tasks masked in the all-pervasive grey.

'When can we leave, Papa?' Pepito's dejected little face brightened at the prospect of leaving this horrible place.

'Soon. In a day or two. Come, we'll find somewhere for you to sleep and something to eat.'

It was time for the evening meal, such as it was. The women were laying out what remained of the food, listlessly, not caring that the plates and beakers were still dirty from the previous meal. The fish had been spitted and grilled; Milagro was grudgingly given a tiny portion but she could hardly swallow it, the resentful eyes of the woman who served her made the food stick in her throat.

*

She did not know what to do. La Palma must be a long way away, much further than Arrecife. How could she bear such a trip, several days in the small boat with a bitter and grieving family? Her imagination ran riot: fights, tears and blows, Rosa throwing Pepito over the side in a fit of jealous rage, herself struggling with Inés' sister and all the time Felipe saying nothing, letting the women get on with it. He was too craven to intervene, she knew that now; she had realised at last what a weak man he was, how he always tried to evade responsibility. He would never decide between his two families.

She lay awake all night, restless and miserable on the rough bed of palm fronds they had been allotted, watching the lightning of the volcano's outbursts through the many gaps in the roof. When the clouds began to turn from black to brown, she made her decision. Felipe lay beside her, heavily asleep, oblivious, like a man unconscious rather than merely asleep, barely breathing. He had risen twice in the night to check on Inés; she had heard voices outside the hut, the deep surly tones of Bentor and the higher voice of one of the women, though she had not been able to make out what they were saying. Now he lay exhausted and she was able to get up and wake Pepito without fear of disturbing him.

She was used, now, to making her escape; it took her only a few minutes to collect her few belongings, steal a hunk of bread from the unappetising dusty larder at the back of what seemed to be the main hut and dip the leather water bottle into the cracked cistern.

There was some light in the sky, a faint paling before dawn making the grim, ash-veiled huts even more bleak in appearance. There was no one about, no sounds of movement, not even a moan from the dying woman. Perhaps she was already dead. Milagro did not delay to find out but hastened up the cinder-strewn track, a nodding Pepito in her arms, glad to get away from the village before anyone noticed her escape.

*

She did not know where she was going, but there was only the one path. When she was above the squalid huts, she looked back down the hill. There was no way along the shore, the narrow track at the end of the beach led nowhere, blocked by a pile of jagged rocks. The path she had chosen must be the way out, across the plain and up towards a craggy gap between the brown and grey hills which dominated the end of the island. Pepito was a dead weight; she set him down and made him walk, despite his sleepy complaints.

She could see the volcanoes now, ragged peaks belching out smoke and fire, the path seeming to lead directly to them. There must be a way through. She could not think where Arrecife was, perhaps it was on the other side of the volcanoes; there had to be a path somewhere, Felipe had come by land; unless he had lied to her again.

The path got steeper, Pepito wailed behind her but she ignored him. The air was heavy with smoke and fumes and they made slow progress. By the time they got to the pass, it became more and more difficult to breathe and the air was thick with the smell of sulphur, the choking foetid breath of the volcano. The ground quaked under their feet. She had never seen the work of the devilish eruption before and she began to think they were on their way into the mouth of hell—just so must it look, flames licking up in the distance, reeking cinders, the air full of ash and foul vapours. She more than half expected to see a demon rise up from the piles of slag to seize her and Pepito and drag them down below.

They reached the top of the pass and the monster lay before them. A monster with many mouths gaping upwards, some belching smoke, some spitting fire, some quiet, edges spiked and black like rotten and broken teeth. They did not dare to go on: in front of them was a trackless expanse of solidified lava, to the left a wilderness of smoking rubble, in front of them the bulk of the nearest beast. From its summit, smoke billowed sluggishly and a dribble of molten red wormed its way down the flank of the hill, bubbling and hissing, flowing relentlessly towards them.

The only possible route seemed to be off to the right, across an inhospitable but seemingly flat patch of cinders. She stepped hesitantly off the path. The cinders were warm under their feet but not burning hot. She could not carry Pepito, the cinders cut into her feet even without his weight in her arms. He cried and screamed as she dragged him over the rough ground which began to move ominously under them: the tongue of molten rock had reached the spot where they had hesitated, cutting them off, and the mountain rumbled to itself, meditating an outright attack. They were lost.

She heard a shout: a figure was scrambling up through the pass on the other side of the stream of lava, a figure carrying a long pole. He used it to vault across the lava and caught them up, gasping and coughing and spitting in the foul air.

'What are you doing?' Felipe was too out of breath to do more than croak. 'Are you trying to kill yourself? Where do you think you're going?'

Milagro faced him defiantly. 'I won't be what you want me to be, I'm not your wife's nurse, your family servant, your children's nanny. They don't want me and I don't want them. I'd rather die here in Lanzarote than be a serving maid in La Palma.'

'You stupid girl!' Felipe grabbed her and shook her. 'You

will die here and so will Pepito, you've been walking straight into the volcano. Let me carry the boy and I'll show you the way back.'

'No!' She clutched Pepito who began to scream, the quarrel between his parents even more frightening than the threat of the volcano.

'You're not having him, I'm going to take him back to Arrecife, he's mine, not yours and he's not going to be brought up as a Guanche.'

'Let him go, you fool, I'm only going to carry him for you, back down to Playa Blanca. You can't survive in Arrecife anyway, you know that, do you want Pepito to die too? To hell with my relations, we'll dump them in Gran Canaria and go on to La Palma by ourselves.'

Milagro shook her head. 'You won't dump Rosa.'

'Rosa? Of course not, she'll stay with us.' Felipe was exasperated at Milagro's refusal to understand. 'She's my child, just as Pepito is. I meant Inés' family, they can go hang, I couldn't live with Bentor telling me what to do all the time.'

He went to pick the child up but Milagro screamed at him again and pulled Pepito free of his grasp. Her voice was hoarse in the fumes and smoke which came swirling down towards them. The top of the volcano had disappeared in the murk but it could be heard muttering with increasing urgency. The smoke stung her eyes and she could feel tears trickling down her face. Tears of rage.

'You can't see, can you, Rosa's the one who hates me the most. What are you going to do? Take us back to Playa Blanca, wait for Inés to die and tell Rosa she's got a new mother, never mind about the old one?'

'You're crazy.'

'No, you're the one who's crazy. You always think I'm going to obey you, you always know best, you never see what other people want. Rosa hates me and Pepito. How could we possibly live together?'

'Why shouldn't we live together, you're my family, how can it not work? I need my family with me.'

'Words! That's all you are, words with nothing behind them. I don't believe in you any more and you're not taking Pepito.'

The little boy was between them, pulled this way and that by his desperate parents, until Milagro managed to kick Felipe so hard that he lost his balance. He let go of Pepito and fell, rolling back into a dip in the ground which had started to smoulder ominously. As he tried to get to his feet, the thin crust of cinders started to break up. Cracks appeared and flames leapt up through them. Felipe could not get a foothold; every time he tried, the ground disintegrated under him. His shirt caught fire and as he endeavoured to beat out the flames, a terrible spurt of scarlet burst from the earth in front of him, showering him with drops of liquid crimson rock. Lava snaked out, flowing down the hill, bearing him with it, screaming. He did not scream for long. His writhing body, jerking help-lessly in the grip of the lava, melted into the glowing stream and disappeared.

*

Milagro stared in horrified disbelief, rooted to the spot, hands reaching out vainly towards the spot where Felipe had van-ished. Pepito gaped after his father, quite unable to understand what was happening. Almost too late, Milagro realised their own danger. The whole hillside was cracking up.

They ran, falling and stumbling and crying. Flames roared up out of the rocks, snatching at their clothes, lava from count-less crevices began to seep across the whole area but somehow they succeeded in reaching firmer ground. Pepito was unharmed apart from his cut and bleeding feet, but the whole of Milagro's left leg was burned when she tripped and fell almost straight into a puddle of molten rock. She managed to roll away from it in time but the white heat seared her leg from ankle to thigh. Her skirt caught fire, too, she beat out the flames frantically with her hands and ran on.

They did not dare stop, even when the black cinders gave way to sand and solid rock. Milagro could hardly put her left foot to the ground but she made herself keep going and at last they came to some kind of man-made path. The slope of the hill was gentler here, the path sandy rather than rocky, though still strewn with cinders, and when she looked down into the valley away from the volcano, she was sure she could see the sea. There was a ruined hut just off the path lower down; part of a wall and traces of some foundations were all that remained but it seemed like some kind of sanctuary. She dragged herself and Pepito to the illusory shelter of its ruins and collapsed.

Pepito was utterly silent once they stopped, gazing back at the flaming mountainside where his father had disappeared. Milagro put her arms round him but he did not seem to notice. Her hands were blistered and her leg was agony, burned by the molten lava then scraped raw by falling again and again as they fled down into the valley. She had lost their only remaining possessions too; somewhere in their flight she had dropped the small bundle, and her mother's gold bracelet was gone as well. Now they had nothing, nothing at all.

She moved her leg and cried out, but she was glad of the pain in a way; it distracted her from thinking of what had just happened up there on the dreadful slopes, stopped her seeing Felipe's burning, thrashing body melting into the lava flow, stopped her hearing his screams.

She did not dare let them rest for long; they seemed to have evaded the volcano's fiery tentacles for the time being but the earth continued to heave, and though the fatal red streams snaked away from them now, disappearing down the other flank of the hill, she could not be sure that the fire would not come spurting out anew under their very feet.

They crawled now, making their way painfully towards the sea, the ground was cooler here and not so steep. Milagro could see the sea clearly beyond the line of low cliffs but every move she made felt as if her leg was being set on fire all over again.

Soon she had to stop altogether. She lay on the black ground completely exhausted, coughing feebly, eyes swollen almost shut, her tongue and lips coated with ash. Pepito squatted mute beside her, his eyes fixed on the sea in the distance but not seeing it, tears rolling silently down his face, making furrows in the ash on his cheeks. She could not believe what had happened; the idea that Felipe was dead, that he had died such a hideous death right in front of her would not fix itself in her brain, yet when she closed her eyes the vivid images tore at her relentlessly. She moaned aloud, pressing her hands to her head to squeeze the nightmare pictures out of her mind, but they would not go.

Dimly, she heard voices. An elderly couple were leading a camel along the edge of the cliff; by chance they noticed the fugitives huddled on the ground and hastened up towards them, exclaiming in horror when they realised their plight.

'How did you get here? Where have you come from?'

The old man was bald and wizened, he could have been the brother of the old farmer she had encountered all those years ago the first time she ran away. She began to sob hopelessly; past and present memories were all jumbled up together, everything, every way led unerringly to grief and disaster.

The woman tried to help her to her feet but she could not stand. They loaded her on to the camel like a sack of grain, lifting Pepito up beside her. She seemed to manage to hold on as the animal lurched and swayed along, but she could not have said where they were going. When at last the movement stopped, she raised her head but she could see nothing. Her eyes were blurred and sore with tears and fumes but it was not just that. It must be night already—how could time have passed so quickly? She could hear the sea too, they must be down on the coast again.

Her burnt leg scraped along the rope which held the camel's pack in place when they got her down; she heard her own voice crying out in agony, she too was a burned, pain-wracked, penniless refugee now.

Hazily, her vision cleared, it did indeed seem to be night. She saw a priest bending over her and she knew she was about to die and go to hell. Felipe had gone before her, she had seen hell fire consume him and the same fate awaited her. It did not matter that she had lost everything, she did not need worldly goods where she was going. I'm already burning, she thought confusedly as pain flared through her leg and took over her whole body. The old woman was dabbing ineffectually at the oozing burns with a corner of her dirty skirt.

'Where have you come from?' The priest sounded concerned, as if he was giving her a last chance, as if forgiveness for her sins was not an impossibility, but she was too disorientated with pain and wretchedness to answer him.

'You can't stay here, you know,' he said gently, 'We have nothing to treat your burns and no water.'

She managed to speak at last, her throat rasping and sore. 'I'm from Arrecife.'

'Is your family still there?' The words were kindly meant but Milagro could only reply with sobs. How could she say my husband is dead, I've just seen him die; the truth was inadmissible even in her head.

The priest patted her shoulder. 'I understand, I'll say a prayer for them. Do you have friends left in Arrecife who can care for you?'

Friends? Who was left there? Nura, crazy Nura, she realised how Nura had gone mad, she was going the same way herself. El Moro? Why should he do anything for her? The throbbing in her leg made her break out in a sweat and her befuddled brain began to have the fanciful notion that she had the choice between two kinds of death: if she did not die here on the spot, if she appealed to El Moro, she would be putting herself into the power of someone who was in league with the devil. Hell would merely be postponed. God had just sent her a warning, shown her a foretaste of what was in store for her, but he had left it up to her; he had not bothered to show her the way out.

Pepito was squatting beside her, still silent, clinging to her hand in desperation. His gritty little fingers clutched hers so tightly that she was in part recalled to her senses. She had to survive, to do whatever was necessary, she had to save Pepito. He was all she had left, all that remained of Felipe.

'Where am I?'

'Tifiosa.' The priest was relieved that she seemed able to speak rationally, despite her distress. 'It's not far from Arrecife, but I don't think you can walk that far. The old man says he will take you on the camel tomorrow or send for someone to fetch you home.'

'Tell him to look for El Moro,' she said. 'He lives outside the town, towards Naos, the other bay. Tell El Moro I've been hurt and ask him to help me.'

The priest frowned, the name of El Moro was clearly not unknown to him. 'What is your name?'

'Milagro.'

She ought to ask him to hear her confession but she could not. She belonged in the world of evil and despair now, and an outward show of repentance would not help. The absurd notion of him praying for Felipe, the idea of saving his soul when it had already been consumed by infernal fire and she was doomed to follow him—she was wandering off into feverish fantasy, drifting in and out of consciousness, aware from time to time of the unbearable pain in her leg, in between periods of flame-filled dreams in which she saw again and again a tortured, writhing figure sinking slowly into a pool of fire.

Chapter IX – El Moro

El Moro came: the devil was swift to claim his own. He propped the semi-conscious girl up on his mule, commanded Pepito to follow behind and took them to his house.

There followed a time of leaden despair. A prisoner of her injuries and her dreadful memories, Milagro recovered very slowly. Nightmares filled her sleeping hours, long painful days stretched out endlessly between the periods of unconsciousness.

Felipe had gone, he was dead, burned to nothing. Gone so completely, she could not believe that his actual physical existence could so easily disappear without a trace. Her memories of him were hopelessly insubstantial, fading day by day, blotted out entirely by the terrible images of his last moments. She tried to pray but had she not seen Felipe disappear into the fires of hell? Would she not be next? It was her fault, after all; if she had not fled yet again, he would not have had to come after her and he would still be alive.

Bitter regret made no difference, he was gone. When she looked back, it seemed that he had been a part of her life for such a short time, it was no wonder her memory refused to record his existence in any permanent way. They had spent more time apart than together; he had come up to Teguise so infrequently and when they lived together in Arrecife he was all too often away at sea. As for the months he had spent in the south after the eruptions, caring for Inés, oblivious of what might be going on in Arrecife, this prolonged absence had been the beginning of his obliteration from Milagro's memory. Now Inés did not have him either, nor did Rosa. He was dead.

She had thought, when she first learnt of Inés' existence, that she would rather have him dead than in the embrace of another woman. Not so. She would give anything to have him still alive, share him with half of Lanzarote if need be, but it was too late. Her chance of happiness had gone for ever, melted away into a scarlet stream of lava and she was left with just one reason to survive—her son, the only possession left to her in the world.

She lay for days on El Moro's bed, trying not to move since each movement sent such bolts of agony through her leg. She looked at her filthy hands and arms, at the ragged remains of her clothes, at Pepito's skeletal limbs barely covered by the tattered shirt which was all he too had left. They now resembled all the other destitute refugees in Arrecife, grimy, covered in ash, with matted hair and haggard, desperate features.

Her nightmares were almost destroying her—their wild and terrible images passing in front of her eyes as soon as she slept: fire, flames, Felipe burning, burning, herself being pushed into the fire after him by a triumphant Don Miguel, El Moro standing by to rescue her at the last minute, sneering as he did so. She knew she would have to pay the price for his help, either in this world or the next. Or both.

Her leg did heal at last, helped by El Moro's magic potions; at least she thought of them as magic, what else could they be, but she did not care by what means she was healed. She realised little by little that she was not ready to die. God had deserted her but Pepito deserved to have at least one parent alive to take care of him. She survived slowly, sluggishly, more as if she did not have the will to die than as if she truly wished to live.

El Moro's conscience rarely pricked him these days. It was a long time since he had felt sorry for anyone except himself and though he could not say he was attracted to Milagro, or that he pitied her in her despair, it was a long time since he had had a woman. The girls in Arrecife had never attracted him, they were mostly afraid of him in any case, but Milagro had not yet lost all of her beauty. Cleaned up and well instructed, she might still arouse his lust. He found the idea quite appealing and made a few experimental sexual overtures, taking the precaution of drugging her first, though this was to avoid any unpleasant struggles as much as to spare her feelings.

He intended to leave Lanzarote soon, indeed he had already been making plans to do so; perhaps he should take her with him, not from any concern for her welfare, but she was a good housekeeper and it might be pleasant to have a regular bedmate again. He did not reveal these thoughts to Milagro. When he asked her to accompany him to Gran Canaria, she did not question his reason for asking her: grateful to him for saving her life and that of her son, she did not immediately consider the implications. She should not have been so naïve but she had forgotten what men were like.

Pepito never referred to Felipe's awful death; whether he really understood what had happened, Milagro did not know. She was too crushed by her own feelings of despair to make much effort to find out if he actually realised what had happened to his father. In the end she cravenly said nothing.

To her surprise, El Moro seemed to like the child and would take time out to play with him. He left her alone at first; she slept in his bed and he slept on the floor until her leg was well on the mend and she was shocked when, shortly after he proposed to take them to Gran Canaria with him, he decided to call in his debt.

'It's time you earned your keep.' He knelt by the bed and lifted his robe, revealing his erect penis. She stared at it, it was long and thin, quite different from Felipe's. His had been a short, thick club, El Moro's was a rampant snake. She tried to back away but he seized her by the hair.

'Let's see what you can do.'

She took it reluctantly in her mouth, trying to hide her revulsion but she was at his mercy. She knew what to do, she had done it for Felipe, but a stranger was different and El Moro's coldness and remoteness seemed so at odds with his obvious state of sexual excitement, the only sign of humanity he had so far revealed. She was almost choking as he thrust deep into her throat but he held her head and she could not escape. After a few moments, he released her.

'Your Guanche lover hasn't taught you very well, has he. Maybe he didn't have very much imagination in the first place.'

He explained precisely what she should do with her tongue, guiding her lips, forcing her fingers to caress and squeeze his balls. She did what she was told, trying to cut her mind off from what her body was being made to do, but she had nothing to distract her, nothing to think about except damnation. She did not dare spit out the horrible bitter liquid when it came spurting into her mouth, glad that it was too dark for him to see the expression of revulsion on her face.

El Moro was quite pleased. 'With a few lessons, you could become extremely proficient. You deserve a reward yourself.'

His hands were smooth, not like Felipe's hands, so rough from the nets and the sea. His fingers probed and teased and pinched until she felt herself melting, melting away and crying out helplessly at his touch. It was not like it had been with Felipe; El Moro knew how to arouse her physically but it was not pleasure she felt, it was an extreme, painful release from an intolerable stress, and she wept. She had betrayed Felipe twice: not only had she caused his death, she had also bedded another man shortly afterwards. Fire ran and flesh sizzled in her dreams that night.

El Moro made her suck him off again just before dawn.

'Don't think this is the only way I like it.' She could hear the contempt in his voice. 'When your burns have healed, I'll be able to show a great many other ways, but you'll have to get better first. Some of my ideas are quite strenuous.'

His words made her shudder but she did not dare to say anything. She was caught, trapped by her own weaknesses and the force of circumstances.

She could walk a little now and she went back to her old hut to see if there was anything worth salvaging, but a family of refugees had already taken it over and she felt too weak to challenge them, even though she could see they were using the big pot she had had to leave behind. If El Moro decided to throw her and Pepito out into the streets once her burns had healed, they would be totally destitute and she would be forced into prostitution, real prostitution, just to feed them—one of the ragtag and bobtail who could not afford to leave Lanzarote and who had lost every single thing, home, possessions, self-respect.

He did not throw her out. She did her best to do what he wanted of her each night, lying to herself as she did so. This was not prostitution, it was survival.

They had to go to Gran Canaria with him too; she could not bear to think of her son as just one more ash-streaked refugee wandering the streets of Arrecife, begging a crust or a bruised prickly pear. She made ready to leave when told, packing up their remaining food and his belongings. They had nothing to pack themselves.

El Moro would not let her touch his books but she would have been afraid to touch them in any case, because of the magic in them. She watched him as he wrapped them first in linen, then in the elaborate mat he used for prayer; she longed to dare to go to church herself before they left, to offer up prayers for Felipe's soul, but she was too frightened of Don Miguel. The priest had not deserted his post, he was still there, exhorting his reduced congregation to repentance, but God had closed his ears to her, no prayers of hers would make any difference.

*

At the last minute before they left, El Moro prised up the stone in front of the hut's fireplace. There was a hole beneath it from which he extracted a small leather bag. She heard the chink of coins as he hung it from his girdle.

The ship waiting in the harbour was a trading ship from

Spain, not very large, one which was built only to run to the Canaries and back, not to cross the Atlantic. It seemed big enough to Milagro, much bigger than Felipe's fishing boat had been. She was able to stand more easily now, without her leg getting too painful, and she leant on the rail looking at the harbour she was about to leave, perhaps for the last time. As usual, the day was grey and smoky with a veiled sun barely visible through the clouds; the volcanoes rumbled in the distance and flashes of fire showed fitfully through the smoke, obscuring the hills behind the town. The warehouses on the quay seemed dingier than ever with their accumulation of ash and the handful of passengers boarding the ship had few people to see them off. There were not so many left in Arrecife now and the governor had recently issued a decree forbidding anyone to leave except on the most urgent business. She wondered how El Moro had managed to get permission; bribery, no doubt, he seemed to have the money. On the other hand, perhaps the governor did not consider him a desirable citizen and was glad to see the back of him.

The last passenger toiled up the gangplank, his heavy sack of belongings raising clouds of ash as he dragged it behind him. The wind was rising, blowing debris hither and thither, the sailors coughed and choked in the clouds of ash coming off the mooring lines as they were hauled aboard. The mainsail creaked up, showering all those on deck with flakes of grey, and the ship swung out from the quay, turning her head towards the harbour entrance and the cleaner water outside. A bloated dead rat bobbed up between the hull and the quayside, grey and scummy, but even rats were becoming scarce in Arrecife.

Pepito, in the company of two other children nearly as ragged and dirty as he was, ran noisily up and down the deck, getting in the way of the sailors, as Milagro watched him anxiously to see if this second departure brought back any memories. He paused by her and tugged at her skirt.

'Are we going to see papa?'

She knelt beside him and held him close, too choked with distress to reply. Did he really not remember what had happened up the mountain? Before she could think what to say, he twisted out of her grasp and ran off again, his question apparently forgotten. She crouched inside the bulwarks, sobbing, still having no idea how to explain to Pepito that his father was dead; if he did not remember, how could she find the words to tell him?

The ship had cleared the heads now and was moving out into deeper water, rolling in the swell which ran down the coast. Milagro felt her stomach heave and she only just managed to stand up before she was sick over the side. She was not the only one and the sailors laughed at the line of vomiting landlubbers.

The island faded away into the brown haze; she was leaving again, with nothing but the bitterest of memories, but what lay ahead held little promise. God was merely about to punish her in a different way.

*

By that evening the sea had subsided; also they were running down-wind and the movement of the boat was steadier. Lanzarote was just a glow in the clouds astern of them now and the neighbouring island of Fuerteventura a dark shape on their right. As they drew away from the malevolence of the volcanoes, the sky cleared and she began to see stars above them, the first she had seen since the eruptions began.

'What a dirty girl you are.'

El Moro's sarcastic voice sounded behind her. He wiped the grit and ash from her face and ran his fingers distastefully over her lips. She shrank back from him but it was no use.

'You have to learn to keep yourself clean as well as to give a man what he needs.'

He made her kneel beside him on the deck and put her hands underneath his robe, regardless of the other passengers,

[162]

though it was quite dark now and no one could really see what they were doing. His breathing was harsh and ragged in her ear as his penis hardened in her fingers and she began to realise that this might be the way to control him. The pleasure she was able to give him put him in her power.

Not at all. His orgasm once done, he was in charge again.

The voyage was not a long one. To her surprise, by the next afternoon they were tying up in the great harbour of Las Palmas. It was such a strange place: boats everywhere, many of them much larger than the one they were on, hundreds of smaller craft, fishing boats, skiffs ferrying people and goods to the ships at anchor. The port seemed immense compared with Arrecife and everything was so clear—no smoke, no ash, the sea shone in the sun, she could see every detail of the distant quays. The water itself was foul. Rubbish of all sorts floated on its surface—dead rats, several of them this time, ropes, fragments of planking, bits of fruit, half an orange that someone would have killed for in Arrecife. But it was blue, not grey and leaden, not filled with scummy ash and the strange floating stones which came out of the volcanoes.

And on the shore, trees. Date palms, oleanders, figs, tamarisks, she did not know what most of them were. The hills behind the harbour were green too, with more trees and a profusion of bushes. Felipe had not lied to her about that at least. Milagro stood open-mouthed, staring at the extraordinary spectacle. El Moro tapped her on the arm.

'We're going ashore.'

She made her way gingerly down the gangplank: bracing herself against the movement of the ship at sea had opened up some of her burns again and it was painful to bend her leg. Pepito skipped and jumped down in front of her, tripping her up as soon as she got onto the quay. She fell awkwardly onto her bad leg and almost fainted with the pain.

El Moro either did not notice or did not care; he disappeared with Pepito into the seething mass of people.

Passengers surged around her, claiming their possessions, shouting for carters and porters, donkeys and mules trudged past her to be loaded. Girls, far less tatty than those around the port in Arrecife, decked in ribbons and gaudy colours, shouted promises at the eager crew on deck. Some passers-by gave her odd looks as she dragged herself up to sit on a bollard: her tattered ash-stained clothing and gaunt features marked her down as a refugee from Lanzarote.

*

Las Palmas was a rich city, richer than Teguise, richer than Arrecife by far, with sumptuous buildings in stone, not white-washed plaster, elaborate churches with towers and ornamented façades. Even the poorest people seemed to be dressed in the sort of clothes that were only worn by the wealthy on Sundays in Arrecife. A man in silk stockings and silver buckled shoes was standing on the dock not far from her, shouting instructions about his merchandise to a seaman on deck, fancy carriages trimmed with leather and velvet rolled along the wide road which ran past the harbour, richly dressed women in fantastical wigs peered out from them. Doña Constancia must have cost Señor Perez a pretty penny when they arrived here. Milagro gazed anxiously around, hoping yet fearing to see her stepfather. They must be somewhere here in Las Palmas, though how to find them was quite another matter.

She saw a turbaned man in the distance but it was not El Moro. There were men about, dressed as he dressed, but they all appeared to be servants rather than masters, dancing attendance on silk-clad ladies and their children. She became increasingly aware of her own shabbiness. It was all very well for El Moro to criticise her but she had no money now, nothing to buy new clothes with, and she could do little work in her present state of health. Was he intending her to beg on street corners? Or worse, much worse, were his instructions in sex, in the art of pleasing men, simply to enable her to earn money on the streets? She shuddered and a lump rose in her throat. I will not do that, I will not do that.

It was only since the eruptions had begun, surely, that she had been so neglectful of her appearance. There had been no point in trying to keep clean, the ash fell faster than it was possible to clear up.

*

El Moro had been gone for a long time, the ship had disembarked all its passengers and the throng on the quay had almost dispersed. The sun was hot and dazzling, the more so as it was so long since they had felt its real heat in Lanzarote. Lost and helpless, sweat running down her face, she used her skirt to wipe it off and clean away some of the streaks of dirt. She ran her fingers through her hair, trying to comb out the tangles. Some of the stitching on her bodice had given way, a detail she had not noticed. She must look like the worst of the girls for sale now, displaying her grubby wares in the hope that some man might find her worth a few coins for a few moments of relief. She huddled forward, her head on her knees so as to reveal as little as possible, more and more convinced that El Moro had abandoned her to her fate.

A shout from Pepito roused her. El Moro had found a carter and Pepito was helping him to load their luggage. The carter himself, cheerful and red-faced, did not miss the gaping bodice. He helped Milagro to climb up into the back of the cart, pinching her bottom largely as he did so. Clearly, he took her for a serving girl, he would not have risked such a familiarity otherwise. Anyway, what else was she?

The cart rumbled and jerked down the cobbled quay and off through the town out into the countryside, palm-lined boulevards and carved stone mansions giving way to plainer whitewashed houses, more like those in Lanzarote but still surrounded with such a profusion of green that Milagro was dazzled. They began to climb up above the town, up a rocky track into wilder vegetation with pine trees and scrubby bushes, but still green, green, green. The carter's mule strained and panted, the wheels jolted over the stones and they came to a sudden stop. Waves of pain shot through Milagro's leg as she fell onto the bottom boards.

*

She could hear water running. She thought at first it was a ringing in her ears but when she managed to scramble to her feet she saw that they had stopped in a small, cool clearing, outside a dilapidated stone hut with a palm-thatched roof. Bushes with berries on them, little red berries, and a neglected vegetable patch with an extraordinary number of ears of corn pushing through the weeds surrounded the building. A stream ran down the hill and away through the pine trees. She stared fascinated at the glittering flow, the water splashing and flashing over the stones, cool, unending, the precious liquid just running away, unchecked and ignored.

The carter lifted their belongings down from the cart and he stretched out his arms to lift her down as well. She smelt the foul breath from his toothless mouth and glared at him so fiercely that he did not dare fondle her as he had intended to do as he set her on the ground. Her leg was agonising and blood had seeped through her skirt, not that one more stain was going to make any difference to that, but she managed to hobble to the door of the hut. It was bigger than the one they had left, but more than that she could not determine. The pain in her leg made her feel light-headed and she had to sit down. El Moro examined her leg before he did anything else; he searched for his ointment and gently applied it to the worst places. She was surprised and touched by his solicitude; only much later did she realise that all he did for her had an ulterior motive. The sooner she was healed, the sooner she would be able to do his bidding.

Life became so easy in Gran Canaria—it was water which made the difference. Everything grew just like that, fruit was there for the taking, she could grow what vegetables she wanted and never worry about how to water them, washing could be done without thinking, even the animals never went short. Life was not real any more, it was too effortless. God had let up but he must only be biding his time, she was still in the employ of the devil and the bill would have to be paid.

She did not deserve this life of ease, yet she could not tire of their green paradise. She would bathe in the stream every day, splashing the water over her face in sheer delight at the coolness of it, she would walk around the clearing touching the leaves on the bushes, feeling their soft freshness, she would kneel enchanted in front of the tender shoots of corn, marvelling at the effortless way they grew and grew.

She was no less afraid of El Moro than she had been. Living with him had not lessened this fear; any illusion of having a sexual hold over him was just that—an illusion. He had none of Felipe's fragility of character: she was less than his servant, she had become his slave. He owned her and at night she was drawn into a world of sin and sex. She could not help herself, even if she had been physically able to escape him it is doubtful whether she would have done so. Felipe had never given her sexual satisfaction like El Moro could. His pleasure always came first and only when she had given him an orgasm to his satisfaction would he consent to make her come, working her over, using his fingers to set her body on fire till she begged for mercy. Then he would laugh and turn over to go to sleep, leaving her wide awake, her body wracked with the spasms of her climax, unable to think of anything but the next time. This was not lovemaking, it was wrong in any case, of course it was wrong: fornication was a sin, particularly with such a one as El Moro, but she could not pray for deliverance when all she could feel was the sting of this hideous desire, blocking off her prayers and rendering her dumb.

*

Time passed. Milagro tried to work up some affection for El Moro but he was not a likeable man—cold, calculating, demanding. She did not expect to come to love him: he was part of her daily life, the worst part in a way, the part over which she had no control. She had made the choice to go with him of her own free will and she had to remind herself of this: she had done it for Pepito, not for her own sake, though her sacrifice (if it could be glorified by the name of sacrifice) became more meaningless every day.

Pepito was growing tall like her vegetables, he seemed to grow even faster than the corn. He was seven, then eight, but the little boy she tried to love and cherish was rapidly turning into someone else and she could only watch as her son, Felipe's son, was transformed. El Moro treated him as a kind of pet, letting him trail around after him all day, taking him down to the city, teaching him to read even, turning him into a little Moorish boy before her eyes, and she could do nothing about it. Physically, he grew more and more like Felipe every day, but Felipe seen through foreign eyes. Pepito seemed to have forgotten all about his father and Milagro did not know how to go about teaching him to remember. El Moro was always Señor, though, never Papa.

Then she made a mistake. Quite unwittingly: it had never occurred to her that she should ask for permission to leave the immediate surroundings of their house, but El Moro returned from Las Palmas one day to find her not at home and he beat her for it, for not being there when he got back, for not asking his leave to go. She had only walked down the side of the stream to give some eggs to the women in the village down the valley, less than a mile away, but he punished her all the same.

Carefully, craftily he beat her, with a small switch through her clothes so that he left no marks, but that was not the worst. When he tired of beating her he raped her, forcing her on to all fours and sodomising her brutally as if she were an animal, tearing her anus on purpose it would seem, so that she could not sit down for a day or more. There was no reward for her that time, no pleasuring of any kind and she did not dare move when he had finished with her in case he should beat her again. He did not speak a word the whole time.

She crept around for the next few days, bleeding, weeping with pain and shame. What a fool I am, she thought, to put up with such treatment. If I went to the authorities and complained that I had been sodomised by an infidel, surely they would put him in jail and I would be free. But she could barely walk around in the hut, let alone escape down the hill into the city. Free to do what, in any case? And where? And how?

Pepito became very quiet all of a sudden, so pale and wan that she wondered if he was sickening for something. Then she realised that he must have witnessed his mother's degradation, but she could not bring herself to say anything to him. She was losing touch with her son; he too was being affected by her sinful way of life but it was quite beyond her, she knew, to put matters right.

El Moro ignored her after that, he did not touch her at night for a week. This was worse than the beating; she had come to need him so much sexually, she needed to be subdued by him, to have him touch her and reduce her to that pathetic state of helpless physical gratification which was her reason for being. On the third night of neglect, she ventured to reach out and caress him as he had taught her but it did not work.

'Don't bother,' he said coldly after a few minutes and a new thought struck her—perhaps he had another woman, in the village or down in Las Palmas. It was so strange that all desire should be snuffed out so suddenly. A ridiculous spasm of some- thing like jealousy shot through her.

Then it all started again, but much less intensely, as if he was indeed tiring of her. She redoubled her efforts to please him, abasing herself, assiduously performing acts she had previously considered abhorrent in order to earn her reward, the evil nature of their relationship made flesh night after night.

By contrast, her days were pleasant and calm, now she knew her place in this green and alien spot with its undemanding way of life, so different from the dust and sand of the island she had left. When El Moro at last took her down to the city, its busy opulence frightened her.

Yes, she was allowed out at last, to work, escorted through the crowded streets to this, that or the other extravagantly wealthy mansion to sew. There were so many smart ladies in Las Palmas with an ever-unsatisfied desire for new clothes and linen and she was a success, sought after for the fine quality of her needlework and embroidery and generously paid.

She never saw the money, of course. El Moro was always with her, delivering her to the door and collecting her and her payment at the end of the day; she was rented out as a mule would be, and with as little respect. She learned, quite by chance, what people thought of her. A voice in the corridor outside the housekeeper's room where she was working one day, sewing a great set of velvet curtains for the alcalde's ballroom, loud, quite careless of whether she might be listening or no: 'Ask la puta del Moro if she can mend this right away.'

The Moor's whore. She stopped, aghast, in mid-stitch. Here they looked down on her even more than the stuffy matrons of Arrecife had. La puta del Moro, his housekeeper, his cook, his whore. He was her master and everyone knew it and there was nothing she could do about it. Crazy fantasies ran through her head, of drugging him with his own potions, stealing the money that was rightfully hers and fleeing. Running away again. She could not face it. Anyway, where could she go? The thought of fleeing aimlessly into the maelstrom of Las Palmas with a small boy in tow was unthinkable. Gran Canaria was an island, far bigger than Lanzarote certainly, but still an island. He would be sure to find her and if she did not manage to kill him, he would kill her. The death of a whore would not cause much comment.

Felipe had dreamed of starting a new life on the other side

of the ocean; maybe she could take ship with Pepito for the Americas one day. Poor Felipe, his dreams were ashes and such a dream must remain just that—a lone woman with a child would have even less chance of survival in a strange land than a couple. Perhaps when Pepito was older; a few years more and he would be grown up and able to take care of his mother. Then they could escape.

*

Three years passed, then four. She worked long and hard, true, but she had regained much of her former beauty with good food and the easy living. Her hair was glossy and black now that she had time to take care of herself, it was not matted and caked with ash, her skin smooth, not dry and scaly with dust. She had put on a little weight but men still watched her with eager eyes as she walked into town behind El Moro; she could feel their lust like waves of heat on her back. As they had back in Teguise when she was a girl.

El Moro himself had lost interest in her altogether. Only occasionally now would he command her sexual attentions and she would lie beside him unsatisfied night after night, aflame with illicit, shameful desire. She learned to do things to herself to quench these flames but it left her feeling soiled and guilty.

He caught her at it one day. She was sitting on the bed they still shared, legs apart, eyes closed, dreamily rubbing herself. Oblivious, in a haze of lust, she had not heard him come in. The first thing she knew, she was flung backwards roughly onto the straw mattress and he forced himself into her. The surprise and violence of the attack did not lessen her own pleasure and she came almost immediately, crying out with the intensity of her orgasm. When he had finished, he rose to his feet and left; she could see the expression of sneering contempt on his face. His own orgasm had meant nothing to him, no more than the relief of pissing against the wall. She did not understand why he despised her so, except that she was a foolish woman, only too obviously governed by her emotions.

She was alone, she seemed to spend most of her life alone, no family, no friends. She had rejected her own family years ago and had not been able to make one of her own. A dead lover, one son the sole survivor of all her babies, that was all she had, and Pepito was growing up, he would not want to stay with his mother for ever. She had found no trace of her mother and stepfather in Las Palmas; every time she went to a new house, she would ask the maids if they knew of a Señor Perez but no one had ever heard of him.

So she was alone. She had made no friends either, though other families lived close by. After her punishment, she did not dare say more than a few words to the women she met at the washing place down stream and she was never allowed to stray in Las Palmas. A maid servant in one of the grandest houses in the city told her why: it was because she was a woman.

She was making a complete set of embroidered sheets for the marriage of the youngest daughter and the bride-to-be's maid was a great gossip. Muslims, she told Milagro, don't let their women out of their sight unless they're veiled and some-times not even then. They are so jealous that they will kill a woman who even looks at another man.

How idiotic, thought Milagro, stitching away, listening to the girl's idle chatter. But she was probably right. That would explain El Moro's unreasonable and possessive attitude. One could hardly watch a woman all the time, though. Take her case, for example. There she was all day, left to work on her own. What was to prevent her having a quick encounter with a suitable man one afternoon—a nice young valet or one of the footmen? It could so easily be arranged without El Moro ever coming to hear of anything suspicious. Not that the men servants she had met were up to much. More than one had his eye on her, that was obvious, but they were all either lecherous old men like Señor Perez, or green boys who would not, she was sure, give her the satisfaction she now craved from a man.

El Moro would never find out, would he? Or was he using

his magical powers to keep an eye on her? He would pray five times a day, getting up at first light just to renew these powers and he might well have ways of discovering what she did when he was not there. More prosaically, and more practically, he could have bribed someone to inform him if she showed signs of straying and she was too afraid of him to risk it. She was still in his thrall even though his brutality and indifference had loosened his hold on her to the point at which she realised she could not spend the rest of her life as his slave. A solution had to be found, but she would have to be very, very careful and ingenious to free herself from his domination.

Time passed, unreal time in isolation in a foreign country. They had been in Gran Canaria for over six years when Milagro heard one day that the eruptions in Lanzarote had ceased and some people were returning home. She had an odd feeling of regret that she was not one of them but she must be mad to want to go back to that life of hardship. It had been bad before and it must be worse now.

Home—Gran Canaria had never truly felt like home, was that what was wrong? Was misery and constant toil really the only way to salvation, would God forgive her if she returned to the struggle, would He help her to overcome the rage of physical need which everlastingly flared up inside her? El Moro had fanned the flames of something which had always been there; as a young girl, this rampant sexuality had been the source of her restlessness, only she had not recognised it as such until Felipe had brought it to life so disastrously. Now she was stuck with it, seemingly for the rest of her days.

She had not thought of Felipe so much lately. Her life with him, her past life was like a troubled dream which her conscious mind had succeeded in blotting out quite effectively. She was living in an emotional void, totally separate from her physical involvement with El Moro; visions of Felipe's terrible death still came back to her but they had lost their ability to drive her to despair.

*

Sometimes she was not even sure she knew what he looked like; if she had Pepito in front of her she would remember—his eyes, the curve of the cheek, the way his hair fell across his forehead, yes, that was Felipe. In looks only. She had thought that Pepito was the one part of her life which had not gone wrong but he had gone over to the enemy now. If she spoke to him, he would look at her as if she was of no importance and ignore anything she asked him to do, though he would obey El Moro. The boy and the man were forming a kind of conspiracy against her, sharing experiences in which she could not participate. When El Moro went down into Las Palmas, he would take the boy with him but Milagro could not gather from Pepito what they did or where they went.

'There are other boys and we play games,' was all he would say; when asked what sort of games, he was vague. Secret games, and the men talked and gave the boys presents. He had good clothes now, finer than her own, and jewellery too, a small gold ring. El Moro cared for Pepito, she realised bitterly, even though he did not care for her.

The lush tranquillity of the house in the clearing was no longer as appealing as it had once been: an easy way of life did not make for ease of mind. Everything was all wrong, it always had been. When she was fifteen she had run away rather than be forced into a loveless marriage, finding herself in a life of poverty and hardship which only love had made worthwhile, yet when forced to make comparisons between Felipe and El Moro, she had to admit that Felipe would not have made a life for them in Gran Canaria the way El Moro had. His fecklessness and carefree approach to things would have left them starving on the beach. She could see how love might evaporate entirely in the face of adversity, but it was not her fault that love had let her down. She had not caused the eruptions which had sent her life off in such a different direction, but her recent prosperity, at least compared with her time with Felipe, was not the answer. The loss of love had almost destroyed her soul entirely and the devil's concubine, la puta del Moro, did not know the way back.

The old, old errors: when she first met Felipe, when she first failed to associate physical pleasure with sin, when she did not stop to reflect on the course of action she was taking, these had caused her downfall. She had been an innocent, ignorant young girl then, but ignorance was no excuse. Don Miguel had told her that—being a child does not mean you are free of sin, if you do not recognise that what you do is sinful, it does not mean that you are innocent.

She came to no conclusion except that denying her love for Felipe, finding it only evil, was like denying that she existed. El Moro the evil side of love, Felipe the good side, they could not both be evil, they were so different, yet they must be. This, then was her punishment: the realisation that the physical pleasure which brought her the most joy was the most evil.

The more she thought about it, the more confused she became, but the idea that return to the hardships of Lanzarote might be part of some kind of atonement for her sins took hold of her and would not let go. It would be even harder to escape from El Moro's clutches in Lanzarote, though, and she feared (she had come to know herself only too well) that she would end up in another man's bed if she did manage to set herself free. Perhaps God would account her sin less if she lived with a man who was at least nominally a good Catholic. But who would have her? Who would be willing to take on la puta del Moro? No one who knew her past; even a widower searching for a housekeeper and a mother for his children would draw the line at such a woman as her.

She could get another man easily. She was not so young any more but she was experienced in the ways of men, goodness knows, and when they stared at her as they still did, recognising the red tide of physical excitement which rose inside her, she knew she could get anyone she wanted. She could get another man, yes, but not one who could redeem her, not a respectable, churchgoing man whose example would teach her to sin no more. She was now irredeemably corrupted, her prayers to be delivered from this terrible curse had gone unanswered. God was silent on the subject, he had left her to burn like the island of Lanzarote itself.

She did not know how to suggest going back to Lanzarote; it seemed such a foolish thing to do, one which El Moro would condemn out of hand. One night, after a number of days of abstinence, he demanded her services and she hastened to obey, to give of her best, to prolong his enjoyment as well as she knew how and put him in a good mood. He bent over her to give her the reward for good conduct and she said, making her question sound as casual as she could,

'Have you ever thought of going back?'

He said nothing for a while, merely continuing what he was doing, kneeling over her, stimulating her with a little polished, rounded stick he kept for that purpose. She felt herself boiling up and flowing away in the inevitable climax as he moved the stick in and out, faster and faster. It was not until her moans had subsided that he answered her question with one of his own.

'Do you want to go back?'

'I don't know.' She tried to define what she really felt in an acceptable form. 'I don't feel I belong here in Gran Canaria.'

'It would be hard, you know, as hard as it was before we left.'

'Had you thought about going back then?' She was surprised. He did not answer her directly, though she failed to notice his evasiveness. She was still dazed with sex.

'I think it would be better for Pepito if we moved from here. There are some girls down in the village whom he sees too often. I would like to put a stop to that before it's too late.'

'Girls!' Milagro was astonished. How could her son have

grown up so quickly? 'He's far too young.'

'He's thirteen.'

Milagro could hardly believe it but it was true. Pepito had been four when Felipe was killed and they had been in Gran Canaria for something like nine years. She was well on the way to old age herself and her son was on the verge of manhood.

*

El Moro had no intention of revealing to her why he himself would prefer to return to Lanzarote; it was not in his nature to confide in a woman and Milagro was no exception to the general rule. Volatile, weak of purpose and untrustworthy, she would never see things the way he did. He was not amazed and dazzled by the wealth of Gran Canaria as Milagro was and Felipe had been right about him: he was a spy for various pirate vessels, but this was not so simple as it used to be.

In Lanzarote, it had been easy—every few months a pirate ship would pause off the north of the island. There were few fishermen up there and those that struggled to make a living in the turbulent waters of those northern headlands liked to keep themselves to themselves. A ship could put innocently into the main port of Arrecife to carry out its legitimate trade, then heave to in the north to pick up a secret haul of promising-looking young boys and girls who would fetch a good price in the slave markets of Tangier or Casablanca. It was El Moro who would prepare the clandestine human cargo, and for this he would be paid handsomely in both goods and gold.

In the sophisticated society of Gran Canaria, however, there were no secrets, prying eyes were everywhere and the pirates were more reluctant to approach such a well-policed stretch of water as that off Las Palmas. Moreover, it was two extra days beat to windward back to the African coast. El Moro had barely made ends meet, even with what Milagro earned for him. He had considered putting her on the streets but in the end he preferred to keep her for himself; besides, her earnings as a seamstress were more certain and more discreet. There was no lack of organised and well-armed pimps in Las Palmas.

'If you want to go back, we'll go.'

It was too dark to see the expression on his face but the idea of El Moro doing something because she wished it aroused her suspicions; she had anticipated arguing with him, though she knew this would be futile, but she was obliged to suppress her doubts in the face of his sudden acquiescence.

To go home. That was what she wanted. Not to run away but to go back to the island where she had been born, not to cross the ocean to face even more unknown hazards but to go home, and home was Lanzarote. Perhaps she might even find her mother back there, not that she could bear the thought of meeting her mother in her present circumstances; la puta del Moro—she could see only too clearly the expression on her mother's face. My daughter, whoring for a living, just as I predicted. Señor Perez was sure to have returned, he would be selling grain at inflated prices to those who could barely afford it at the normal price.

Grain, they would need grain themselves, seeds, animals, everything would have to be taken with them. There was no time for fantasising about her long-lost family, the next few weeks would be busy.

Now that the decision had been taken and she had not had to plead with El Moro, to abase herself endlessly, she felt that her burden of sin had lightened already. It was more and more clear to her that she would not be forgiven while she stayed away, lolling at her ease in the soft living of Gran Canaria. She could not yet see how to rid herself of that terrible plague, how to control her physical cravings; even as such thoughts ranged through her troubled brain, she could feel the heat welling up inside her, the intolerable itch between her legs. This was ridiculous. She was past thirty, far too old for that sort of thing.

A bizarre thought struck her. Doña Constancia had been older than Milagro was now when she had been conceived.

Had she inherited this senseless urge from her mother? The idea of the corseted Doña Constancia unlacing her bodice and rolling about on a bed with the portly Señor Perez did not bear thinking about. Laughable, disgusting, totally improbable.

*

It was in fact several months before they were ready to leave.

'I have arrangements to make.' El Moro was as enigmatic and uninformative as ever. What arrangements? Milagro often wondered how he made a living. She never knew how much she was paid for her needlework; the price was agreed by El Moro out of her hearing and he always collected the money, but it could not be that much. She had only a vague idea of how commerce worked but he must be trading in something, men made money out of trade. She remembered Señor Perez's boastful speeches over dinner about the profits he had made out of this or that cargo but about El Moro she still knew little or nothing. Other men were easy to read, sex and money were all they thought of, but El Moro was a blank wall.

He was not extravagant; the food on the table was mostly what they, or she rather, produced, though he would occasionally bring back luxuries from the city—fruit or a choice cut of meat—and they had no silver tableware or fine glasses like those in use in the grand establishments she visited in Las Palmas. Of course he did not drink, he would not, like so many men, like Felipe, drink his money away regardless of whether it was needed for more important things.

No, he was not like other men, not at all, and she was more in thrall to him than she had ever been to Felipe. Perhaps he really was some devil if not Satan himself—she was at a loss to explain the strange hold he had over her. Love had nothing to do with it. She feared his oddness, his contempt for his fellow men in general, for women in particular, his brutality, mental and physical. Yet, when he touched her, or even when she imagined him touching her, this set her ablaze. It could

[179]

only be devilry, but when it came down to it she was always too frightened of him to denounce him; he was capable of killing her before she had time to seek out a priest and make her confession. Then she would go straight to hell.

Witchcraft, devilry, was he putting something in her food? He collected herbs from the woods, he would bring back boxes of strange powders from the apothecary, mix and brew peculiar-smelling potions which he would sell, discreetly, to those who came to enquire about them. He treated burns and fevers (she was a witness to that), he would sell medications for various aches and pains and she had seen him set broken arms and legs. He could easily have made up some brew which put a spell on her, certainly something was causing her to burn so insatiably. She watched him carefully for several days to no avail; in any case she, the servant, prepared and cooked everything.

One of the oddest things about him, to her, was that he had taken pains to cure her burns and he would treat the sick, notwithstanding his contempt for his patients. If she had understood his motives, she would have been all the more puzzled. He did despise the people of the Canaries, for their ignorance and lack of imagination, and he only stayed there because this feeling of superiority had become essential to his existence: he enjoyed his power over them, it amused him to see the glances of apprehension as he walked down the street, both in Gran Canaria and in Arrecife. He exercised his medicinal skills, not because of any concern for his patients but for scientific reasons. He did not care whether they lived or died, they all expected to die in any case so he could experiment on them with impunity and learn much from their reactions, which he could not have done if he had been obliged to act with more circumspection in a more sophisticated and knowledgeable society. He toyed with the idea of writing a treatise on primitive reactions to medicines; one day he would, in his old age, return home to Turkey and civilisation.

Milagro was still a more or less agreeable addition to his life. He did not despise her particularly; as a woman, she was naturally a lower class of being—weak, impulsive, not given to any kind of rational thought. Sexually, she was so easy to manipulate: he experimented with her sexual reactions much as he did with his sick patients and derived considerable pleasure from observing her helpless writhings under his ministrations. He looked forward to continuing his experiments when they arrived back in Lanzarote. He had plans for Pepito too, which he had no intention of revealing to her, and he did not want the lad learning bad habits from some ignorant little village girl.

Chapter X – 1756 – Diego's Story

The schoolteacher is waiting for Rodrigo, a man somewhat older than Rodrigo himself and not as tall. He has greying hair but his skin is fair, with a broader nose and thicker lips than Rodrigo is accustomed to seeing in Spain and he wonders if, despite his light complexion and blue eyes, the man has African blood. An educated man nevertheless.

'Diego Hernández, Señor.' He sounds incongruously pompous. 'I'm the schoolmaster here, for what it's worth. Most of the children come from families too poor to send them to school; they consider education an unnecessary refinement, but I do my best. My house is not large, not what you're accustomed to, no doubt,' looking at Rodrigo's well-cut coat, 'but it has a spare room and my wife is a good housekeeper. The only alternative is the tavern with its disease and lice, or the whorehouse which is even worse.'

He leads the way along the crumbling quay and up a side street. Two youths who have been struggling with Rodrigo's luggage trail after them, the heavy trunks balanced uncertainly on a two-wheeled cart. Diego's house is a short way from the harbour and close to the church. The street is deserted, the houses shuttered against the sun and the dust, but the shutters are freshly painted, the doors stout with brass knockers. This must be the better part of town: most of the houses have more than one storey, too. Diego's is one of these but the view from the bedroom to which he is shown reveals the other side of the picture. The room looks out onto a tumbledown collection of shacks. Scrawny hens scratch among the prickly pears and ragged shoeless children kick stones at each other. Goats stray at will in and out of the huts.

By contrast, the room itself is, though sparsely furnished, neat and tidy, the bed linen appears to be clean and an appetising smell is coming from the kitchen. He sets about unpacking his belongings, laying out his geological equipment on the floor. Most of his clothes he leaves in their trunk, taking out only a few shirts and his stoutest boots for scrambling over rocks, the ones stained yellow by the sulphur springs of Vulcano.

The weather is mild for October, much warmer than it was in Cadiz, and he will have no need of the heavy winter attire he has brought. Not knowing what to expect and hearing that there are mountains in Lanzarote, Fernando has packed a considerable amount of clothing more suited to the Pyrenees: worsted breeches and heavy leather jerkins, Rodrigo not having thought to tell him that the mountains were only a few hundred metres high.

He meets the rest of the family at supper: Rosa, Diego's wife, and their children, three solemn boys between ten and fourteen, little copies of their father, and a small girl much younger, about four or five. When he sees the whole family together, Rodrigo notices they all have the same eyes: not dark brown like those of Spanish or Moorish descent he has been expecting to encounter, but much lighter in colour. Now that he comes to study Diego and his children more closely he is at a loss to explain their origin, but then he is a geologist, he reminds himself. The ethnic origins of native populations are not his subject, though M. de Buffon will no doubt be keenly interested. He stares at the children and they stare gravely back.

Rosa has prepared a simple stew of kid which they eat with cakes of a primitive kind of corn bread. There is only fruit to follow: desert fruit, dates and prickly pears; a peasant meal, but a delicious change from the stomach-churning shipboard fare. He is offered a beaker of thin local wine; neither of his hosts are drinking it, he notices, and he tastes it warily. By Spanish standards it is undrinkable, contriving to be both vinegary and too sweet at the same time, but he manages to swallow some without grimacing. He is bursting with questions about Lanzarote and the wine provides a good opening. He enquires, as tactfully as he can, if it is made on the island.

Diego smiles, pouring a little into his own beaker.

'It's not very good, is it. You wouldn't believe how much it's improved over the last few years, though. We had to bring everything with us when we came back, you know—seeds, vine cuttings, animals, there was virtually nothing left here. Almost no rain for six years and pollution by volcanic ash killed off most things except for the cacti and a few palm trees. And the prickly pears, you probably call them Barbary figs. Nothing kills them.'

'You mean the volcano changed the climate of Lanzarote?'

'For a time, yes.' He turns to Rosa as if seeking her permission to continue, as if the subject of the eruptions is bringing back unwelcome memories. Rosa says nothing but her face has lost its pleasant smile.

'We dare not depend on rain for crop irrigation but we desperately hope for some from time to time; there are a few springs on the island, like the one at Famara in the north, but not enough. During the eruptions the rain became poisonous, it mingled with the ash in the sky and came down as mud. We have special ways of growing crops here now, of conserving dew and keeping in the moisture, of protecting seedlings and young trees from the wind too. We make circles of stones and cover the roots of the plants with sand. I'll show you tomorrow, if you're interested. We have camels and goats, of course, they're easy to feed, and our cheese is not bad, better than our wine in any case.'

Diego pauses in his pedantic explanations and Rodrigo has some difficulty in keeping a straight face; the man is a schoolteacher, true, but does he have to sound so much like a pompous professor labouring a point?

*

'What's interesting to me,' Diego has not noticed Rodrigo's

wry expression, 'is why a man like yourself should want to come to Lanzarote. You're not a merchant or a farmer, obviously, or even a soldier. There's nothing for a soldier here now, even the pirates leave us alone these days, the pickings are far too slim. Are you descended from one of the old Spanish families who came with de Bethencourt?'

Rodrigo cannot believe his luck in happening so quickly upon someone who may be able to answer many of his questions. He is not interested in the history of the island, he remembers the name de Bethencourt vaguely as the conqueror of Lanzarote in the fourteenth century but that does not concern him; the unique geological history of the island is what he is here to research.

'I want to know everything that happened here during the eruptions.' He disregards Rosa's increasingly troubled expression. 'I want to talk to anyone who was there and actually saw what happened, how such a catastrophe changed the face of the land.'

He is not prepared for the reactions of his hosts: Rosa's cry of distressed protest and Diego's scowl of disapproval take him completely by surprise.

'No one wants to remember that time.' Diego's muttered rebuke is hardly audible. 'So many people died, the crops were ruined, houses buried under the floods of lava. Even the survivors were in danger, the air was poisoned with ash and gases from the eruption. Only a few lived and fewer escaped, the lucky ones who could afford to leave and go to other islands.'

Completely distraught, tears streaming down her face, Rosa rushes precipitately from the room. Rodrigo is alarmed, and also intrigued; it has not occurred to him that personal tragedy might, after so many years, be so fresh in the minds of the islanders. When he visited Vesuvius, the villagers who still lived on its slopes were only too eager to pester him with ghoulish tales of disaster.

'I did not mean to upset your wife.' He hastens to

apologise. 'I certainly did not come here to gloat over your misfortunes; my interest in the eruptions is purely scientific.'

'Perhaps.' Diego is not mollified. 'We did not survive those disastrous years merely to find ourselves the object of some wealthy dilettante's morbid curiosity.'

Rodrigo bridles at this; his lack of sensitivity was quite unwitting and he does not let Diego get away with such an unfair criticism.

'You yourself must be better off than many of the people here, your house is larger, your clothes are better. You've chosen to teach the poor. I'm sorry, I've no such inclination, good works are not for me. You may despise me for being wealthy but it's as much an accident of birth as being poor, you know.'

Diego says nothing and Rodrigo hurriedly continues before the man can think up some further reproach.

'How can I explain the fascination volcanoes have for me? I can understand how, living on top of one, you consider it a constant menace and bringer of calamity, but when you think how and why they erupt, where all the molten rock and poisonous vapours come from, how their furnace burns under the earth not so far beneath our feet, you must realise there is so much to be explained—they are a mystery which demands to be investigated.' He is the one who is lecturing now.

'I have discussed vulcanology with Monsieur Buffon, the famous French naturalist. I heard him speak on the subject in Paris a few years ago and I thought here was a field of study I could do something with, not so much to justify my idle existence as to give some point to my life, to prove to myself as much as anything that I'm more than an empty-headed fool with more money than sense. I was a soldier once, but I've seen more than enough killing and I certainly didn't come to Lanzarote to research human tragedy.

'I've explored many other volcanoes of course—Vesuvius, Stromboli, Vulcano, Etna, I've even been as far as Thira in the

Cyclades, in Greece. I admit being rich is a great help, I can afford to charter ships and take a good deal of valuable geological equipment with me, but I like to think scientific discovery will benefit all mankind in the end. I was really excited, though I don't know whether you can understand this, when I discovered Lanzarote was a volcanic island not many savants know about.'

'You have to understand us.' Diego's expression is as severe as ever and he does not seem to be at all impressed by Rodrigo's voluble explanation. 'Rosa saw many of her family burned to death and her father disappeared completely; she has never been able to find out what happened to him. I was fortunate, I had gone to Seville to study and I was safe, but I'm the only survivor of my family.'

'I had hoped,' persists Rodrigo, 'to talk to people who were here at the time to get an accurate account of events and to visit Timanfaya myself, of course. It's very unscientific to go merely on hearsay and not make one's own observations.'

Another callous statement.

'No one goes to Timanfaya.' Diego's face is like a thundercloud. 'No one wants to trample on the graves of their families and friends. Whole villages are buried under the lava fields, there's not one family on the island which did not lose someone. It was hard to believe God would allow such a thing to happen.'

Rodrigo has no intention of becoming involved in a theological discussion as well as a moral one. 'You're still here,' he observes, 'you could have abandoned Lanzarote, gone to Tenerife or Gran Canaria where the living is easier.'

'Most of us did leave, it was almost impossible to survive, but we came back when the eruptions ceased.'

'Why?' Rodrigo is completely mystified. 'Why not stay away? Surely the difficulties of starting again here must have been almost insurmountable.'

'This is our home,' says Diego simply. 'When you've lost

your family and your possessions and you live in exile, if you can at least go home you can fool yourself into believing you've not quite lost all there is to lose.'

An interesting point, one Rodrigo is not prepared to challenge. He studies Diego's singular features. 'Are you really native to Lanzarote? It's not often one sees someone with eyes like yours in Spain.'

'We're Guanches, we're not of Spanish descent, but I'm sure you've never heard of the Guanches. No one has except those who live here in the Canaries.' His contemptuous expression is that of a teacher who has a poor opinion of his pupil's abilities, but Rodrigo is obliged to admit that he had no idea who the Guanches might be.

'The Guanches are the original inhabitants of the Canaries. We came from North Africa. There are only a few of us left now, your ancestors took most of us into slavery when they conquered the islands. You won't know the story; even the people of Lanzarote don't know their own history, even those who can read are hardly interested in it.'

'I should like to hear it.' Rodrigo's curiosity is genuinely aroused by this unknown aspect of the island's past. 'I never thought of the islanders as being anything but Spanish, I must confess, I was only interested in the natural phenomena. Please go on.'

Diego pours some more wine into their beakers and leans back in his chair, settling down to continue the lecture on his favourite subject.

'The first Spanish came to Lanzarote more than three hundred years ago, led by a man who was not in fact Spanish but Norman, Juan de Bethencourt. Priests came with him, sent by Castile to convert us heathen natives to Christianity. The island was not called Lanzarote then but Tytheroygatra and it was ruled by a king, Guadarfia. He was not a king like the king of Spain, naturally, but he was king of Lanzarote nevertheless. Our people hid from the Spanish when they landed. The

Guanches were no more warlike in those days than they are now, even though we knew that conquerors would have only one aim: to enslave our men and rape our wives and daughters. There was actually very little fighting before a truce of sorts was made.'

Diego's manner is strange, his face full of animation; he talks of 'we' not 'they'. The history of his people three hundred years in the past is as real to him as the tragic events of recent times, if not more so.

'Under the terms of the truce, the Spanish were permitted by the king—not that he had much choice in the matter—to build a fort at Guanapay, near Teguise, the old capital of the island. It is a fortified town itself, Teguise, fortified against the pirates. We've always had a bad life here; sometimes I do wonder myself why we decided to stay here in the first place. If the Spanish were not attempting to enslave us, it was the Ottomans or the Berbers coming over from North Africa. We used to hide in the caves in the north of the island if we could not reach Teguise in time.'

He adds, his voice heavy with sarcasm, 'You should find the caves of great interest, they're huge blow holes, it seems, made by molten lava. They have underground lakes and some extraordinary rock formations.'

Rodrigo does not rise to the bait; he is finding the lecture quite intriguing.

'In those days, promises were just words and truces with native peoples were made to be broken. I suppose things have not changed too much today. One of de Bethencourt's lieutenants, Bertin de Berneval, took advantage of his leader's absence to capture some of us to sell as slaves and we took our revenge on those of you who could not reach the fort in time.

'Of course it did not end there, reprisal followed reprisal; there was a good deal of fighting but we had no chance against the well-armed soldiers of Spain. Guadarfia was not a particularly heroic leader and there were traitors among his own men willing to betray him to the enemy. Moreover, he had little experience of the greed and duplicity of invaders when confronted by a naive indigenous population. We were all enslaved in the end and forcibly baptised as Christians, though this did not stop us preserving a great many of our old customs.

'Lanzarote was too barren to be of much interest to the Spanish except as an emergency staging post on the way to the Americas. They turned their attention to overrunning the other islands and there was much worse fighting in Tenerife and Gran Canaria. The Guanches survived by hiding in the hills or the volcanic blow holes and gradually the Spanish left us in peace.

'Us' again. Rodrigo cannot suppress an expression of scepticism and scorn. Diego is an educated man, yet here he is, believing in an ancient legend of dubious veracity. Diego notices his reaction.

'You're surprised. You can't understand how I can be so well-informed when I come from a race of people you would consider savages.'

'I can't understand,' Rodrigo cannot help saying, 'why you believe in such legends. They sound like the stories you tell little children, deeds of heroism and treachery which have little basis in truth.'

Diego frowns. 'They're not legends, they're the history of the Guanche people. You've never been conquered, you don't know what it is to have your origins denied and obliterated. We are Guanches and we still exist. We're not Spanish. Admit it, you yourself noticed we're different, not like the mainland Spanish to look at. We came from North Africa many hundreds of years ago and we brought our own language and customs with us. We still use many words which are not Spanish, the last remnants of our original language.'

Rosa returns, recovered from her outburst of grief. Rodrigo studies her lined face—what he has taken for the usual ravages of a hard, peasant life are the signs of a deeper tragedy.

'I can remember our family being different when I was little, different from the other villagers,' she says. 'My grand-parents wore the traditional clothes, long-tailed shirts and tall hats. I remember as a girl sitting down to eat, on the ground, round a palm mat covered with a white cloth instead of a table.'

Rodrigo is eager to introduce the subject of Timanfaya and the volcanic eruptions again, now that Rosa seems to have calmed down, but he does not dare—he has upset his hosts by his lack of tact and then thrown doubt on their origins. How-ever, he has come to Lanzarote to find out about the Montañas del Fuego, not to listen to obscure folk tales. As he is wonder-ing how to reintroduce the subject with more finesse this time, Rosa herself, to his astonishment, brings the matter up.

'Señor, there is a woman here who can tell you about the time of the volcanoes.' Her voice is hesitant, it is a visible effort for her to get the words out.

'No,' interrupts Diego, 'he doesn't need to see her.'

Rosa puts her hand on his arm.

'I think I have to stop grieving. Nothing can change the past or bring my father back, I know that, at least when I think clearly about things; but she might just tell a stranger how he died, someone who doesn't know the story of her past and won't blame her for his death.'

Diego sighs in disbelief. 'Why would she speak now? If she can still speak.'

He turns to Rodrigo. 'This woman, Milagro, she was Rosa's father's... mistress.' He too seems unwilling to talk about her.

'She lived in Arrecife. It was only after the eruptions began that Felipe brought her down to Playa Blanca where Rosa and her mother had taken refuge.'

'Felipe?'

'Felipe was Rosa's father. He intended to take them all, Rosa and her mother and Milagro and her child, to Gran Canaria to safety, but then he and Milagro disappeared one morning and he was never seen again. When I brought Rosa and the children back to Arrecife six years ago, we found Milagro here. She was a drunk, living on other people's charity. We found her a hut and Rosa takes her food but she won't speak to us.'

'She's mad,' Rosa breaks in, her eyes filled with tears once more. 'I'm sure she killed my father but she won't tell me what happened to him. She hasn't spoken to anyone for years. I hate her, I always have, but she knew my father and she's the only one left who did, my only link with the past. My uncle and I did escape, the others, my mother, my sisters, my cousins, they all died. I can still remember running through the fields, the hills melting, the corn crackling as it caught fire behind us, the horrible choking smell.'

She is unable to go on. Rodrigo sits, fidgeting with embarrassment, and Diego holds her in his arms as she sobs helplessly. It is some time before she recovers enough to continue.

'I didn't recognise Milagro when we came back. I'd only seen her once, when I was ten, and I didn't know she was here. I heard rumours about this mad woman and her wild tales about the past but it wasn't till someone mentioned her name that I knew who she must be. I begged her to tell me about my father but she wouldn't say a word, she just spat on the ground. She's crazy, all the evil things she's done have affected her mind. Why couldn't she have died and my father have lived?'

Diego puts his arm round her again. 'I'm sure, my dear, she's not happy. You've got a family of your own, you've got me and the children, she has nothing. She must wake every morning grieving over her past.'

He turns to Rodrigo. 'It seems she came back to Arrecife soon after the eruptions ceased with a Moor, another of her lovers, and when he died she became a whore. She had no other way of earning a living. She had a child, Felipe's, a son, but he seems to have disappeared years ago. Everyone despises her for her past and you would think she has no reason to go on living, if even half the tales about her are true. Unfortunately, one does not necessarily die when one has nothing left to live for. We can see her tomorrow if you wish, but don't hope for very much. She may only spit at you too.'

Rodrigo yawns involuntarily. 'Please don't think I'm finding what you're telling me at all dull,' he hastens to assure his hosts. 'It's just that the voyage from Cadiz was very exhausting. I'll retire to my room, if you'll excuse me.'

He accepts the candle Diego holds out to him and makes his way thoughtfully upstairs. There is much more to Lanzarote than he first thought, this barren rock has bred human violence and tragedy as well as geological drama. The moonlight floods in through the window and he has no need of the candle as he sits down to write up his diary, using the top of his trunk as a table. His tiredness seems to vanish, temporarily at least, as he mulls over the events of the day. He has totally neglected his diary, inevitably, on board ship and it takes him some time to recall and describe the past few days to his satisfaction.

When he has finished, he goes to the window to look out at the eerie landscape: black and silver now, it has taken on a certain beauty in the moonlight but he cannot picture himself living in such a place. He would miss trees and flowers and the sound of running water, things taken for granted at home in Seville and even in the driest parts of the Estremadura. He can ill imagine a people choosing to live in such a desolate place. The wind blows most of the night, clattering shutters and palm branches, but he sleeps soundly, exhausted by his ordeal at sea, at last in a bed which stays level on a floor which is not moving.

Chapter XI – 1741 – Return

Milagro and El Moro left Gran Canaria in the September. It was important, he reminded her, to arrive back in Lanzarote before the rainy season (if there was one) to prepare or rebuild a cistern and plant vegetables so that they would be watered at the right time. Now they were on their way, Milagro had desperate misgivings; it seemed so foolish to give up so much on what now seemed a whim. She might just as well be damned in comfort.

The voyage back was unpleasant. The ship was not really a ship, it was quite small, a fishing smack doing some part-time trading, and it still smelt strongly of stale fish, but there was more than enough room for all their belongings—furniture, clothes, seeds, roots, a cage of hens, a young nanny goat, ten times what they had originally arrived in Gran Canaria with. They were the only passengers, sitting awkwardly on sacks of grain in the stern while the boat bucked and tossed, tacking back and forth endlessly up the channel and round the bottom of Fuerteventura.

It took them nearly three days. Milagro was fully prepared to die, so sick was she, so much worse than ever before. Even going to hell could not be as bad as that, she thought, and Pepito was thoroughly cowed, crouching pale and silent in the shelter of the sacks now covered by a smelly old sail to protect them from the flying spray. Everything was encrusted in salt: they had left Lanzarote caked with dust and ash, they returned like Lot's wife, pillars of salt. El Moro was, of course, unmoved, at least if he felt sick he did not show it. He gave Milagro and Pepito small pieces of a pungent root to chew on; the taste was not unpleasant and Milagro could feel the warmth of the juice calming her heaving stomach. Pepito spat his out in disgust and was almost immediately sick but El Moro refused to give him another piece.

On the third morning, the wind and sea died down and

they drifted slowly in and out, up towards Arrecife. The hills of Lanzarote stood out clear in the early morning light. A faint plume of vapour rose in the distant sky but the hideous pall of smoke had gone. The island had not changed: white, grey, black and brown, the ruined landscape was only too familiar and it did not welcome her back. Arrecife itself was even shabbier and dustier than she remembered. The pall of ash had gone but the buildings surrounding the port were in a desperate state of dilapidation, though the occasional palm tree had survived, showing up optimistically green among the dismal houses. A miserable homecoming.

The ship lurched across a sand bar; the harbour was much shallower than it used to be thanks to six years of upheaval and off the only remaining quay a couple of boats still lay stranded. They docked not without difficulty and the captain warned them to disembark their effects before the tide began to recede.

They went ashore. El Moro hastened off to see what had become of his house and Pepito ran after him but Milagro lingered to look around the port she had once known so well: much of it was so ruined as to be hardly recognisable. Her queasy stomach and spinning head did not improve on dry land and a terrible thought struck her. Surely she could not be pregnant. She tried in vain to count up the days to see how late she was; she had come to believe pregnancy to be a thing of the past, that she was too old. But no. Her mother had been old when she was born, she remembered with considerable misgiving, she must have been close to forty and Milagro herself was still only thirty.

She stood on the quay, lost in unpleasant thought, oblivious to the cries of the sailors, who wanted to know what to do with their possessions, not to mention the animals. She began to tremble with dread, clutching her stomach, trying to feel if there was anything growing inside her—some tiny being with horns and cloven hooves.

There was a shout from Pepito; he had returned and was

calling her to organise the animals whilst he took charge of their baggage. The house was still intact, it appeared. She forced herself into action, there were too many things to be done to worry about herself for the moment. The goat they had brought was quite definitely pregnant and needed to be coaxed gently ashore, while in the crate of chickens one had died, pecked to death by its fellows. She rescued the corpse and tied it to the outside of the cage, to be plucked (properly) and eaten later. She grasped the string of the shivering goat. It was in a much worse state than she was, clearly not far from giving birth. She dragged it up the rough track towards El Moro's old house.

When they had left, this track had been a smooth path, paved with lava slabs, but there had been no one to see to that sort of thing for a good many years; the slabs had been hacked out and taken away for other purposes and the path was merely jagged stones and dust. A few weeds had made their appearance along the edge nevertheless. Lanzarote was showing some signs of coming back to life.

*

By the time she reached the house she felt different, no longer sick and dizzy but bent double with stomach cramps. With immense relief, she felt the familiar sensation of blood trickling down her thighs. She bled copiously over the next few days, more than usual, but at least, if she had been pregnant, she now no longer was.

The house was filthy. An old man had been living in it who soon, on beholding El Moro, fled, leaving most of his meagre belongings behind him, crossing himself as he ran away. They had to sleep outside the first night, the interior smelt so bad, and it took Milagro hours of disgusting hard work to clean out the old man's mess.

It was exhausting work for months—digging, planting, tending the goat which was delivered safely of its kid but turned sickly afterwards, soothing the disturbed chickens so that they would start to lay again. She had forgotten how hard it was just to stay alive in Lanzarote, but she had to bear it. It kept her from thinking, from remembering Felipe and her few years of happiness. He was gone, long gone, and she had to make the best of what she had. She put her repentance aside with the excuse that she was too busy to go church, too tired. El Moro forced himself on her only rarely and she was less eager herself, often so exhausted at the end of the day that her body could not rouse itself to any kind of sexual desire at all.

Pepito could do the heavy work now, rebuilding the cistern under instruction from El Moro, digging the recalcitrant rocks out of what was to become the vegetable garden. Rain came down plentifully in November and everything began to look green once more.

*

Pepito. Almost grown up and El Moro's constant companion, adopting his ways of dressing, aping his habits. His physical resemblance to Felipe was as striking as ever, but it was like seeing a well-known face in the street only to find out it belonged to a stranger. He had betrayed his mother completely: he was El Moro's son now and he had even learned some of his language. The two of them would converse in this incomprehensible tongue, shutting her out altogether. Pepito had joined the man's world, the one from which women were excluded. She was on a downward path, as she had always been, sinking lower and lower, and even her son was being taught to despise her.

There were a few familiar faces left in Lanzarote and some half-recognised ones, grown much older with hardship and misery, the poorest people, the ones who had stayed because they could not afford to leave. The wealthier citizens were trickling back but, more often than not, staying only briefly, just long enough to stake a claim on their abandoned properties before retreating again to one of the more salubrious islands. Of her mother and stepfather there was no sign, but she did not expect to hear any news of them unless she went up to Teguise, and she did not have the time to do that. El Moro would not let her go in any case.

Then in January something happened, something so bad that it kicked her right down to the bottom of the ladder of despair and degradation she had been hoping to climb up.

*

Four months of toil and an adequate rainfall had transformed the house and garden into something approaching a civilised dwelling and Milagro had time to go to the market once or twice, though she generally returned empty-handed. There was little to buy but it got her away from the stifling atmosphere of the house and the oppressive thoughts which thronged incessantly through her head.

The day was warm, the air was clear, but Milagro decided against going yet again to the market and its almost empty stalls. She wandered down to the port to gaze out to sea, as she had so often done when she waited for Felipe to return. A sail was visible far out, a lateen sail, perhaps a pirate ship, even though they had not come near Lanzarote for years. She ought to visit the priest and go about repenting her sins before it was too late. El Moro prayed regularly, it would not be so hard for her to slip away while he was at his devotions.

Before she had time to change her mind, she made her way back to the house to check on him; it was about time for prayer. She was ill-prepared for the scene which greeted her and she stood in the doorway, transfixed in amazement. Not one but two figures were bowed to the ground on the elaborate prayer mat.

'What's this?' She could not repress a cry of dismay. It was her fault, of course, she should have gone back to the church as soon as they arrived in Arrecife and obliged Pepito to go with her.

El Moro paid no attention except to pull Pepito severely back onto his knees as he tried to get up. Only when the prayers were completed did they turn their attention to the distressed woman in the doorway; she had stood helpless, wringing her hands, not knowing what to do or say.

Full of excitement, Pepito leapt to his feet and embraced her.

'Mama, I'm going away, I've got a berth on a ship.'

Milagro ignored his exhilaration. 'What are you doing, praying like that? You're a Christian, not a heathen Muslim.'

She realised, belatedly, what he had said. 'What ship? Where are you going? I don't want you to be a fisherman and leave me, like your father did.'

'No, mama, you don't understand, it's a trading ship going to Africa. The captain's a friend of El Moro and he wants a cabin boy. They're coming to fetch me any minute.'

He was hopping up and down with anticipation and Milagro noticed his clothes: a robe of fine linen, like El Moro wore, and a new gold chain round his neck.

'You can't go.' She did not recognise her son in this barbarically strange attire .

'Mama, why not? I'll be rich, I'll wear fine clothes all day long. I know just what to do to make the captain like me. El Moro's taught me everything. And the prayers, well, some of them anyway. It wasn't easy at first but he says I'm really good at it now.'

Milagro did not really understand what Pepito was talking about but a cold feeling of dread spread through her. She began to sob.

'Mama, I'll come back to see you, I'll bring you new clothes and jewellery too. Let me go.'

She grabbed hold of him, crushing him tightly to her, glaring at El Moro in defiance. He stood, arms folded, surveying her with his usual scornful expression.

'You shan't have him, he's staying here with me,' she

[199]

screamed at him. 'He's a Christian.'

Pepito wriggled out of her grasp. 'I can't stay here, how can I? There's nothing here. You made us come back from Gran Canaria for what? Dust and dirt and poverty. I'll be a man soon and I want to get rich, not stay in a filthy hole, struggling to be a fisherman or a farmer, poor all my life. Why should I? It's my chance of a future on this ship, with a man who'll buy me jewels and gold. I'll be living in luxury, not sitting in a hovel dressed in rags, covered in dust and sand.'

'You can't go,' sobbed the wretched woman, 'you're my son, you belong with me. What shall I do without you?' She had still not grasped the implications of what Pepito's future life would involve, but she clung to his arm, refusing to let go of him. He twisted out of her grasp.

'Please mama, don't make such a fuss. I'm grown up now, you can't expect me to stay here forever.'

'It's decided.' El Moro's voice was harsh. 'You have no say in the matter.'

'No!' Milagro screamed in despair. He had done his best to destroy her, now he was taking her son away from her forever. She flung herself at Pepito's feet, clinging to his ankles, wailing and crying. A voice sounded behind her, a foreign voice speaking in an ominous alien tongue, the one El Moro had taught Pepito.

'Say goodbye to your mother,' commanded El Moro. Pepito bent down to help his mother to her feet and kissed her.

'Don't worry, I'll be all right. I've got so much to look forward to now.'

She gazed, horror-struck, at the man in the doorway who had come to take her son from her, a dark, unshaven man. His clothes were rough and salt-stained but he had a heavy gold ring in one ear and gold rings on his fingers. He grinned at her, showing two gold teeth among the rotten stumps in his mouth.

'Very good.' He patted Pepito's cheeks and squeezed his buttocks familiarly. His words were so accented as to be barely comprehensible. 'Say goodbye to mama.' The money-bag he took from his belt chinked heavily as he handed it to El Moro; he put his arm round the boy and began to lead him away.

Milagro screamed again and flew at El Moro, reaching for his eyes with her nails, but he hit her on the side of the head so hard that he knocked her across the room. She fell to the floor again, dizzy with the blow, but she managed to scramble towards her son as the man urged him out. El Moro stood in the doorway, barring her from following and kicked her in the stomach, winding her so that she could hardly gasp out her words.

'You've sold him,' she moaned, 'you've sold him as a slave.'

'You are such a stupid woman. He's not a slave, he's not like the rest of them. He'll be the captain's pet, a handsome boy like that, a valued member of the ship's company.'

She gaped at him. 'I don't understand.'

El Moro sneered. 'What do you think men do on these ships when there are no women onboard? Pepito will be privileged, the captain's favourite, not just any cabin boy to be handed round among the deck crew. He really has a gift for it, you know.'

'What? For what?' Then she realised at last what sort of life her son was going to lead, the enormity of what El Moro had done to him. She spat in his face and he smashed her across the room again, then, before she had time to pick herself up, began to punch and kick her systematically until she was all but unconscious.

'Have you learned obedience at last?' She could not even whimper yes or no and he dragged her over to the bed by her hair. 'Now my bum boy has gone, you'll have to take his place.'

He threw her onto the bed, face down and knelt over her, parting her buttocks and ripping into her. The pain and the humiliation seemed to go on forever, made all the more unbearable by the realisation that this was what Pepito would have to suffer.

He let her go at last and she heard him leave, slamming the door of the house behind him. She lay helpless, it was too painful to move, and in her tormented mind the thought of what had happened to her son was even worse than the anguish of Felipe's death. She longed to die herself as she had after Felipe was killed; in fact, had she been able to walk, she would have gone down to the harbour and thrown herself into the sea. After many hours, when she was able to control her tears and the pain had abated a little as long as she did not move too much, she found that she still needed to stay alive. She could not let El Moro get away with what he had done.

*

She had seen enough of the cruelty and indifference of one man to another in Lanzarote during the eruptions, she knew only too well how little regard people had for their neighbours in times of crisis, but to corrupt children like that... All the rumours she had heard in the past about El Moro were probably true—the tales of kidnapped children and young women sold as prostitutes in the slave markets of Tangiers. The vague stories of what men did together when they could not find a woman began to make horrible sense to her at last, too. The idea of a rough, strange brutish man forcing her poor little boy down into the depths of degradation... she dared not picture to herself what Pepito might be doing. Bile rose in her throat, the very thought made her vomit. El Moro had just given her a demonstration of how terribly he would suffer.

But Pepito had gone willingly. What had he said? I know what to do to make the captain like me—it was not her little boy who had gone with the pirate, it was some other, depraved, youth. In her misery and despair over Felipe's death she had failed her son, she had not shown him enough love, she had not bothered to keep him safe and this was the result. Barely two years younger than she had been when she first embarked on her own life of sin and degradation. The thought that Doña Constancia might have despaired over her in much the same way came to her. No, it could not be—Doña Constancia had always been cold and distant in a way that Milagro was not. Milagro's fault was in showing her emotions all too readily, being constantly led astray by them, not a fault one could ever ascribe to her mother.

It was late, she did not know how many hours she had lain there, paralysed with pain and grief, but it was dark outside and the moon had set. She heard El Moro's step and she cringed, shrinking to the far side of the bed, pressing herself against the wall. It was no use pretending to be asleep, he would merely wake her up to do his bidding. He threw off his robe and lay down beside her, wrenching her towards him.

'Suck me off.' He was too strong for her to pull away, he grabbed her hair with one hand and forced her mouth open with the other, ramming his penis so far down her throat that she choked.

'You don't want me to take you from behind again, do you?' He released her hair and probed her anus roughly with his thumb, laughing at her shriek of pain.

'The choice is yours.'

Tears streaming down her face, she did as she was told, hoping it would not take long. As she mechanically performed the necessary actions, a tiny spark of something like her former spirit remained alight inside her—there must be some way of hurting him, he had to have some vulnerable spot.

She heard him grunt, his penis leapt in her mouth spurting the disgusting liquid down her throat. She was nearly sick and had to spit it out, hoping he would not notice in the darkness. Then with an enormous effort of will, she dared to ask him a question. Surely Pepito could not be his only victim

'How many children have you sold?'

He turned away from her as he always did; the sexual act

over with, he never wanted to touch her till the next time the urge took him, unless it was to reward her for good behaviour, to stimulate her to orgasm in order to demonstrate his power over her. After a while, he replied.

'It's not so easy now. They want older children in Tangiers this year, children who can work hard as well as please their masters. Little children are too difficult to control. I have to go further afield too, up beyond the volcanoes. Before the eruptions, there were many villagers who wanted to send their children off to find employment in the towns because they could not feed them at home. Life is much harder now, even if they have no food for the children, they need them to work in the fields.'

He made a curious sound in the dark. Milagro could not believe it but it sounded like a laugh.

'Someone offered me a baby the other day. What was I going to do with it, feed it till it grew up? The Moors aren't interested in babies, the girls must be old enough to breed and the boys have to know what it's all about. There's no pleasure in taking pleasure unless one can give it as well.'

His callous, disgusting description of his machinations was almost too much for Milagro. Only fear held her back from striking him, fear and an instinct of self-preservation, the beginnings of a desire to stay alive and avenge herself and her son.

'How can you sell people?' It took great control not to sound too upset, merely curious.

'Why not? What sort of life is it here in Lanzarote? A slave in Tangiers has a better life by far—fed, clothed, well-treated by and large, not starving in a ditch in rags, eating mouldy bread and rotten prickly pears. What's the difference between selling a child and marrying one's son or daughter into a wealthy man's family? You told me yourself that you ran away from Teguise to avoid just such a marriage.'

She had no answer to that, though she knew instinctively that there must be a flaw in his reasoning; being married off and being sold as a slave were not the same thing at all and never could be.

The next morning, he behaved as though nothing had happened: a minor episode which was now over, that was all selling her son was to him. She sat at the table beside herself with grief, tears flowing uncontrollably down her face on to the piece of needlework she was trying to complete, watching him make his ablutions and say his prayers as he always did. How could he pray, what sort of god would listen to a man like that?

The thought came to her that he was the demon sent to punish her for her evil life, for her sins, for refusing to help Inés, for causing Felipe's death. But, if he was the instrument of God's revenge on her, then she would turn the tables. She would destroy El Moro one way or the other; if she bided her time, eventually the moment would come when she would be able to kill him, wreak her vengeance on God's avenger. Thou shalt not kill, such were the teachings of the religion she had been so anxious to rejoin, but the church did not want her and God had disowned her. She had nothing to lose.

Chapter XII – Revenge

She spoke when spoken to. She did as she was told. She had been afraid that the memory would fade like her recollections of Felipe, that her resentment would become less bitter, but it was always there, it ran alongside her every day with undiminished force. The opportunity for revenge would come, but she had to be patient and let it provide itself.

She obeyed orders, in and out of bed, like an unthinking domestic animal. There were few rewards for good behaviour now but she did not want them so much these days. Her body's fire was burning low. She waited, she spied on El Moro, when he was in Arrecife at least; she could not follow him when he went out of the town, she would have been too conspicuous and she could not hope to follow his mule's trot on foot.

Now she knew what he really did, it was not hard to see. She should have realised why he had behaved in such a friendly way to Pepito in the first place. Little details constantly recurred to her—the presents, the clothes, the games which Pepito was so reluctant to describe to her. Secret games, he had said. She should have guessed.

She observed El Moro when he talked to children. Newly-arrived families were becoming more and more plentiful, families who had fled came back in increasing numbers and Arrecife began, if not exactly to prosper, at least to become less of a ghost town. Ships called in to trade again, a few fishing boats used the silted up harbour, there was even talk of clearing away some of the sandbanks and repairing the outer wall properly.

El Moro always talked to the boys first, those over the age of ten. Milagro never warned any of their mothers, why should she be the only one to suffer? She observed, listened when she could, noted how clever he was. He never made too much of a child, just a few words, an occasional fruit. Then, a month or so later, the boy would disappear, quite casually; one evening he would not come home.

A shirt was washed up on the beach once, belonging to a boy whose family had been one of the first to return. Milagro had noticed him for a couple of years, watched him grow tall, come to the brink of manhood, just as Pepito had done. She was sure the boy had not drowned, but she did not disillusion the grieving parents.

She found out what El Moro did with his gold. It was no longer under the stone in front of the fireplace, she had already ascertained that. After each child's disappearance, and there were not very many in fact, only four or five a year, El Moro would inspect the cistern rebuilt at the back of the house. She climbed up one day to look inside, when she was sure he would be absent for some time; he had gone on his mule with a pack of food and clothing. She pushed the cover of the cistern aside; there was a string going down into the water, tied to a peg in the wall just below the top. She pulled on the string and a heavy bag came up from the depths, clinking. She laughed to herself, she was not the stupid woman he took her for, oh no.

*

She bided her time.

El Moro was not particularly interested in money for its own sake. One needed it to live, unless one was prepared to break one's back every hour of the day in the fields, but it was the difficulty and the challenge of illicit trade which appealed to him. He wanted to be paid for the children he sold, obviously, but he was not too greedy and he had no intention of being found out and executed, as he surely would be if he were caught. Arrested, summarily hauled off to Spain on the next boat and burnt at the stake, no doubt, or some equally horrible fate. The children meant nothing to him—the spawn of the unbelievers, whose miserable souls were damned anyway.

Milagro was something of a disappointment to him now. He had cowed her into such dumb, total obedience that the game was not so amusing. He could not play on her sexually any more. She had been like a musical instrument—touch her here or there, get this or that reaction to his fingers till she was writhing at his feet, completely at his mercy. No longer. Perhaps he was growing too old himself. He contemplated throwing her out but she was useful in a way. The mere drudgery of scraping a living from the soil was a dispiriting experience. Breaking one's back over the rocky soil to clear a patch of ground, chasing the hens to collect their eggs, milking the goat and spending hours making cheese—why do all this if one had a servant to do it?

Perhaps he should send her down to whore in the docks now that her sexual attraction for him had gone. Even beating her and sodomising her had lost its appeal. She would do whatever he commanded her to—sullenly, mechanically, giving him little pleasure, simply the carnal relief which was still necessary. A slack, submissive body and greying hair did not compare with the taut flesh and lithe young limbs, the screams of pain and delight when he was breaking in a promising boy. Thoughts of such moments, now so rare, still roused him from time to time and he would make use of Milagro then; a convenient hole, that was all.

He ceased to notice what she did or did not do; as long as she was there when he wanted, he did not care. He ate the food she cooked, she kept the house clean and occasionally she would do some needlework for a woman who could afford such a luxury. Needless to say, he collected the money for this and Milagro never saw a single coin.

She observed and waited. He did not detect her watching him, she had become part of the background—a haggard, grey-haired woman in a patched dress, like so many of the women in Lanzarote.

He would sleep in the afternoons now, old age was creeping on him and it was too hot to do much else that third summer of their return. It was sweltering, no wind day after day, the whole island withering under the lash of the sun's rays.

Trade was slack in the summer in any case; less wind meant becalmed ships. It was better to wait till the autumn when the trade winds picked up again.

It was far more agreeable on such afternoons to lie in the shade of the fig tree than to ride along a dusty track all the way to Arrieta or Orzola, the ports in the north-east of the island. El Moro had long ago devised a foolproof means of communication with his pirate customers. They would row a man ashore to leave a message in the trunk of a certain tree on their way down island (there were only three trees in Arrieta and it was hardly a harbour), letting him know the likely date of their return. He would be there to signal them on the appointed day.

There was a convenient cave, too, barely half an hour's walk up into the hills; there, he would corral the children he had lured away from their families until the pirates arrived. It had the added advantage of being well away from any settlements, there was not even a camel shed close by, no one to hear the cries of those he chose to instruct in the carrying out of their new duties, no one to hear the weeping at night. He had found the cave increasingly useful in recent years. Before the eruptions, the pirates had boldly come into Arrecife itself to do a little legitimate trading as well, but since the island's slow return to life had begun the authorities had become rather too vigilant. Pepito, of course, had not been a problem, he had been a willing victim. Only too willing—there had been something disturbingly corrupt about that boy. However, dragging four or five howling children through the middle of town was quite out of the question.

This summer was a summer to do nothing, to count one's money and think of cooler weather, to make up a few medicines possibly, to dream of returning home but above all to enjoy the afternoon siesta, fanned by one's servant.

The servant had brooded and planned, generally fruitlessly, for nearly four years. She knew she would have to kill him outright, it was no use merely wounding him. Though she would like to see him die a lingering, agonizing death, this was, in practice, not a possibility. She had no intention of being charged with murder. The governor might not think El Moro's death anything other than a good riddance, but she could not be sure of that; she knew for certain that he had reason to be grateful to the Moor. A serving girl he had got pregnant was spirited away into slavery without the governor's wife ever knowing anything of it.

*

Milagro had become privy to many of El Moro's secrets now. She contemplated poisoning him with one of his own brews, one of them must surely be lethal but she did not know which one. He kept many notes, written in a book which he did not bother to hide, but she could not even read Spanish, let alone the curious dots and wavy lines he read from. So that was out of the question; if she simply made him sick and he guessed what she had done, the consequences would be frightful. She intended to get away with it, to live in triumph, and on his money, after his death.

Siesta time. El Moro snored, Milagro fanned, the new mule tethered to the fig tree by the door whickered and kicked. They had only had it for a few weeks and it was a troublesome beast, young and frisky and unwilling to be mounted. Half asleep herself, Milagro's eyes roamed vacantly over her surroundings, and the perfect solution at last came to her. Round the base of the fig tree were small lumps of stone, jagged yellow sandstone, pumice, white and weightless, black rounded clots of lava. There was one particular piece of sandstone, curved and sharp-edged like a hoof.

She laid down the fan and waited to see what would happen. El Moro grunted and stirred but he did not wake. She rose quietly to her feet and took a tentative step towards the rock border, looking round her apprehensively. There was no one in sight. She felt quite relaxed; her heart was thundering in her breast but her brain was working calmly and sensibly, figuring out exactly what to do. She knelt by the tree and began to prize the piece of sandstone out of the ground. It came away easily. She looked round again. El Moro was most decidedly still asleep, on his back, his mouth open.

She raised the lump of stone over his head, taking aim with great care. She had only one chance and it must be right. She brought it down hard, with both hands, smashing it into his temple and his right eye. It made a frightful hole, his eyes flew open and his body convulsed. Blood spurted all over her; she had not been prepared for that, nor for the curious gurgling noise he made. He lay on his back, his eyes still open and staring at her as she frantically wiped the blood off her hand and arm with her skirt. Knees knocking, she thrust the lump of rock back into its place, then she noticed the blood on it. She pulled it out again and pushed it back in the other way round.

She bent over her victim. He was staring upwards, his right eye a mass of blood, the left one open but not focussing. A puddle of blood was forming under his head. She touched him, at arms length; he did not react at first but then his body jerked horribly once or twice, twisting and arching as she retreated aghast. At last the body flopped back onto the ground. He was dead, she was sure he was dead. She had killed him.

She ran to the mule, set it loose and gave it a kick. It trotted off down the hill towards the centre of town. She waited a few seconds before running after it, screaming,

'Help me, help me, please, someone help!'

The streets were deserted, the houses shuttered fast against the afternoon sun, and no one bothered to come out and enquire what all the fuss was about. The mule had disappeared. In front of the tax office was a guard, half asleep in the shade.

Milagro seized his arm and he came to, recoiling from this wild, bloodstained figure.

'It's El Moro,' she cried. 'The mule kicked him on the head. I think he's dead.'

'So what?' The guard was not that interested. Then he realised exactly what she had said. 'Dead? Perhaps I had better come and have a look.'

He ambled up the hill, oblivious of Milagro's agitation; she did not need to put on an act, the awfulness of what she had done had begun to sink in. One or two curious inhabitants had emerged from their houses, roused at last by Milagro's cries, and it was a little procession of seven or eight people which arrived to view the body. Milagro did not dare look; fearful that he might not be dead after all, she stopped some way away, hiding her face in her hands.

'He's under the fig tree.' Her words were barely audible but the townspeople surged forward and thronged around the body, with more turning up every minute. It had not taken long for word to go out of this welcome distraction on a hot, dull afternoon.

Though she did not dare look, Milagro edged closer to hear what was being said.

'He's dead, weally dead.' The guard had a loud coarse voice and a speech impediment, not an R to his name. 'Good widdance too, if you ask me.'

'Did she say the mule?'

'Yes, the mule kicked him. God, look at that hole in his head.'

'What about the woman?'

Someone came up to her and took her arm. It was an old woman, a net-mender whom Milagro had known years ago. When Felipe had been alive, when she had been, if not respectable, at least on the verge of respectability, when the future had been full of hope, before everything had gone wrong. She was trembling uncontrollably, the gravity of her deed overwhelming her.

'I want to lie down.'

The old woman helped her into the house. Milagro stripped off her bloodstained dress but there was blood on her arms underneath. Regardless, she used all the water in the pot by the fireplace, a whole day's supply, scrubbing and scrubbing at the marks, but she could not feel clean. She had killed a man. A Muslim, an evildoer, a corrupter of the innocent, but did that put him on a par with the animals? How could she have thought that it was her task to exact revenge on such a monster?

The gossiping continued outside the door.

'Shouldn't someone fetch the priest?'

'What for? He wasn't a Christian.'

'He might disappear in a puff of smoke if Don Miguel reads the last rites over him.' There was laughter at that.

'Be serious, the man is dead. He'll have to be buried, even if he can't go in the church cemetery.'

Milagro threw herself down on the bed, trying not to listen as the conversation turned to the inevitable. What about the woman? What about the woman, what was she going to do now?

No one suspected her of killing him, at least. She was summoned by the Alcalde the next morning to give her account of the accident; he believed her story, he had no reason not to. The death of a highly undesirable inhabitant of Arrecife was not one which was worth investigating in great detail. The man had been kicked in the head by his mule, he had died and that was the end of it. Except that the body had to be buried. The judge studied the distressed woman who stood in front of him.

'Was he your husband?'

She shook her head.

'He can't have a Christian burial, you understand. His grave is being dug outside the cemetery wall.'

She nodded. She understood perfectly well, in fact she approved. Felipe had no grave, Pepito wherever he was would not have a Christian burial, why should El Moro be favoured?

Pepito had never come back. Of course not. He might even be dead himself now, drowned or killed in a raid. She began to cry, the pent-up emotion of the last few days overflowing in a torrent of tears she could not stop. Even the disagreeable thought that the judge must assume she was mourning El Moro did not halt her outpouring of grief.

The Alcalde patted her on the shoulder. She was, or could still be attractive, he noticed, her breasts filled out the simple dress in a most desirable way. He dismissed this unworthy thought as far as he could, and he spoke more kindly to her.

'He is being buried now. Do you want to come to the grave?'

She recoiled at the idea but then, she thought, why not? Seeing his body in the ground covered in earth would make her quite sure that he was dead. He could no longer do her any harm. She had had a terrible dream the previous night, in which he had come back to life: he had raped her and all the while blood from the wound in his head had poured into her mouth. She had woken up dripping with sweat and, worse, with the old familiar feeling of sexual desire flaming up inside her yet again.

He was dead, she had killed him. She watched the body being lowered into the dusty hole just outside the cemetery wall. There was no one there, except the gravediggers, the judge and herself. And Don Miguel. The priest had come, reluctantly, despite himself. The man was an infidel, suspected of some heinous crimes, a dabbler in witchcraft, in league with the devil but, presumably, he had a soul. The powers of evil should not be allowed to triumph unopposed and the devil would find it just as uncomfortable in heaven as sinners did in hell. He muttered a short prayer.

To Milagro he did not speak; he stared grimly at her as he turned away from the graveside and she had the dreadful feeling that he knew what she had done. Unrepentant sinner, fornicator, devil worshipper, now a murderess, she had truly damned herself. She gazed at the earth being shovelled hastily over the body, dust and stones showering down on the white shrouded form, stilled forever by her criminal act.

She shuddered. Life could come to an end just like that. He was alive, then he was dead. She had had the power to kill him and no one knew except God. The judge made to leave but she ran after him.

'What shall I do with his things? His books, his clothes, all his medicines?'

'Is there anything of value?'

'How should I know? The books perhaps.' She did not mention the cache of money in the cistern.

The Alcalde accompanied her back to the house. El Moro's house but not hers now, it appeared.

'You'll have to leave here. This is a good house, the town could use it for some poor family. There will be taxes to pay but the value of the mule should cover them.'

The guilty animal had been found and returned to her. She did not want it, she did not want a reminder of what she had done. But taxes?

'I don't want the mule, but I thought I could have the house. Didn't it belong to him?'

'He's dead and he was a foreigner.'

The judge poked around inside the house, peering doubt-fully into the books, surveying the shelf of herbs and powders from a safe distance. His eyes lit up when he saw the prayer mat, which he rolled up and put under his arm.

'You must find some other lodging by the end of the week. The books, all the other stuff—get rid of it. Burn it.' He gestured at the dead man's clothing. 'And all that. No one wears such heathen stuff round here.'

He felt he was being generous, letting her dispose of the dead man's goods as she would. She had admitted that she was not his wife, so she did not have a right to anything at all. He felt sorry for her in a way; how had she come to be the Moor's woman? She could still have some appeal for a man—if she wiped the dust from her face and hair and had a new dress, she might rival many of the women of Arrecife. He relented a little.

'If you need some help, just ask me.' It was not by chance that his hand lingered on her arm and his fingers discreetly caressed her breast. She moved away from him, shocked but not really surprised. Men took her for a fallen woman, she was a fallen woman, why should a judge be any different? He was a man too.

She began to go through what El Moro had left. It gave her an odd feeling, handling the robes he had worn when he was alive. Clothes were only objects, she told herself and the cloth would be very useful. If she had shared his bed for so long, she could wear his clothes.

She had never really known him, that cold, secretive man. Thirteen years she had been with him, far longer than she had been with Felipe, yet his real self had been sealed off from her completely. Felipe had been so transparent, so easy to understand, so stubborn and yet so weak, while El Moro was so totally the opposite. Next time, she must find herself someone in between. Next time: what was she thinking of? There would not be a next time, the time now was for reform, for repentance, to think about how to live a virtuous life.

She turned to the books. She was really afraid to touch them, afraid that the magic in them might scorch her fingers. She poked them from the shelf onto the floor with a stick. Pages of cursive writing fluttered across the room but they settled where they fell, not flying up again of their own volition.

There were many drawings as well as writing, of men and women with their guts showing disgustingly, their parts labelled and numbered, drawings of plants and trees too, but few that she had ever seen. She pushed them all into the fireplace. Then she took down all the boxes of powders, the bundles of herbs (using a piece of rag to handle them so as not to touch them with her fingers) and threw them on top.

They burned easily, one spark from the flint and everything was alight. She coughed and choked in the smoke that

[216]

arose, her head spinning. It must be the burning medicines which made her feel so odd. She collapsed on the bed, light-headed and euphoric, as if she had no more cares at all, as if everything from now on would be different, better. She would begin life all over again.

The smoke cleared, the fire died down and she prodded the heap of smouldering parchment to make quite sure every page, every last scrap and magical word was consumed, ending El Moro's malign influence over her forever.

She was free, but at a cost. As the feeling of artificial well-being evaporated, she began to think about what she had done. She had killed someone, with her own hands. Death was not anything so unusual, people were dying all the time, even without the help of the volcanoes' destructive force. Felipe had died, her babies had died, but she would have saved them if she could. El Moro had been different. She would not have saved him: even if it had been a genuine accident, a real kick by the mule, she would not have called for help until she was sure it was too late. She had crossed the line, taken a human life, a much graver sin by far than merely never going to church and living a life of fornication. Of those, one could repent and make amends. Not murder.

She spent her first nights of freedom sleepless, in dreadful apprehension, waiting for God to strike her, for a fiery pit to open up for her, there in the middle of Arrecife, as it had done for countless innocent people on the island.

It did not happen; though she wished to die, to leave the life of hell she had been living in even for the real hell, she continued to live and, to all outward appearances, she was the same person as she had always been. At first light, the day she was due to leave El Moro's house, she retrieved the bag of money from its hiding place in the cistern and secreted it in the bundle of cloth that had been El Moro's robes. Worldly considerations, at least, were taken care of for the time being.

Chapter XIII – Degradation

The act of revenge had lifted a weight from her shoulders and set another one there in its place. She ought to go to church once more, now she was truly free, to confess but she was too afraid. Who knows? Don Miguel might feel that murder freed him from the secret of the confessional, it might be too serious a crime to conceal from the judge.

The deep feelings of guilt lessened as the weeks went by, the killing of El Moro merely another disastrous episode in a life already ruined by ill-fortune. Materially, she had no worries, with all El Moro's savings to live on; the tavern keeper offered her a room and a job, just serving, he said, but she was able to refuse it. He knew her reputation, he was the same tavern keeper who had been there for twenty years and just serving was not what he had in mind for her. He had remained in Arrecife all through the eruptions, there was always someone who needed a drink or two and a woman and could pay for them.

Milagro found a room herself, with an ancient fisherman's widow; La Graciosa she was known as, since she and her husband (now long drowned together with their three sons) had come from the little island of Graciosa off the north-western corner of Lanzarote. She was very old, rather deaf and almost blind, but she had a shack on the seashore to the east of the town, with a separate storeroom, and she was happy to let Milagro sleep there for nothing, provided she cooked for her and kept her company in the evenings.

Milagro was subjected to many wearisome and confused tales of what life had been like in Lanzarote in the old days; though she made an effort to be pleasant to the old lady (this is part of my penance, she reasoned to herself) it came to seem a high price to pay for free board and lodging.

She resented being thrown out of El Moro's house, though. It would not have happened if she had been a respectable matron rather than the Moor's kept woman. She would often walk past the house, casting bitter glances at the family which now occupied it. A Guanche family—they had the all too familiar round faces and light-coloured eyes. There were still Guanches in Arrecife but she kept well away from them, it would be opening old wounds. The old habits continued, she noted: the long shirts and tall hats, the white cloth spread on the ground for meals instead of on a table, the old-fashioned vocabulary.

Alone in bed at night, she would often cry for no particular reason. The avenging act had left her empty, without a future—everything gone, husband, son, no purpose left at all. She was reminded of her crime every time she took a coin from the money-bag, now carefully buried beneath her makeshift bed in the store room, but it did not stop her spending the money. This was merely a continuation of her revenge; in any case, some of the money was what she had earned and never been paid.

It was fortunate that La Graciosa was virtually blind as well as deaf and could not see what Milagro was doing, for she was very nosy and would continually follow her around, demanding to know what she was up to, had she stoked the fire, were the figs ripe yet, was there any fish for dinner, why did she not go down to the harbour to see if the fishing boats were in? There were occasions when it was all Milagro could do not to hit her.

*

She did go down to the harbour quite frequently. It had been so much a part of her life and she liked to look at the sea and at the boats entering and leaving, even though the memories they brought back were hardly pleasant ones. Part of the main quay had been roughly repaired, though most of it was still silted up, and few efforts were being made to relaunch two boats stranded by the movements of the sea bed during the long years of the eruptions.

The sailors and the workmen still stared at the women walking along the quay as they always had done, though naturally she avoided their lecherous glances. She was a reformed woman, she had left all that behind her. She had managed to tidy herself up too, the lethargy of the years following Pepito's terrible departure seemed to have gone and she wore new dresses now, made from the cloth of El Moro's robes, as fine as she used to have in Teguise all those years ago. She would take pains over her hair, looking at her appearance in his small silver mirror, another of his involuntary legacies. She had always assumed he used it for arranging his turban, an article of clothing he had abandoned by the time she came to live with him. If she had known what he really used it for, she would have thrown it in the harbour. It had been for signalling to the pirate vessels; from the hill above Arrieta, the flash of light could be seen well out to sea and the pirates would know that this was the night to put into the coast and pick up their cargo of weeping children.

Men did look at her, older men of course now, but she was older too. Not old enough; the brazier still smouldered within her; like the island itself, the fires were there under the surface. She felt them as she rubbed her legs together when she walked, when she was in bed at night and had to use her fingers to bring relief. She wished she had kept the polished stick which El Moro had used to stimulate her, but that had been one of the first things she had put on the fire. She took to using the pestle for grinding corn, pushing it back and forth inside her while her other hand rubbed and pinched her nipples till she came. She felt no shame doing this, though it must be wrong, like everything else that brought pleasure.

*

A trading ship came down from Spain one day and the bosun noticed the woman sitting on the harbour breakwater. Later, out of curiosity, he climbed up to sit beside her, his eyes gazing hungrily at her breasts and the curve of her hips. She turned to look at him: a tough, scarred man about the same age as she was, with calloused hands and broken nails from handling sails and ropes.

'Is your husband away?' He assumed this to be the reason for her vigil there, watching the boats entering and leaving the harbour. She seemed a pretty woman, though sad and careworn like so many of the island women..

'I have no husband.' He seemed agreeable enough and her body was reminding her that she had not had a man for a very long time. A reformed woman did not have such feelings and she tried to suppress them. In vain.

'Dead, is he? Drowned?' The sailor moved closer to her.

'He was killed by the volcano a long time ago.' It *was* a long time ago, some fifteen or sixteen years now, wasn't it? She had lost count.

'A lovely woman like you is still on her own? I can hardly believe it.'

He was very close to her now, his thigh touching hers. His physical nearness was thoroughly unsettling and despite her best intentions she could feel the wetness starting between her legs, her nipples hardening in anticipation and what was threatening to become uncontrollable desire. She glanced down at his breeches, it was clear that he had an erection and it was all she could do not to reach out and feel his penis. He'll think I'm a whore if I do that, she told herself, I must not let him know what I'm really like.

He put his hand on her arm, then his arm round her shoulders. He had been at sea for ten days and restraint was hardly on his mind either. She must be willing, she would have cried out by now and fled from him. He kissed her; still she did not pull away from him, on the contrary, she kissed him back. Even better, she pressed his hand to her breasts and he could feel the hardness of her nipples through the thin linen of her bodice.

His broken nails snagged on the light material as he fondled her and she groaned, abandoning herself to the thrilling feelings she had thought gone forever. Her hands reached for his breeches, loosening the string which held them up and he wasted no time, pushed her back on the rocks and lifted her skirts. He did not question why she was so eager, why she was so hungry for him, why she was spreading her legs so easily, arching her body up to receive him, then moaning and rubbing herself after he had finished till she came as well.

He had mistaken her. Housewives did not behave like that, certainly his wife in Spain did not. She merely lay there passive, sighing with impatience if he took too long. From her wanton behaviour, this woman must be one of the tavern girls, though her clothes were all wrong. Outwardly, she appeared decent and modestly dressed but as he did up his breeches she still lay there on the ground, eyes closed, stroking herself and sighing with satisfaction.

He studied her more closely: still attractive despite the grey hair and wrinkles, the scarring on her legs. If she was a tart, she was a very successful one; he had not had such a good screw in a long time. He reached out to caress her breasts, with a view to beginning again, but she opened her eyes suddenly, sitting up in confusion, as if she had just remembered where she was and was embarrassed by what she had been doing.

She was. She was overcome with shame. It was so long since she had had a man, a man and not a beast, that she had been carried away with physical longing, oblivious to how immodest her behaviour must seem to this total stranger. As she scrambled, blushing hotly, to her feet, he said,

'Will you be in the tavern tonight?'

'I don't go to the tavern.'

He had found out the worst in her, right away, and she dare not meet him there, not in front of half the population of Arrecife, she had to stop this before it went any further. It was true, in any case, she never went to the tavern.

'Where do you live?'

'You can't come there. The old woman I live with is blind but she's not all that deaf.'

Milagro could feel herself succumbing, despite all her good resolutions; it was just as it had been when she first met Felipe. She could not refuse.

'Come to the tavern then.'

'No, I'll come back here later, after dark.'

Shocked, horrified even, to find that her physical instincts were still so rampant, she still came to meet him later, and again the next night, and every time he came back to Arrecife. His name was Enrique, she did keep her wits about her sufficiently to find that out, though little more.

*

She showed him all that she had learned; she meant to bind him to her so he could not want another woman and in this she succeeded, but the years of shame and humiliation had left her with only the empty physical need—El Moro had destroyed any chance of a new love. Enrique himself obviously had no requirements beyond the physical but he was so impressed by her sexual expertise that he was not put off when he found out how she had acquired it. They met secretly, or so Milagro fondly imagined, but he could not resist boasting about her skilled lovemaking to his fellow sailors, and the men in the tavern were not slow to inform him of her past.

'I see la puta del Moro has found herself another man,' remarked one of the fishermen, during Enrique's second visit to the island.

'What do you mean?' Enrique was not so much outraged as puzzled.

'Milagro, the one you spend all that time on the beach with, she used to be one of the Guanche fishermen's women, years ago that was. He disappeared about the time of the eruptions and she went with El Moro after that. He came here from an African trading ship, put ashore with a broken leg. Years ago that was, too.'

Someone else chipped in, eager to spread the gossip.

'You'd see him limping around in his long robe and great big turban. He sold medicines and a few other things as well from what one heard. He went off to Gran Canaria, took Milagro with him, in the first year of the eruptions I think it was, but they came back when everything quietened down again. There was a son, the Guanche's son, but I don't know what happened to him. He must have gone to sea like his father.'

'What about the Moor?'

'Oh, he died, kicked in the head by his mule, I believe. Is she hot stuff, Milagro? I bet the Moor taught her a lot of harem tricks.'

So Milagro was a tart, but it did not trouble Enrique too much. Sex was sex and he did not repeat the tavern gossip to her. She was good, in any case, really good, she didn't have the pox, yet at any rate, and she never asked him for payment. What more could a man ask?

*

La Graciosa died. It was Milagro's third murder. Not really a murder this time, she could not have saved the old woman's life. Bedridden and feverish, La Graciosa lay helpless for days, calling feebly for Milagro all the time, and Milagro's patience began to wear thin. She brought water, she changed the soiled bedding every day, taking it down to the sea to rinse it out. The rainfall in Lanzarote had reverted to normal when the eruptions ceased, barely enough to survive on for drinking and agricultural purposes, certainly not enough water to wash anything on that scale.

The old woman would not eat, she was hardly conscious in the end, sweating with fever, her chest crackling every time she drew a feeble breath, gasping for water even when Milagro had only just put the beaker to her lips.

Enrique's ship was leaving the next day and Milagro was desperate to get away. He did not know when he was coming back and Milagro's fever was far worse than La Graciosa's, the irresistible fire between her legs was so bad, she felt she could hardly walk to the shore where Enrique would be waiting for her. The old woman wailed, grasping her arm with a hand that had by no means lost all its strength, muttering nonsensically about some episode in the dim and distant past. Milagro shook her arm free and ran out, disregarding the cries of distress and the smell which came from the bed. The old woman had soiled it again, let her lie in it. She was hardly aware of what was going on around her now in any case and Milagro had had more than enough of playing nurse that day.

There was a convenient boulder of black lava not far from La Graciosa's hovel, where they had taken to meeting. Not many people came that way and they could enjoy each other without fear of interruption. Milagro ran down the beach, fearful that Enrique might have got tired of waiting, but he was still there, though rather the worse for drink. He usually brought a flask of wine with him and he had drunk most of it while waiting for her. He offered her the last dregs but that was not what she wanted. She fell on him, feeling his erection through the coarse stuff of his breeches (drink did not normally affect him too much) and wasted no time in dragging them off him. His penis was hot and smooth, so much better than a stone pestle, and she needed him desperately, needed him so that she could forget she was damned.

It was some hours later before she returned to the hut. La Graciosa was dead, her emaciated body sprawled across the floor, tangled in the filthy bedding. Milagro had let her die alone for the sake of a few hours of illicit love. Her third murder. She stooped, conscience-stricken, over the motionless body, shaking it in the vain hope that the old woman might still have some spark of life in her. It was useless.

Milagro went for the priest, that was the one thing she

could do. There was a new priest now, young and kind. Don Miguel had died a few months back, struck down by his unjust God. Haranguing a cringing penitent one day on the steps of the church, the burly, red-faced cleric had paused in mid-cry, clutched his chest in agony and fallen like a log, tumbling down the steps to lie lifeless in the dust of the plaza.

There is no hope for me, thought Milagro when she heard the news; how can such a devout man incur God's displeasure and die so young? Don Miguel was not even fifty, it seemed, though he had always appeared older.

His replacement was not a local man. Don Miguel himself had been born in Lanzarote and lived there all his life, apart from a brief period of study in Salamanca. He had considered it his duty to save his fellow islanders, rather than leave for another island, which would have brought him far more money and much more comfort.

The new priest, Don Jaime, was from Tenerife; he knew something of Milagro's past, one of Don Miguel's acolytes had been quick to inform him of the shortcomings of his parishioners. He knew about El Moro and even of her liaison with a Guanche fisherman, he was in fact part Guanche himself. He never reproached her for what she had been and he seemed to be sincerely concerned for her, both body and soul. He did what was necessary for La Graciosa and asked Milagro to walk back to the church with him.

'I'm worried about you,' he told her. 'Why don't you start coming to church again, I know you used to once. I won't shout at you and preach at you like Don Miguel; El Moro is dead and you are free of him now, he can no longer prevent you from rejoining your God. You have much to confess but God is always ready to pardon a sinner.'

'Why should I confess? The only things I repent are those which God would not pardon in any case.'

'You can't be sure of that, it's not for you to judge. God's mercy is infinite, it's never too late to repent. Here we are, right outside the church. Why don't you let me hear your confession?'

Milagro shook her head. She did not believe in God's mercy any more. Innocent people died through no fault of their own, the most devout man in the whole of Lanzarote had been struck down prematurely while she, who had killed three people, remained unpunished.

Felipe's death was most on her conscience. It was her stupidity which had been entirely responsible—if she had not run away and tried to get back to Arrecife, losing her way among the volcanoes so catastrophically, he would not have had to try and rescue her. She had not killed him with her own hands, but it was directly because of her that he had died.

El Moro was a criminal, he would have been executed by the authorities if she had denounced him. The fact that he died at her hands instead of on the gallows made no difference; no matter which way one looked at it, she would have been the cause of his death, but he deserved to die.

La Graciosa was dying anyway but she should have stayed with the old woman, called the priest in time; she had left the dying woman uncomforted to wallow in sin with her lover. If she were only guilty of selfishness that was shameful enough: she could not forgive herself for being so heartless and she could not bear to confess to Don Jaime the other events of that night.

Everything seemed to have happened as a result of something else. The string of events had started all those years ago in Teguise with a Guanche fisherman looking for a market for his fish and a foolish girl, too naïve to say no. What should I have done, she asked herself, walking back to the hut which was hers alone now. Should I have stayed in Teguise, been married against my will to a man I did not love, condemned to a life of sanctified misery? What did I have instead? Poverty and hardship but with such moments of love and joy that it made all the hardship worth while. I feel more like giving thanks for the ecstasy of physical love than doing penance for my many sins.

When Felipe was killed, was he being punished for what he did, for having two wives and trying to make them both happy, for attempting to save his children? I had no choice then, I had to survive to bring up Pepito, or so I thought till that all went bad and it turned out I had been sharing the bed of a disgusting criminal to preserve my son for a life of corruption.

Her muddled brain could not sort out her degree of culpability. Don Miguel said she was a sinner. So she was, but whose fault was that? Why had God allowed so much of the devil into her and not shown her the way to deal with the evil part of her? If it was truly evil. Why was she condemned to be damned right from the start? Why was she so weak when it came to men that the physical part of her took over so totally and obliterated the rest of her, which should have been her conscience? Why, why, why? She was damned, she knew that. Where there should be sorrow and torment in her soul, there was a dull void which the words of priest and church could not penetrate.

She would have liked to go to confession, it would be easy to reveal the extent of her sins to such a sympathetic young man as Don Jaime, but the words would not come. She could not say to him, any more than she could have to Don Miguel, Father hear my confession. Was this what it meant to be damned? Did the devil seize one's tongue and will, dry up one's tears so that one could not confess? Did it start in the cradle, so long ago that she could not remember? What sort of sin could a baby commit that would condemn it to eternal damnation? She tried to explain some of these thoughts to a shocked and distressed Don Jaime. One did not question the ways of God like that, he admonished her, advising her to resort to prayer.

She was by no means the only person in Arrecife who had difficulty in coming to terms with the enormity of the catastrophe, he knew, but others had, by and large, dumbly accepted the unfathomable workings of God's will. He was genuinely worried by her state of mind and he did not know how to counter the obvious breakdown of her faith. Even a Jesuit would have been hard put to offer her any convincing reasons for what she considered to be God's thoughtless cruelty to man, and prayer and repentance would not come. She was indeed like the island of Lanzarote itself: a mindless force which flared up for no reason, spreading destruction wantonly and randomly.

*

Milagro had much time to brood; she went looking for work to occupy her mind as much as anything but work was still scarce. There were few nets to mend and not many people with spare money for new clothes or bed linen. She began to wonder how much longer she would live; was the time approaching when she would learn the answers to all her questions? She was on her own again; Enrique's ship had sailed for Spain early the morning after La Graciosa's death and he never came back. She never found out whether he could not or would not; he could have learned of her callous behaviour towards La Graciosa and been too disgusted with her ever to come near her again.

The emptiness of her life began to prey on her mind and, at last, she decided to go up to Teguise, to discover what had become of her mother. She did not relish such a meeting but this seemed to be the one thing left in an existence devoid of everything that made life worth living. She begged a ride up with a farmer who came down regularly to sell his produce in the market. She did not recognise the road as the mule toiled up the long dusty hill and she barely recognised the town itself. It seemed shabby and small, its walls crumbling, its big gates no longer able to close on their broken hinges. The fortifications had not withstood the innumerable earth tremors. When she found Señor Perez's house, it was deserted: shutters closed, what was left of them, doors barred. At the back, one of the shutters was partly ajar and she peered inside. There was nothing there, just dust and piled rubble where a ceiling had given way.

'What do you want?'

A voice behind her made her jump. She blinked at the man who had spoken. His face was vaguely familiar, he must have been just a boy when she left, the same age as she was, but the years had given him pinched adult features.

'I used to live here. I wondered what had happened to Señor Perez.'

He had no idea who she was. 'He left, took a ship to Gran Canaria. It sank, at least it never arrived. One of his daughters came back a few years ago and cleared everything out. She didn't want the house, didn't want to stay in Lanzarote and I can't say I blame her. I'd go if I could, I should have gone long ago but I didn't have the money.'

His voice trailed on in a familiar recital of misery and deprivation.

'Señor Perez is dead?'

The man paused in his tale of woe. 'I suppose so; drowned and all those with him.'

It was as if she had been punched in the heart. In all those years, it had never crossed her mind that her mother might be dead. She stumbled off down the street, dazed, her last link with the past severed forever.

She walked out through the sagging gates, down the hill into the evening sun until it was too dark to see the road. She fell over a rock, landing in a ditch and she lay there on the rough ground, bemused, befuddled, unable to keep hold of reality. It was getting cold but she could not see the way down the hill, so she spent the night in the open, huddled close to the ground, sharp stones digging into her side, shivering and crying.

She was not sure, in the end, why she was crying. She had

never loved her mother and Doña Constancia had not loved her, but now she was dead, had been dead for years, and Milagro never knew it. She had cut herself off from the past when she fled from Teguise but that had been her own decision, not so much of a decision as a confused instinctive reaction of compelling necessity, and the thought that an invisible fate had sheared away her roots without her knowing was intolerable.

*

Dawn came at last and, chilly and stiff, she roused herself and made her way back to Arrecife, to La Graciosa's hut, a place to sleep, to shelter from the weather, nothing more. Not a home, she would never have a home again. Everyone she had ever shared her life with, gone: Felipe, Pepito, now her mother.

During the days that followed, she realised at last how fully she was damned; she had already gone to hell even though she was not yet dead. She felt hunger and thirst, the heat of the sun, the need to relieve herself, to sleep, but it was not life that she was living. She began to drink. Felipe had often gone to the tavern but he never brought wine home and El Moro, of course, never drank, he scorned such foolishness. Enrique had always had a flask of wine to hand and she remembered the lift of doubtful pleasure the alcohol had given her.

She took to visiting the tavern, spending what few coins she earned through mending nets on wine. El Moro's stock of wealth was disappearing rapidly but Milagro felt a numbness now, she no longer cared what happened to her and she found the way to earn the price of a jug of wine only too easy. A few minutes in the dark of her hut or on a pile of nets in the hold of a fishing boat and she would have enough for wine for a week. She would sometimes try to work out how she had sunk to that level, where the slide downhill had begun, but it was too confusing, not worth bothering her head with.

There was a disadvantage, just a slight one. The fire in her had not gone out, the curse was still upon her, and the brief, stabbing, quick release for a drunken sailor would rekindle her own desires. After the man had left, she had to work on herself, rubbing and pinching and probing, clawing her way to relief in an undiminished frenzy. She could sleep then, she found, a dreamless, easeful, drunken torpor.

She could not concentrate sometimes; there were days when the sunset took her by surprise. She would not remember what had happened that morning, that afternoon, there would be a gap of several hours. It was not like being drunk, time would simply pass by without her recording it and she was often hungry, with her money virtually gone and little or no work available. She would get in a muddle mending nets, her fingers no longer seemed to know what to do at times and it took her so long that few fishermen would trust their repairs to her.

She seemed to be two people: the inner one a dull lump of stone, a volcanic rock with little or no substance and no connection with the other part of her which went about its daily business, such as it was. Her stony heart and mind watched her walk down to the harbour, sit on the quay to observe the life of the port, talk. Talk to strangers, telling them tales of what life had been like during the eruptions. Not her own story, not Felipe's death, Pepito's desertion, El Moro's treachery, of course not—all that was imprisoned for ever in her petrified core, in case any residual emotion should seep out and force her to reflect on her present state.

No, she could hear her other self rambling on, relating borrowed memories, tales of other people's disasters. In fact, her real past was more than a little vague now; bits of it would float to the surface from time to time but it was an effort to remember in what order things had happened. El Moro for example, she knew he had been kicked to death by his mule, at least she thought that was how he had died. She felt she could have prevented his death but she could not really remember why. When had he died? After Pepito left, surely. Thinking about Pepito always made her cry but there again she was not quite sure why. She did not bother to sort out her memories in the end. What was the point? Life drifted by and one day it would stop.

Don Jaime came to see her regularly; he felt he had some-how failed to get through to her when she still had all her wits and it pained him constantly to see what she was reduced to, pained him even more that she seemed to have no idea how low she had fallen—a once beautiful and spirited woman, now a dirty ragged whore, old before her time, rapidly becoming so repulsive that even the most drunken of sailors would have nothing to do with her. He often brought her food, he was con-cerned that she might starve to death and not even notice. He listened to her ramblings; sometimes, they did make sense and he would have the uncomfortable feeling that she was deliber-ately trying to shock him, that she was not truly as mad as she appeared to be.

*

Time passed and men's memories were short, even without the excuse of madness. A crazy old woman, one of the many who were not right in the head after the events of the past, living on charity, who cared? If the priest wanted to help her, let him. Charity was more widespread now, with the return of more and more of the original inhabitants, anxious to pick up where they left off, to track down distant relations who might have survived.

Another seemingly endless summer drought was coming to an end, the fourth since El Moro's death, though Milagro had long since lost count. When she heard the rain, she went outside to let the heavy drops spatter her face and rinse some of the dust out of her hair. She never bothered to wash any more, it was a waste of time. The rain trickled down her face and a dull flash of memory came to her: La Graciosa, she had smelled really bad towards the end. Momentarily aware of the comparison, she stood up rubbing at her face with her ragged skirt in a half-hearted attempt to get rid of some of the accumulated grime.

A woman had come to see her that morning, with Don Jaime, and Milagro had naturally assumed that she was one of the parish do-gooders, come to save her soul. But she was damned, there she was sitting in her filth, living out her damnation if not exactly comfortably, at least with few worldly cares and there was nothing anyone could do about it. She had told Don Jaime years ago—God had rejected her and now she was rejecting God and his salvation.

The rain seemed to be clearing her head as well as washing away the dirt. The woman had said her name—Rosa. Rosa? Rosa, a small cross child, so many years ago, standing scowling on the beach in Playa Blanca. Was that woman Rosa grown up? Milagro had still had hope then, love had still been alive, fading yes but not yet gone, still worth living for, till Rosa ruined it all.

Now she had come back, if that woman was that Rosa. She had the typical Guanche features but Milagro could not now recall Felipe's face, or Pepito's.

It must be the same Rosa. She came back day after day, always asking the same questions. Who else but Felipe's daughter would ask them—where is my father, what happened to him, when did you last see him? She would not tell her. Rosa blamed her for Felipe's death, but it had been Rosa's fault too. It was her hatred which had driven Milagro and Pepito to flee so fatally. Another change of direction in her life, prompted by what? God? Fate? Chance? Which one of them was responsible?

Defying Rosa gave her some revived interest in living. She had really only been passing the time for years but now she could take a malicious pleasure in Rosa's grief. She pretended to be deaf as well as mad, and much madder than she really was, for things were often quite clear now, the fog which had lain over the past seemed to be lifting. The painful memories which had been hiding behind it re-emerged but she could also recall some happier moments without the years of misery intervening too much. Felipe's death, the loss of Pepito, they were bitter to recall but seen as if through a gauze, the details less distinct than they used to be. The most distressing thing about remembering was what she could no longer remember: how she had felt as a young girl, why it had been so essential to run away from home and risk all for Felipe. She found it hard to credit, so many years later, that she could have been so foolish.

She tried to work out how old she was, she thought she must be well over forty but dates and numbers, so long unused because there had been no necessity for them, would not fix themselves in her head. She was perhaps not even as old as her mother had been the last time she saw her.

What would have happened if she had never met Felipe? If she had stayed in Teguise and lived a life of virtue as a good wife and mother, she might well be dead in any case, drowned on the way to Gran Canaria, killed in the eruptions or dead in childbirth. So many people died, from natural or unnatural causes, why was she still alive? There seemed no sense to it.

The return of memory caused her to understand, in part, Rosa's desperate need to know her father's fate. It was Milagro's own shock at discovering her mother's death so long after the event which had finally turned her into what she was now. Her stony core was softening, she could weep for her past, for her present state, but she was used to despair by now. She would tell Rosa nothing, though, not yet; she might even make her wait for a deathbed confession.

Chapter XIV – 1756 – Truth

Rodrigo wakes with the light into a strange calm and lies listening to the land sounds outside—a hen squawking tentatively, a dog barking, a baby wailing somewhere close at hand, down in the hovels beneath his window, no doubt.

What am I doing here, he thinks for a moment. He has slept soundly enough but his dreams have put him back on board the Concepción, tossing and turning in an imaginary bunk, with the roar of the sea and the wind in his ears. Early morning land noises seem unnatural, a crowing cock and a bleating goat rather than the raucous cry of a seagull and the creak of the rigging and the ship's planking as she labours through the waves.

He gets up and goes to the window. The wind has gone and the sun is just coming up, turning the hills from grey to ochre once more. No one stirs in the yard below and the dusty leaves of the fig tree beneath his window are motionless. As he gazes idly down at the broken roofs, the door of one of the shacks opens and a frowsy young woman appears, leading a goat. She squats down to milk it into a bucket which has been lying on its side by the sagging door, pausing only briefly to shake some of the dust and gravel out of it. A child stumbles out behind her, naked and scratching, then a smaller child carrying a baby. They too squat down in the dirt next to their mother, to watch the milking. The girl squirts milk from the goat's teat into their open mouths and their squeals disturb the baby. It begins to wail and the girl is obliged to arrange it at her breast in order to continue milking the animal with one hand.

Rodrigo watches the double milking process with some amusement. The girl would appeal to him if she was cleaner and clad in something other than the torn and stained shift, which appears to be her only article of clothing. But the curve of her grimy breast and the tangle of greasy dark curls cascading down her half-naked back do not arouse him in the slightest. When planning his expedition to Lanzarote, he did not give too much thought as to what kind of female company might be on offer when he reached his destination. If the young woman in the yard below is typical of what is available, he can look forward to many days of abstinence.

One of the children has noticed him at the window and is pointing up at him. He withdraws, embarrassed at having been caught spying, so to speak. He dresses quickly and sits down at his makeshift table, turning his attention to the organisation of his research. He must find out about the climatic changes which the eruptions have brought about too; this is an aspect he has not previously considered. He must collect eyewitness accounts, preferably from reliable citizens such as priests or schoolteachers, not just from crazy old women, to convince the critical M. de Buffon that he has accomplished a serious study of the island. Most imperatively, he must see Timanfaya for himself and observe the devastation which the Montañas del Fuego have wrought; he needs to inspect the still smoking calderas, to make detailed drawings and collect samples of the rocks. From what he has learned at supper the night before it will not be easy to find a guide, and he has no map.

He has a book, though. Amongst the treatises on volcanic phenomena by Guettard and by himself which the French naturalist has furnished him with is one given him by a professor of mathematics just before he left Seville, a book written by an Italian engineer some hundred and fifty years before, purporting to give some detailed descriptions of the island. Rodrigo intended to glance at it onboard ship, but the weather decreed otherwise and he has not even opened it. He picks it out of his trunk and begins to flip through the pages. The author, one Torriani, came to Lanzarote to improve the fortifications of the island and was apparently struck by the idiosyncrasies of the inhabitants. Rodrigo comes across a number of references to 'natives', to their odd customs and dress. Are these the Guanches from whom Diego and Rosa claim to be descended? Absorbed in the text, he does not notice the little girl venture timidly into the room and he starts when he feels a tug on his sleeve.

'Señor, my mother says come.'

She leads him downstairs and watches, round-eyed, as he consumes the flat bread, dates and goat's milk set out for him on the table. If the milk is from the goat he has just seen being milked, Rosa has at least taken the care to skim the dust from it before offering it to him. Of Diego and the boys there are no sign, but Rosa sits down opposite him as he eats.

'If you want to see this woman,' her voice is carefully controlled, 'I'm going to see her now. I generally take her some food each morning.'

Rodrigo studies her face. Her eyes are bleak, the grief of the night before not far below the surface.

'Please, don't do anything for me that might distress you; I'm sure I can find someone else who will tell me what I want to know.'

Rosa shakes her head vehemently. 'I've thought about this all night, you must see her. It could be the only chance of making her speak. She mustn't be allowed to go to her grave with her secrets, I have to find out what happened to my father. Please, come with me now.'

Rodrigo does not wait to finish his breakfast; the chance may not present itself again. He clearly cannot expect the deluge of dramatic eyewitness accounts he collected on the slopes of Stromboli and Vesuvio—indeed then he accumulated too much information, each story being more sensational and unlikely than the last—but this woman's story may be a beginning. He runs upstairs to collect his writing materials and eagerly follows Rosa.

The woman lives in a mean-looking hut on the outskirts of the town, more of a shack made of palm fronds and one ruined lava block wall. In the doorway (it has no actual door) a bent figure sits on a flat-topped lump of lava. The woman's face is hidden by a curtain of long dark hair, heavily streaked with grey. Black sleeves hide her arms, but as they approach the woman hitches up her dusty skirt and extends a scarred hand to scratch her leg, which is a mass of ulcers and healed burn tissue. She seems defeated, hopeless.

'Milagro!' Rosa addresses her in a loud voice. 'She seems to be deaf, too, Señor Rodrigo, you'll have to shout at her. Milagro, someone has come to see you.'

Milagro does not move. Rosa bends over her and shakes her shoulder.

'Milagro, this man wants to know about the time of the volcanoes. He's come from Spain to talk to you.'

The woman raises her head and stares at Rosa. Years of dust have worked their way into the furrowed skin of her grimy face and into the matted hair which hangs round her sunken cheeks. When she opens her mouth to cough, her lack of teeth is obvious. Her eyes are half-closed against the morning sun.

Rodrigo looks from the grotesque figure before him to Rosa, tall and graceful by comparison, despite the lines of hardship in her face.

'You say she was your father's mistress?'

Rosa smiles bitterly. 'She's not even ten years older than I am and she was beautiful once, so they say. You can see how her evil life has left its mark on her.'

She turns to the old woman again. 'Do you hear? This is Don Rodrigo. He's come to ask you about the eruptions.'

She puts the basket of food down at the woman's feet. Milagro does not move but she stares first at Rosa then at Rodrigo. She says not a word, though her mouth opens in a kind of sneer, revealing her toothless gums again.

'You see, it's hopeless. I think she's forgotten how to speak, even if she wanted to. She's completely unhinged.'

Rodrigo is not so sure. Milagro seems to him, though old and wizened before her time in appearance, to have retained her sanity to some degree. Her eyes are not the dull vacant ones of the senile, they seem to be full of cunning, as if she is mocking Rosa.

'Do you think some wine would loosen her tongue?' He speaks loudly, observing Milagro closely. He is sure he can detect a flicker of interest in the old woman's eyes at the mention of wine.

Rosa shrugs. 'Perhaps. I don't give her wine but I've found her drunk occasionally. Someone brings her a jug from the tavern from time to time, I think.'

'Show me the tavern and leave her to me.'

Dubiously, Rosa leaves him at the tavern door and he returns to the dilapidated hut bearing a jug of the same thin brew he drank himself the night before. Milagro has not moved from the doorway but now she raises her head at the sound of his step.

It is so hard to believe that this wrinkled crone could ever have been a beauty, but her eyes light up at the sight of the wine jug; he catches a glimpse of the passion they must once have held. She reminds him, incongruously, of a girl in the back streets of Granada, a girl who half-killed him with her lovemaking.

The old woman reaches out eagerly for the wine.

'First you must promise to talk to me.'

She mutters and coughs; perhaps she has truly forgotten how to speak.

'Give me the wine.' Her voice creaks in her throat like a rusty hinge long unused. He allows her to drink briefly before snatching the jug back. Milagro coughs again and spits on the ground.

'What do you want to know?' She straightens up, less of an ancient grotesque now.

'Everything.'

Astonished at the difference in her bearing, Rodrigo hands the jug quickly back to her, in case she changes her mind and falls silent again. The woman takes a longer drink this time, then sets the jug down on the ground.

'I won't talk to her.'

Her voice grows stronger and less hoarse. 'She despises me. It wasn't her fault, but it wasn't mine either, though she seems to think it was.'

'Are you talking about the eruptions?'

Milagro laughs, cackling and gurgling. 'The eruptions? The priest blamed them on me too. No, it was Felipe. Everything changed when I ran away to be with him. It was his fault. If he hadn't been what he was, it would all have been different.'

Rodrigo waits. Slowly, confusedly, hesitantly at first, Milagro tells him her story. It takes a long time and many more jugs of wine, not all of them for her.

Chapter XV – Closure

The sun is setting. Milagro's long and rambling tale has taken all day. Rodrigo stares at the ragged, exhausted figure in front of him. She has frequently got to her feet, paced limping around, crouched weeping in despair, but now she sits on the stone in front of the sagging door once again. Her voice has tailed away, she had nothing more to tell him.

What ought he to be saying? How terrible? What a tragic life you've had? Some mundane and futile comment like that? He watches her in silence, a silence he is at last obliged to break himself.

'Will you tell Rosa what happened to her father?'

Milagro's eyes are closed, her head rests against the splintered door jamb.

'You tell her if you like. I don't care any more.'

Her voice is cracked and almost inaudible. Rodrigo clears his own throat, racking his brains for some suitable pronouncement.

'Thank you. Thank you for telling me what it was like.' A stupid and pointless remark. He presses on hurriedly, 'I didn't think the eruptions could affect everyone's lives so much. I understand now.'

Her story has confirmed in awful detail what Diego told him the night before. Hitherto, Rodrigo has been able to devote himself exclusively to geological matters, blithely disregarding the personal aspect. Round Etna and Vesuvio, people moved away for the short time that the eruptions lasted as a matter of course, then they moved back again. A few were killed, he was told, those too stubborn to believe that the lava would ever reach their farms, but a mere handful of casualties. Not hundreds of unsuspecting peasants whose livelihood had disappeared forever. How indeed could one believe in a god who let such terrible things take place? Rodrigo might well have lost his own faith in such circumstances.

Milagro's face seems relaxed and calm now, despite her obvious fatigue; there is almost a smile on her lips and Rodrigo can see for a moment the beauty behind the ravages of evil and disaster.

'Perhaps I should go to confession after all. Telling someone else is such a relief.'

'Shall I ask Don Jaime to come and see you?'

'No.' Her toothless mouth twists in a grimace. 'Far too late. What can he do for me now? All my sins, all my sins... I can't go back and undo them, any more than I could have saved Lanzarote by simply renouncing Felipe.'

'The eruptions are a natural phenomenon, they have nothing to do with the shortcomings of the islanders.' Rodrigo has heard this kind of thing before.

'That's not what Don Miguel said and he was right.' She rambles on. 'Like Lanzarote, I couldn't stop, I had a fire inside me that burnt the island all up.

'That's just fantasy. Why, the volcanoes may well erupt again, in a few years, after your death for example.'

Milagro shakes her head. 'The fire has gone out now, it won't happen again, at least not because of me.'

'Is that what you've been thinking all these years? It's not true, it's just not true.'

She clings to her delusions. 'True? Of course it's true. Telling you the whole story has made sense of everything. Why me, I don't know, but I understand the fire that won't go out, that destroys without thinking of the consequences.'

She must be quite drunk, it is the wine talking. Four or five jugs he has brought for her to keep the narration flowing, no wonder she is not making any sense. She is falling asleep now, her head lolls and she lets herself be helped inside the hut to lie down on the malodorous pallet which is practically all it boasts in the way of furnishings.

Rodrigo leaves her lapsing into a wine-induced torpor and steals away. He is not proud of himself. He should not have insisted on hearing her story, should not have plied her with so much wine to keep her tongue loose. He feels burdened with some of her guilt himself as a result.

But he knows that this is nonsense. She may have killed El Moro, but should she really carry all the blame for his death, such an unworthy character, a real monster, a man who raped and abducted young children, who richly deserved to be hanged? Rodrigo himself has killed—in war, and two men who tried to rob him in Seville. Merely defending his purse did not give him the right to kill, he thought too late, yet the priest who heard his confession at the time made light of the whole matter.

A veteran soldier would have to spend half his life on his knees atoning for the violent acts perpetrated in the name of religion and justice. Rodrigo has always considered himself a religious man, a God-fearing man, but his faith has never been seriously challenged. Seeing the utter devastation of the islanders' way of life wrought by the six years of eruptions, surely any sins committed, even such as those of Milagro, must be atoned for by now. Original sin, does that really account for so much pain and distress? Why has he never thought to ask such questions till now?

He feels only pity for the grotesque figure snoring lightly in the miserable hut. The ugliness of old age, it comes to all, sinners and penitents alike. He makes his way slowly back towards his lodgings, sombre, tumbled thoughts swarming through his head: life, death, punishment, eternal fire—his own existence has barely been touched by such considerations, except during the brief period when he fought for his country against the French for a few months, many years ago when he was eighteen and fired with ambition for death or glory. He does not remember being troubled by any ideological worries then—it was kill or be killed and there was no choice.

He stumbles on the rough path in the gloom and someone seizes his arm to prevent him falling. Diego.

'Ah.'

Rodrigo opens his mouth to say... what? He owes it to Diego to tell him the truth (some of it at least, Milagro's true sexual nature is none of his business) and let him decide what to tell his wife. He clears his throat. 'About Felipe...'

'Yes?' Diego grabs his arm more insistently. 'What did she tell you?'

'She told me what happened to him. She didn't kill him.'

Rodrigo pauses. Recounting Milagro's harrowing narration of Felipe's death, and her subsequent decline, feels like betraying a confidence.

'No, I'm sure she didn't kill him. Felipe wanted to take her and her son to La Palma with Rosa and the survivors of Rosa's family but Rosa hated her on sight and she hated Rosa. The whole family treated her as an interloper and she tried to make her own way back to Arrecife, taking Pepito with her. She got lost, Felipe came after her and was killed by a lava flow. Milagro was burned too, I'm sure you've noticed the scarring on her leg, but she and Pepito managed to escape back to Arrecife.'

Diego sighs. 'That does seem to fit with what Rosa has told me. Felipe evidently told her that last morning he was going to fetch Milagro and Pepito back and Rosa remembers crying and begging him not to leave her. I never really thought Milagro capable of killing anyone, even in a jealous rage. I'll tell Rosa it was truly an accident and leave it at that. Now Milagro has at last spoken out, Rosa may be able to let go of her resentment; she never had any hope that her father was still alive in any case. I'll go on ahead and break the news.'

Rodrigo hovers outside the schoolmaster's house. He hears a storm of hysterical weeping and it is not until silence falls that he ventures to enter. There is no sign of Rosa. The children are laying the table and there is a smell of cooking fish in the air. Diego enters the room with a dish of some white substance. He proceeds to distribute large dollops of food onto each plate and, as he notices Rodrigo's apprehension, he smiles. At least, he comes as close to smiling as he ever will, a curious twist of the lips.

'Sancocho—salt cod and sweet potato. Try it, you'll find it more appetising than it looks.'

The children are eating with evident relish, spooning a brownish green sauce from a small bowl onto the amorphous white mass. Rodrigo copies them and tries a tentative mouthful. The sauce is the spiciest he had ever tasted, it catches the back of his throat and he feels for a moment as if he has swallowed a burning coal, but the combination of the pungent sauce and the mild, cooling fishy mush is not unpleasant. It is certainly unlike anything he has ever eaten before.

Rosa does not appear at all and Rodrigo tactfully refrains from asking after her; he does not want another reprimand from his severe host. However, at breakfast the next morning she is there, outwardly calm and cheerful.

'Now I look back,' she volunteers to Rodrigo, 'I don't believe my father was a very admirable man. He was hardly ever at home and when he did come it was always only for a few days at a time. I think it was mainly because he was there so rarely that he became so precious to me. He made Milagro suffer too, I can see that now.'

She is silent for more than a moment and there is an awkward pause before she says stiffly, 'Thank you for making her talk. I suppose I should make my peace with her. Sometime.'

Her eyes are still red from weeping, Rodrigo notices, and her hair is not tied back as tidily as it was the previous day.

'If you still want to go, one of Diego's pupils will guide you to Timanfaya, he has an aunt who lives in Uga. The young know nothing of what has happened, of course; they are always daring each other to walk on the hot places in the lava fields, little fools. They've forgotten how dangerous it can be up there.'

Rodrigo is to stay in Uga with the boy's aunt overnight, then carry on up to the volcanic area. He hires two donkeys in the town and he and his guide make their way up miles of dusty track, through an unchanging panorama of barrenness, grey fields giving way to brown fields, dominated all the time by the smooth, innocuous-looking conical hills of the volcanoes themselves. They are not even very high, not compared with Vesuvio or Stromboli, but the thought that they have risen from nothing out of green fields of crops in such a short time, not evolved over many thousands of years, makes them intimidating enough for Rodrigo, their serried ranks crouching over the landscape, just waiting to break out again in renewed mischief.

*

Uga is a new town, the old one lying many feet deep under piles of volcanic slag some miles to the north, and as a result the houses have a civilised, freshly-painted appearance, more or less entirely lacking in Arrecife. But this is an illusion. An unappetising meal of hard bread and rancid cheese, followed by an uncomfortable night on a rough plank bed with a lumpy, bug-ridden straw mattress, ensure that Rodrigo sleeps little that night, and he is up before it is really light. He prods his by now reluctant guide awake and sunrise finds them wading through the drifts of black sand which border the lava fields themselves. The sand is ankle deep and the donkeys are making little headway, so they are forced to dismount. The boy lags further and further behind, eventually offering to wait with the animals on the lower slopes, while Rodrigo goes on towards the summit.

'Go straight up,' he says waving a vague hand towards a gap between two conical mounds. He is clearly no Guanche, this one, his swarthy skin, long hooked nose and lank black hair reminding Rodrigo of a rather shabby crow.

'All right.' Rodrigo is hardly surprised; they are both hot and sweating already and in any case he will make quicker progress on his own. 'If you want to be paid, you'd better be here with the donkeys when I come down again this afternoon.'

He takes a silver coin out of his pocket and waves it under the crow's beak. The black eyes light up but Rodrigo snatches the coin away and puts it back in his pocket.

'Later.'

He takes his bag with writing materials and water bottles. He struggles up the hill, sinking deeper and deeper with every step. The sand is the same colour as the hills themselves, much darker than sea sand, really black in places with patches of red and grey. When he at last reaches the gap between two mounds which the boy has indicated, an astonishing sight lies in front of him.

To his right stretches a series of small craters, like heavy raindrops on sand petrified at their moment of impact, each one a miniature caldera. Above him a clear track, an old lava trail black as ink, a glistening snail trail of obsidian, leads up to a craggy, lowering multi-coloured rock formation, its tormented shapes mute witnesses to the mighty upheavals. He has seen such rock formations before in the Aeolian islands, Lipari and Salina as well as Vulcano, but there they were covered with vegetation, fairly dripping with greenery and flowering shrubs, their brutal forms softened.

Reddish scree gives ominously under his feet as he advances. By digging his heels in and throwing himself on to his back, he avoids sliding more than a few yards down the slope. The ground is warm, a comforting warmth, the same temperature as the palms of his hands as he clambers up to the ridge again on hands and knees. He sits down to contemplate the array of geological marvels spread out before him. Ochre and vermilion, sepia and charcoal, the burnt and mangled rocks seem to be the product of witchcraft or devilry, thrown up from hell; surely no natural forces can have formed them. Twisted granite baked and burned out of all recognition, basalt crags like bizarre monstrous animals crouching over drifts of sand, scarlet and black. The foul stench of sulphur hangs in the air, far more choking than Vulcano, and many of the rock formations are striped with the yellowish green of the mineral. Some of the small calderas are still smoking, wisps of blue arising as if they are the homes of malevolent, cigarillo-smoking spirits.

Rodrigo leaps down the rocks on the other side of the gap, sliding down, scrambling back up, tapping and prodding, chipping and hammering, stowing the specimens he collects in the leather bag which hangs from his neck The smell of sulphur becomes almost unendurable and a sudden gout of flame bursts out of the ground not very far from where he is standing. He beats a hurried retreat from the mountain's foetid breath, but it is only a blowhole—the subterranean gases have momentarily built up to ignition point. The flames soon die away and he sits down again to sketch his surroundings. He is not much of an artist, he cannot hope to do the scene justice. It is more of a personal record. As if he is likely to forget the incredible sights in front of him.

He pauses at last, carefully corks the ink-bottle and blots the last drawing with a handful of volcanic sand. A thought strikes him and he clambers back up to check on his unenthusiastic guide. As he has feared, he can see a small figure trudging through the sand away from the volcanoes, leading two donkeys. The faint-hearted youth has not been that eager to earn his silver coin.

'Damn the boy.' He is now in a quandary. The sun is quite low in the sky: he has been so intoxicated by the mountain's geological marvels that he has failed to notice the passing of time. It is too late now for him to find his own way down the mountain in any safety before darkness falls. The risk of straying into some unstable and perhaps fatally fragile area in the failing light is too great.

The deformed rocks are already casting longer and more ominous shadows on the ground, sinister wild beasts waiting to pounce as soon as the light has gone. He must find some place to pass the night, but where? He moves well away from the blowhole area, contemplating bedding down in the sand, but the idea that some slight movement of the ground during the night might bury him in a choking torrent makes him very wary.

He finds, finally, a patch of smooth ground between two basalt outcrops, which feels perfectly firm when he stamps on it. He will be hungry, the lad has made off with the food as well as the animals, but his water bottle is still half full. He drinks sparingly of the brackish and sulphurous liquid and settles himself, wrapped in his cloak, to endure the long and disquieting night ahead of him. He has the time now, too much time, to begin planning the memorandum he intends to write on the physical phenomena of Lanzarote for the benefit of M. de Buffon.

The ground is a comfortable temperature, but when he lies down he fancies he can hear it murmuring and muttering—magma still not far below the surface, ranging this way and that, seeking a weak point in the surface crust. A vague childhood memory comes to him, of his mother making him put his ear to her swollen belly to hear the stirrings of his younger sister a few weeks before she was born. The warmth, the faint noises (or are they a product of his imagination, heated like the ground?) remind him of that; he hopes he is not about to be the unwilling witness of another hellish birthing from the womb of Lanzarote, but the night, though long and made far longer by his inability to sleep for more than short periods at a time, passes off peacefully enough. Blowholes explode more than once, sending grotesque shadows flickering over the extravagantly misshapen landscape, and in the distance he sees from time to time an ominous reddish glow appear and lingeringly disappear, accompanied by a muted subterranean rumble. The waning moon sets early, leaving him with the occasional light of the island's nocturnal emissions.

Dawn finds him soundly asleep at last and it is only when the sun is well and truly risen that he comes to, his mouth full of sand where he has rolled over in his sleep. Coughing and spitting and very hungry, he is now fully awake. A few mouthfuls of the unpalatable water in his flask revive him sufficiently to think about finding his way back

On second thoughts, he determines to explore further now that he has another whole day in front of him. He can do without food for a few more hours. He sets off to climb the reddish dune to his left in the hope of glimpsing the sea from its summit and, despite sliding back more than once, he soon arrives at the top.

He can indeed see the sea, sparkling and indifferent in the far distance, but in between is an impossibly huge lava plain, mile upon mile of cinder with more outcrops of contorted and mangled rocks, charred and hurled aside and heaped up by the unstoppable force of the lava flows. He starts across the black surface, picking up scoriae of infinitely varying shape and colour, but as his boots crunch over the ground a terrible thought comes to him. No one wants to go up to the volcanoes, Diego said, it would be like walking on someone's grave, and the splintering of the friable rocks under his boots suddenly resembles the snapping of bones. He leaps back on to the sand again: if one has to walk across a recent battlefield, one does not step on the dead bodies left lying there. He has enough specimens, it is time to go, to leave Lanzarote to recover from its past as best it can.

*

It takes him several hours and more than a little backtracking to reach Uga. His erstwhile guide is nowhere to be seen, his aunt denies all knowledge of his whereabouts, but the hired donkeys are tethered outside her hut. Rodrigo repossesses them and makes his way back to Arrecife, his head full of conflicting thoughts, geological preoccupations not being uppermost. The scoriae crunching like crushed skulls beneath his feet, the sinister malformations of the landscape—he understands now the

[251]

reluctance of the people to revisit the blasted remains of their past and he can hardly blame the youth for deserting him as darkness fell.

He goes straight down to the port, to see about arranging some rapid passage home. Bartolomé is not due for another two weeks, weeks which Rodrigo originally, and naïvely, assumed would be spent happily browsing amid the relics of the eruptions, organizing his research on the current geological state of affairs. He has lost his appetite for research, he cannot now pick over the grisly remnants of tragedy for selfish scientific reasons. M. de Buffon will have to be disappointed. Diego's judgement has proved right again: though tiresome and pedantic, his evaluation of Lanzarote and its people is only too correct.

There is some kind of commotion going on round the other side of the harbour: in among the sandstone outcrops in the shallow, reef-strewn eastern part of the port, a small crowd has gathered. As he draws closer, curiosity still getting the better of him, he sees two men hauling a dripping black object out of the water. A dead body, a woman's body, a body with long trailing dark hair. A cold feeling grips Rodrigo and he pushes his way roughly through the crowd to see the face of the dead person.

Milagro. Of course.

'How did it happen?'

The toothless fisherman who is helping pull her out shrugs.

'Who knows? She often walked round the rocks and her legs aren't so good these days, going rotten with old burns, you know. That and the wine.'

He cackles and Rodrigo recoils from the noisome, fishy breath. However, the man bends over to pull down her skirts, rucked up almost to her waist as she is hauled unceremoniously onto the shore. Was he once one of her lovers, he too? As the man smooths the hair back from her face, she moans and water trickles from her mouth. She is still alive. Rodrigo stares at the woman's body, sprawled on the sand, feeling obscurely responsible for her plight. She told him her story, made her confession to him. Did she just give up and let herself fall from the rocks, letting her tenuous hold on life go at last? As he stands irresolutely by, a figure comes flying down the shore. Rosa.

'What happened to her, she's not dead, is she?' She kneels by the woman's side, shakes her shoulder with tears pouring down her cheeks. Rodrigo kneels down next her and Rosa turns to him, grasping his arm hysterically.

'She musn't die, she's all I've got left of the past. Too late, too late, why didn't I think of it like that before?'

The old woman coughs weakly and more water trickles from her mouth.

'Milagro, can you hear me?' Rosa pats her face desperately. 'I know what happened, it wasn't your fault, my father loved you. Don't die, I can take care of you now.'

Milagro opens her eyes. She reaches out and gropes for Rosa's hand, feebly, but time has run out. Her eyes close again and her body relaxes into death.

*

Rodrigo turns to go. He has to find a ship to take him away from this island of tragedy. He cannot be blamed for the death of a woman he had only met once. Can he? There is nothing he can do for Rosa, for Milagro now in any case.

Yes, there is. A priest, Don Jaime presumably, has come to kneel by the dead woman and pray for her. Rodrigo hands him several gold coins.

'See that she gets a decent Christian burial.'

Don Jaime starts slightly, from the abruptness of the stranger's request, or perhaps because he himself is wondering about how Milagro came to fall from the rocks.

'Of course,' he says. 'What else would I do?'

'And say masses for her soul. It can't be too late.'

Pray for her, for Lanzarote and all its people, for their dark and ruined lives.